Edward Robert Bulwer Lytton

Poems

Historical and Characteristic

Edward Robert Bulwer Lytton

Poems
Historical and Characteristic

ISBN/EAN: 9783744713009

Printed in Europe, USA, Canada, Australia, Japan

Cover: Foto ©Andreas Hilbeck / pixelio.de

More available books at **www.hansebooks.com**

POEMS

HISTORICAL AND CHARACTERISTIC.

BY

ROBERT LORD LYTTON.

LONDON:

CHAPMAN & HALL, 193, PICCADILLY.

1877.

CONTENTS.

vi   CONTENTS.

POEMS
CLASSICAL, HISTORICAL, AND CHARACTERISTIC.

"L'Histoire ne commence et ne finit nulle part."
LOUIS BLANC.

v.

CRŒSUS AND ADRASTUS.

" Ὡς φησιν ἐν τῇ πρωτῃ Ἡρόδοτος."

ATHENÆUS, B. XXIII.

FORTUNE, that walks above the heads of men
I' the rolling clouds, the witless denizen
Of airy Nothing, by Necessity
Among the unsteady Hours, with hooded eye,
Subservient to a will not hers, is led :
And, as she passes, oft upon his head
That, underneath heaven's hollowness, doth stand
Highest of men, her loose incertain hand
Lets fall the iron wedge and leaden weight.

Crœsus, the lord of all the Lydian state,
Of men was held the man by Fortune best
With her unheedful blind abundance blest :
Because all winds into his harbours blew
Opulent sails; because his sceptre drew
Out of far lands a majesty immense ;
Because, to enrich his swoln magnificence,
The homage of a hundred hills was roll'd
Upon a hundred rivers ; because gold
And glory made him singular in the smile
O' the seldom-smiling world a little while.

To him, in secret vision, at the deep
Of night, what time Fate walks awake thro' Sleep,
The gods reveal'd that, in the coming on
Of times to be, Atys, his best-loved son,
Untimely, in the unripe putting forth
Of his green years, and blossom-promised worth,
By an iron dart must perish.
                                Then the king,
Long while within himself considering
The dreadful import of the dream,—in fear
Lest any iron javelin, lance, or spear,
Left to the clutch of clumsy Chance, should fall
On Atys,—gave command to gather all
Such weapons out of reach of him he loved,
Safe in a secret chamber far removed.
And,—that the menaced prince no more should take
His wont i' the woods, with baying dogs to break
The rough boar's ambush, nor the lion wound,
Nor flying stag, with dexterous darts,—he found,
And wived to Atys, the most beautiful
Of Lydian women: lovelier than the lull
Of Summer eves in lands where Summer fills
With slumbrous light the slopes of snowy hills
Flusht by a fleeting sun.   So fair was she
Whose claspèd arms should gentle gaolers be
To Crœsus' chiefest treasure.
                                This being done,
The king was comforted about his son.

But while the nuptial feast, at mid of mirth,
O'erflow'd with festival the golden girth
Of the king's palace,—while, with fold on fold
Of full delight, the mellow music roll'd

From Lydian harps a heaving heaven of sound
In the gorgeous galleries, and garlands crown'd
Warm faces in a mist of odours rare,—
There came before the king at unaware
A stranger from beyond the storm-beat sea :
A man pursued by pale Calamity,
With hands polluted ; on whose countenance
Was fix'd the shadow of foregone mischance.
His slow steps up the hymeneal hall
Struck sounds that sent deep silence on thro' all
That swarming revel.   Music's broken wing
Flutter'd and strove against the check'd harp-string :
And he that pour'd stood, holding half-way up
The two-car'd pitcher o'er the leaf-twined cup,
While the wine wasted : he that served lean'd o'er
The savorous fumes of anise-spicèd boar,
With trencher tilted : they whose limbs were dropp'd
At ease on purple benches, elbow-propp'd,
Half rose, and, stooping forward, shock'd awry
From jostled brows, sloped one way suddenly,
Their slanted crowns, blue-boss'd with violet,
Or dropping roses : each with eyes wide-set
In unintelligent wonder on the wan
And melancholy image of that man.
He, moving thro' the amazement that he caused,
Approach'd, unbid, the throne of Crœsus ; paused,
And there, with groans from inmost anguish brought,
The hospitable-hearted king besought
His hands by the Lydian rite to purify
From taint of blood.
                    To whom, when presently
He had his asking granted, Crœsus said :

" Whence art thou, stranger? and whose blood hast
    shed,
That doth so fiercely clamour at the porch
Of Heaven's high halls? What burning wrong doth
    scorch
Sweet rest from out the record of thy days?"

To whom that other :
                " But that Judgment lays
Foundations deeper than Oblivion,
I would my shadow from beneath the sun
Had pass'd for ever; being the most forlorn
Of men! A Phrygian I, and royal-born;
The son of Gordius, son of Midas; who,
Ill-starred! unwittingly my brother slew.
For this, my father from his much-loved face,
And all the happy dwellings of my race,
Me into wide and wandering exile drave :
Whence, flying on the salt white-edgèd wave,
Cast out from comfort unto stars unknown,
My hollow ship, before the north wind blown,
Fate to these shores directed; where I stand
A friendless man, sea-flung on foreign land.
In thus much learn, O king, from whence I came,
And what I am. Adrastus is my name."

The monarch smiled upon him, and replied,

" Thy friends are ours : thy land to ours allied :
If not with kindred, here with kind, thou art.
A frowning fate to bear with smiling heart
Is highest wisdom. In our court remain.
Cease to be sad. Nor tempt the seas again."

So in the Lydian court Adrastus stay'd.
Eating the bread of Crœsus: and obey'd
The kindly king, well-pleased to roam no more.

Now, at that time, a horrible wild boar,
By hunger driven from his lair, below
The dells dark-leavèd, lit with golden snow,
Where Mysian Olympus meets the morn,
Made ravage in the land; despoil'd the corn,
The tender vine in many a vineyard tore,
Each sapling sallow olive wounded sore,
And oft, about the little hilly towns
And stony hamlets, where high yellow downs
Pasture, among cold clouds, the mountain goat
That wanders wild from wattled fold remote,
His fierce blood-dripping tusk foul mischief wrought.
For this, the sorely-injured Mysians sought
At many times the ruinous beast to slay;
But never yet at any time could they
Come nigh him to his hurt. For he, indeed,
Slew many of them, and the rest had need
Of nimble feet in fearful flight to find
Unworthy safety. Thus was ruin join'd
To ruin.
       Therefore, unto Crœsus now
They sent an embassage; that he should know
The damage done them by this savage thing;
Entreating much, moreover, that the king,
With certain of the Lydian youths, would send
Atys, the prince, to help them make an end.
For of all noble youths in Lydian bound
Atys the most high-couraged was renown'd,
Nor match'd in martial vigour.

               Crœsus then,
When he had heard the message of these men,
Made answer to the Mysians :

                 "For our son,
Ye shall not have him.   Think no more upon
That matter.   For, indeed, the crescent light
That was newborn to gild his nuptial night
Is yet the unfinish'd circlet of a moon.
And shall a husband leave a wife so soon,
Ere the first spousal month be sped, to lie
On hill-tops bare, beneath the naked sky,
Neglecting wedlock young, and the sweet due
Of marriage pillows, Mysians, for you ?
But since (touching all else) we love you well,
And fain would see the huge beast horrible,
That hath such havoc made of your fair land,
Defeated, we will send a chosen band
Of our best valours; men that shall not miss
What is to do.   Be ye content with this."

But, when the Mysians were therewith content,
The son of Crœsus, hearing these things, went
To Crœsus, and said to him :

                 "In time past,
Father, or in the chase, or war, thou wast
The first to wish me famous; who dost now
To me forbid the javelin and the bow.
Wherefore?   For yet I deem that thou hast not
In me detected any taint or spot
Of fear, dishonouring one to honour born.
Yet think how all men from henceforth must scorn
Thy son, whom, being thy son, they should revere,
In him revering thee, when I appear

Among them in the agora : I alone
Of all men missing honour to be won
From this adventure !   For what sort of a man
To the coarse general (that is quick to scan
Faults in superior natures) shall I seem ?
Or what to my fair wife ?   How shall she deem
Henceforth of him, who in her white arms lay
No less than as a god but yesterday ?
Wherefore, lest I some memorable deed
Now miss to do, I pray thy leave to lead
The honourable ardours of this chase,
True to my noble name and princely place ;
Or, this denied, vouchsafe, at least, to say
For what just cause I must remain away.
Since I, in all things, would my heart convince
The king must needs be wiser than the prince."

But Crœsus, weeping, answered :

" Not, my son,
Because in thee aught unbecoming done
Displeased me, nor without sad reason just,
And strict constraint to do what needs I must
(Not what I would, if what I would might be !)
Have I thus acted.   For there came to me
A vision from the gods, upon my bed,
In the deep middle of the night, which said
That in the days at hand, an iron dart
Thee from my love, and from thy life, must part.
For this, thy marriage have I hasten'd on :
That, with occasion due, thou shouldst, my son,
Awhile withhold thee from thy wont to seek
The haunts of lions, or with dogs to break
The rough boar's ambush in the rooty earth,

But rest, companion'd, by the pillar'd hearth,
To one new-wedded a befitting place;
For this, did I forbid thee to the chase:
For this . . . O stay, my son, by thy fair wife,
And, in prolonging thine, prolong my life ! "

And his son answer'd :

                      " Wisely, since the dream
Came from the all-wise gods, as I must deem,
Wisely, dear head, and kindly, hast thou done;
Thus, with forethoughted care, to hold thy son
Back from the far-seen coming of the wave
Of Fate,—if him forethoughted care could save !
But I, indeed, as touching this same chase,
Can see no cause for fear.   In every place
Death's footsteps fall.   Nor triple-bolted gate,
Nor brazen wall, can shut from man his fate.
Yet, had the vision prophesied to me
That, or by tooth, or tusk, my death should be,
I had been well content to stay at home;
Leaving the coming hour, at least, to come
By me not rashly met in middle way.
But since 'twas said an iron dart must slay
Me, to black death appointed, I might fear
An iron dart as well, tho' staying here,
As there, in open field, among my friends.
For who can lock his life up at all ends
From charmèd Chance, that walks invisibly
Among us, to elude the dragon eye
Of Policy, and the stretch'd hand of Care?
Wherefore, I pray thee yet that I may share
What honour from this hunt is to be won,
Before death find me.   Since a man may shun

Honour, yet shunning honour all he can,
He shuns not Death, which finds out every man."

Then Crœsus, overcome, not satisfied,
From under moisten'd eyelids, doubtful, eyed
The impatient flushing in the brighten'd cheek
Of Atys. And, because his heart was weak
From its vague fears to shape foundation fast
For judgment, "Since, my son," he sigh'd at last,
"My mind, tho' unconvinced, thy words have shaked,
Do as thou wilt."
                        But, like a man new-waked
From evil dreams, who longs for any light
To break the no-more-tolerable night,
Soon as, far off in the purple corridor,
The sandal clicking on the marble floor
Ceased to be heard, and he was all alone,
And knew that Atys to the chase was gone,
He started up in a great discontent
Of his own thoughts, and for Adrastus sent;
To whom the monarch thus his mind express'd :

"Adrastus, since, not only as my guest
But as my friend, thou hast to me been dear,
If aught of natural piety, and the fear
Of Zeus, whom I by hospitable rites
Have honour'd, honouring thee, thy heart delights
To harbour, heed thou well my words. For I,
When thou, pursued by pale Calamity,
Didst come before me, thee, upbraiding not,
Did purify, and, as a man no spot
Of blood attainted, to my hearth received,
And there with ministering hand relieved.

Now, therefore, follow to the chase my son,
Nor leave him ever till the chase be done ;
His guardian be ; prevent him in the way,
And let no skulking villain lurk to slay
The son of him that hath befriended thee.
Moreover, for thine own sake, thou shouldst be
Of this adventure ; so, to signalise
A noble name by feats of fair emprise ;
Since thy forefathers of such feats had praise,
And thou art in the vigour of thy days."

Adrastus answer'd :

               "For no cause but this
(Since Crœsus' wish unto Adrastus is
Sacred as law deliver'd from above)
In this adventure had I sought to move.
For 'tis not fit that such a man as I,
Under the shadow of adversity,
Should with his prosperous compeers resort ;
And, not desiring this, from martial sport
Among the Lydian youths, with spear or bow,
I have till now withheld myself.   But now,
Since I am bid by him I must obey,
Bound to requite in whatsoe'er I may
Kindness received, this chase I will not shun.
Thou, therefore, rest assured thy royal son,
Dear Paramount, so far as lies in me,
His guardian, shall unharm'd return to thee."

Meanwhile, the huntsmen had with leathern thongs
The lean hounds leash'd, and all that fair belongs
To royal chase appointed, as was fit ;
With pious rites around the altar, lit

To solemn Cybele, at whose great shrines
On wooded Ida, 'mid the windy pines,
Or Tmolus, oft the Sardian, to invoke
The mighty Mother, bade the black sheep smoke;
And Artemis, the silver-crescented,
Adoring whom, a white kid's blood was shed,
And crowns of scarlet poppies, intermix'd
With dittany, among the columns fix'd,
Or hung, fresh-gather'd, the high stones upon.

And now the Lydian youths (with whom the son
Of Crœsus and the Phrygian stranger) blew
The brazen bugles, till the drops of dew
Danced in the drowsy hollows of the wood;
And the unseen things that haunt by fell and flood,
Roused by the clanging echoes out of rest,
Shouted from misty lands, and, trampling, press'd
Thro' glimmering intervals of greenness cold,
To hang in flying laughters manifold
Upon the march of that blithe company:
Great-hearted hunters all, with quiver'd thigh,
And spear on shoulder propp'd, in buskins brown
Brushing the honey-meal and yellow down
From the high-flowering weed, whilst, in their rear,
The great drums throbb'd low thunder, and the clear
Short-sounding cymbals sung; until they came
To large Olympus, where the amber flame
Of morn, new-risen, was spreaded broad, and still.
There, for the ruinous beast they search'd, until
They found him, with the dew upon his flank,
Couch'd in a hollow cold, beneath the dank
Roots of a fallen oak, thick-roofèd, dim.
And, having narrowly encircled him,

They hurl'd their javelins at him.   With the rest
That stranger (he that was King Crœsus' guest,
The Phrygian, named Adrastus, purified
Of murder by the monarch), when he spied
The monster, by the dogs' tenacious bite,
And smart of clinging steel, now madden'd quite,
Making towards him,—hurl'd against the boar:
Which missing, by mischance he wounded sore
Atys; through whose gash'd body, with a groan
The quick life rush'd.
               Thus fates, in vain foreknown,
Were suddenly accomplish'd.   For those Powers
That spin, and snap, the threads of mortal hours,
Had will'd that Crœsus nevermore should hear
The voice of Atys; unto him more dear
Than fondest echo to forlornest hill
In lonesome lands, more sweet than sweetest rill,
Thro' shadowy mountain meadows murmuring cold,
To panting herds: nor evermore behold
The face of Atys; unto him more fair
Than mellow sunlight and the summer air
To sick men waking heal'd.   Now, therefore, one,
Having beheld the fate of the king's son,
Fled back to Sardis, and to Crœsus said
What he had seen :—how that a javelin, sped
By that ill-fated hand,—to nothing good
Predestined, from the blot of brother's blood
By Crœsus purified, yet all in vain,
Since still to bloodshed doom'd,—had Atys slain,
Fulfilling fates predicted.
              Crœsus then,
Believing that he was of living men
Most miserable, who had purified,

Himself, the hand by second slaughter dyed
In the dear blood of his much-mourn'd-for son
(Since by his own deed was he now undone)
Uplifted hands to Heaven, and vengeance claim'd
Of Zeus, the Expiator; whom he named
By double title, to make doubly strong
A twofold curse upon a twofold wrong:
As God of Hospitality,—since he
That was his guest had proved his enemy;
As God of Private Friendship,—since the man
That slew his son was his son's guardian,
To whom himself the sacred charge did give.

Therefore he pray'd, "Let not Adrastus live!"

But, while he pray'd, a noise of mourning rose
Among the flinty courts; and, follow'd close
Out of the narrow streets by a dense throng
Of people weeping, slowly moved along
The Lydian hunters bearing up the bier
Of Atys, strewn with branches; in whose rear,
Down-headed, as a man that bears the weight
Of some enormous and excessive fate,
The slayer walk'd.
           Full slowly had they come,
With steps that ever slacken'd nearer home,
And heavier evermore their burthen seem'd,
As ever longer round their footsteps stream'd
The woeful crowd; and evermore they thought
Sadlier on him to whom they sadly brought
His hope in ruins. When they reach'd the gate
The western sky was all on flame. Stretch'd straight
Thro' a thick amber haze Adrastus saw,
As in a trance of supernatural awe,

The high slant street;. that lengthen'd on, and on,
And up, and up, until it touch'd the sun,
And there fell off into a field of flame.
He knew that he was bearing his last shame;
And all the men and women, swarming dim
Along the misty light, were made to him
Shadows, and things of air, for all his mind
Was pass'd beyond them. So, with heart resign'd
To its surpassing sorrow, he bow'd down
His head, and follow'd up the column'd town
The bier of Atys, without any care
Of what might come : because supreme despair
Had taken out the substance from the show
Of the world's business, and his thoughts were now
In a great silence, which no mortal speech,
Kind, or unkind, might any longer reach.
Meanwhile, with melancholy footsteps slow,
Slow footsteps hinder'd by the general woe,
Those hunters mount the murmurous marble stair
To the king's palace.
                 He himself stood there
To meet them; knowing why they came; with eyes
Impatiently defiant of surprise.
But, when they set their burthen down before
The father of him murder'd whom they bore;
And, when the inward-moaning monarch flung
His body on the branchèd bier,—there hung
With murmurings meaningless, and dabbled vest
Soak'd in the dear blood sobbing from the breast
Of his slain son,—there, dragg'd along the flint
His bruisèd knees ; and crush'd, beneath the print
Of passionate lips, groans choked in kisses close,
Pour'd idly on those eyelids meek, and those

White lips that aye such cruel coldness kept,
For all the hot love on them kist and wept;
And when the miserable wife, whom now
The sudden hubbub from the courts below
Had pierced to, thro' the swiftly-emptied house,
Flew forth, and, kneeling o'er her slaughter'd spouse,
Beat with wild hands her breast, and tore her hair,
And cried out, " Where, you unjust gods, O where,
Between the stubborn earth and stolid sky,
Was found the fault of my felicity?
That such a cruel deed should have been done
Under high heaven, beneath the pleasant sun!"
Then he, that was the cause of that wide woe,
Came forth before the corpse, and, kneeling low,
Stretch'd out sad hands to Crœsus; upon whom
He call'd, to execute the righteous doom
Of death on him, deserving life no more.

When, therefore, Crœsus heard this, he forbore
To groan against the edge of his own fate;
But judged most miserable that man's state
Who, evil meaning not, had evil done,—
First having slain his brother, then the son
Of him that gave him hospitality.
So, letting sink a slowly-soften'd eye
To settle on Adrastus, who yet knelt
Before him, his hard thoughts began to melt,
And he was moved in mind to tolerate
The greatness of his grief; which, being less great
Than his that caused it, stood in check, to make
This tolerable, too.
                    Sadly he spake:
"To me," he said, " thou hast requital made,

v.   c

Most miserable man! on thine own head
Invoking death.   Wherefore, I doom thee not.
Nor deem thy hand hath this disastrous lot
From the dark urn down-shaken.   Rather, he,
That unknown god, whoever he may be,
That long ago foreshadow'd this worst hour,
Hath thus compell'd it to us.   Some veil'd Power
Walks in our midst, and moves us to strange ends.
Our wills are Heaven's, and we what Heaven intends."
Then Crœsus caused to be upheaved foursquare
A mount of milk-white marble: and did there
In trophied urn the holy ashes heap
Of his loved Atys.   And, that fame should keep
Unperish'd all the prince's early glory,
Large tablets wrought he, rough with this sad story.

But when the solemn-footed funeral,
With martial music, from the marble wall
Flow'd off, and fell asunder in far fields;
And silenced was the clang of jostling shields,
And the sonorous-throated trumpet mute,
And mute the shrill-voiced melancholy flute;
What time Orion in the west began
Over the thin edge of the ocean
To set a shining foot, and dark night fell;
Then, judging life to be intolerable,
The son of Gordius sharply made short end
Of long mischance: and, calling death his friend,
He, self-condemn'd to darkness, in the gloom
And stillness, slew himself upon the tomb.
This to Adrastus was the end of tears.

But Crœsus mourn'd for Atys many years.

LICINIUS.

"Quid salvum est si Roma perit?"
HIERONYMUS, Ep. 91.

PART I.

THE TIME.

I.

IT was the fall and evening of a time
In whose large daylight, ere it sank, sublime
And strong, as bulks of brazen gods, that stand,
Bare-bodied, with helm'd head and armèd hand,
All massive monumental thoughts of hers
Rome's mind had mark'd in stately characters
Against the world's horizon. These, at last,
Fading, as darkness deepen'd thro' her vast
Dominion, Rome became mere space, spread forth,
Confused and shapeless, east, west, south, and north;
And, the whole homeless earth thus made her home,
Rome now might nowhere rid herself of Rome.
The heavens were all distemper'd with the breath
Of her old age. She, very nigh to death,
Paced thro' her perishing world in search of air
Unpoison'd by herself; but everywhere,
Like that Greek giant to whose frenzied frame
The blood of his slain foe clung fast as flame,

Withering the mighty limbs he could not free
From their disastrous trophy, so did she,
Choked by her own ensanguined purple, pant.

II.

Rome, in all places earth's inhabitant,
In no place earth's possessor any more,
Was thus by Rome pursued from shore to shore.
And, in that vast and sombre universe
Which was her dying chamber, 'twas Rome's curse
To see the shadows change to substances,
The substances to shadows: and disease
Lengthening the life of death in all that was.

III.

That severe Senate, once by Cyneas ·
To gods in synod liken'd, was become
Mere kennel for the curs that cramm'd in Rome
(Rome,—robb'd in turn by Goth, Hun, Vandal, Gaul,
And, having all devour'd, devour'd by all!),
. Earth's offal,—the filch'd filth of every land :
Mongrels, they lick'd each new-made master's hand,
' Snarling at one another.   Gorged with gore,
The purple gluttons of the globe,—no more
They, whose tremendous sires were fain to tug
For savage nurture at the she wolf's dug,
With Mavors march'd, beneath the Bird of Jove,
To scale the shaken walls o' the world.   Craft throve,
As courage fail'd.   Nor, now, the People rose,
And clamour'd, but the Courtier, plotting close,
Bided his time, and stabb'd.   Thus tyrants, dying,
Made room for tyrants : tyranny thus vying

With tyranny : to suit which, slavery
With slavery, and fear with fear, did vie ;
While Roman swords, for daggers used, were red
With murder, not with conquest.   At the head
Of Rome's worst rabble (ill revering it !)
A new Religion's riddling labarum, writ
On Rome's red ensigns by a Faith unknown
To Rome's stern sires, from Tiber, now, to Rhone,
Replaced her Senate's and her People's name :
Claiming whose sanction, in contempt of shame,
Blood-smear'd Brutality with pale Disgrace
Coupled, like dogs, upon the public place.
Slander, the stylus, Treason plied the knife :
And, preaching peace, Religion practised strife.

IV.

Old things had ceased, nor new things yet begun,
To justify their place beneath the sun.
The Future and the Past, contending, wrought
To wreck the Present, for whose faith they fought :
And, in the barbarous bosom of the new,
Grimly the worn-out old world's vices grew.
Some pure Patrician, in whose veins yet ran
The scornful blood of sires Etrurian,
Saw, newly shrined, as, frowning, past he trod,
The Mother of the Galilean God,
And cursed her : some hook-nosed Antiochene,
Whose great-grandfather Paul's first prize had been
Among the Rabbins, on the other side
Passing, beheld, stark naked, wanton eyed,
Stout-bodied Venus in her ancient place,
And spat, devoutly brutal, in her face :

Some half-bred Cæsar, waiting for his chance,
Bow'd to both goddesses, and, with a glance
Behind him, pass'd, suspicious, on his way.

v.

Rome, in the main, for her part, like some grey
Bedridden beldam, petulant and weak,
That from her own stout firstborn's sunburnt cheek,
And brawny arm, turns, captious, to caress
The sprawling grandchild on her knees, and bless
With mumbling lip the unswaddled infancy
Whose manhood will not dawn before she die,
Less loved whatever rested of her prime
Than the loud childhood of the later time :
And the new creed, as babes are by the nurse,
Fondled and scolded, and both ways made worse,
Babbling, clench'd baby clutches to destroy
Both sun and moon.   An empire was its toy.
Donatus, with fierce fingers dipp'd in gall,
Dragg'd down Cicilien thro' the councils all :
From sultry churches Carthaginian
To convents cold in Arles the echoes ran
Of curses, all pure Christian, in bad Greek :
Cicilien damn'd Donatus.   Shriek for shriek,
And stab for stab, with gladiatorial gust,
And, clamorous, scattering cumbrous clouds of dust,
The well-match'd theologic athletes strove,
While Cæsar, smiling, eyed them from above.
Meanwhile, amid the hubbub, unalarm'd,
That " Christian Cicero," Lactantius, charm'd
Young Crispus ; and in smoothest Latin praised
Those Christian virtues on whose work he gazed ;

Discomfited the Polytheist sore,
And smote the fall'n Olympians by the score ;
Slaughtering, with finely-pointed periods
Of borrow'd Ciceronian, Cicero's gods.

VI.

Then, when Licinius, Rome's last Roman, saw
The gods, his sires had worshipt with grave awe,
By slave, and savage, pimp, buffoon, and priest
Scorn'd and insulted, "Unavenged, at least,
The great gods die not !" groan'd the grey old man.
And, breaking bound from wilds Pannonian,
He, with a remnant rallied to the name
Of Jove the Avenger, cross'd the world, and came,
Camping on Hebrus, to confront the Sign
Of that new Creed proclaim'd by Constantine.

PART II.

THE MAN.

I.

Evening.   At morn the battle.   Met at last,
Stood, face to face, the Future and the Past.
Under the wild and sullen hills of Thrace,
Ominous, wrathful, ruin in his face,
On the last day of his own deity
The sun sunk.   Mystic lights, from sky to sky,
Shot meteoric thro' the startled stars,
O'er regions named from him that, born of Mars,
First reign'd among those snowy mountain tops,
What time grey Saturn by the sons of Ops

Was, in his turn—as, by himself, had been
Cœlus, his sire—dethroned. For Power, not e'en
In Heaven, one hand holds ever. There, while o'er
Rome's antique ensigns, Jove's own Bird once more
Spread his broad wings upon the gloomy air,
The robed Haruspices, with silent care,
Prepared the victim, and asperged the shrine
Mysteriously with sprinkled meal and wine
And frankincense, till all together gleam'd
The altars of the Twelve Great Gods, and stream'd
With fragrant fumes. A shout of pride : a sound
Of shields in closing circle clasht all round
The central camp.: where martial cymbals clang'd
Applause, as old Licinius thus harangued
The legions loyal to the gods he loved :

II.

" Romans, whose pride is by your name approved,
The immortal gods, that to your fathers gave
The empire they now call their sons to save,
From yonder altars on those sons look down,
And all Olympus deems our cause its own. .
With us the gods to battle go : with us
Whatever rests of Rome yet virtuous,
Yet Roman : all of manhood left on earth,
Of godhood left in Heaven. From every hearth
Where Roman sons revere heroic sires
Our hearts have caught hereditary fires.
Each Roman here, to rescue Rome her laws,
Her gods, her memories, her manhood, draws
The sword Rome gave her children. Friends, our foes
Not us alone, but the great gods, oppose.

False to the faith of their forefathers, they,
To change Rome's laws, and chase her gods away,
Have arm'd Dishonour.   Such   their   cause.   Our
    own
To serve, and save, the old worth, the old renown
Of all that made Rome, ROME.   A cause so just
I, with just faith, to the great gods entrust ;
Whose cause it is.   But if, O friends, in truth,
All we now fight for—all that to our youth
Was sacred, all that to our age is dear,
The greatness of the gods that we revere,
The manful Past that manly minds admire,
The immortal name of Rome's immortal sire,
The urns wherein our fathers' dust is laid,
The shrines they built us, and the laws they made,
Ay, even the banners that they bore in war!
—Were all these things less noble than they are,
Yet, where, in fortune's poorest state, is he,
So poor in spirit, that can endure to see
Foul'd by the rabble on his own hearth floor
The meanest garb that his dead father wore ?
Or what man breathes, tho' born of humblest birth,
That hallows not whate'er remains on earth
—Each frailest relic, and each feeblest trace,
His reverent love can rescue from disgrace—
Of her that bore him ?   Direr monster none,
Since Pyrrha's age, hath prey'd on earth, nor done
More impious deed, than this unfather'd Faith!
Man's memories all unmothering by a breath
Which blights the Present, strikes the godlike Past
Godless, and doth the barren Future blast
Bare of the bright presiding Powers that blest
Our great forefathers, gone to glorious rest ;

They in whose names, with pure libations
Full-pour'd, our mothers blest their unborn sons ;
Man's fair familiar Presidencies all,
Whose forms made sacred even a foeman's hall !
These, whom we fight for, are the gods that fought
For great Achilles; are the gods that brought
The wise Ulysses to his island home,
And brought from Troy the patriarch sire of Rome.
Them old Homerus, them Virgilius, sung :
Them heroes worshipt : them we know. This young
New-found half-god, Jew-born and bastard both,
Patron of slaves, and Power of upstart growth,
Where was he when Troy burn'd ? Enough ! We
    know
Whose cause is ours—Rome's cause ! whose foe—
    Rome's foe !
Whose gods—Rome's gods ! In hands, more mighty far
Than ours, the mighty issues of this war
Hang. If we fall, Romans, with us falls all
Romans have lived for. But we cannot fall,
Rome cannot fall, while yet of Rome there be
A score of Romans left to cry with me,
' Honour to our dead fathers ! ' "

III.

                Proud he spake.
And from that armèd auditory brake
The multitudinous echo of his mind,
In human-hearted thunder, the night wind
Roll'd hoarse above the battle-heapèd ground.

PART III.

THE GODS.

I.

But afterward; when, save the steel-shod sound
O' the surly sentinel from tent to tent,
The camps were silent, and the night far spent,
Licinius, rising in the restless night,
Mused by the altars of his gods.

II.

    Faint light
Stream'd from the faded embers, and faint fume.
O'er all his spirit a supernatural gloom
Had fall'n, and that profound discouragement
Which seizes on the soul whose passion, spent
In stormy thought, leaves action half unnerved.
In dead-cold skies the dark east, unobserved,
Wax'd sallow. Dead-cold influences pass'd
About the old man's heart. Licinius cast
His body upon the ground, and felt a Fear
Plant its foot on him in the darkness drear,
And pray'd intensely, as men only pray
When Fear is on them. Terror pass'd away.
A mystic wind was moving in his hair:
And hands unearthly touch'd him unaware.

III.

He, gazing up against the scatter'd gleam
Of the late stars, what time her dragon team

The night's moon-fronted maiden charioteer
Down o'er the dark world's edge was driving clear,
Saw—bright above the black and massy earth,
From cope to base—beyond the utmost girth
Of their wide-orb'd horizons, the intense
And intricate heavens, with silent vehemence,
Burst supernaturally open; as tho'
A bud should in a moment's time, not grow,
But change itself, into a flower full-blown.

IV.

To his sole sight was such a marvel shown.
The fair Olympians, all at once, and all
Together, in the Ambrosial Banquet Hall!
Each august countenance (vast gladness closed
In complete calm) ineffably composed
To an aweful beauty. Unendurably bare
The bright celestial nakednesses were.
And, far behind those Heavenly Presences,
Heaven's self lay bare to the innermost abyss
Of the unsounded azure. Orb in orb
Of what both seem'd to emit and to absorb,
In the same everlasting moment, light,
Space, silence,—sporting with the infinite!
For, to the universe, the universe
Listening, the while it answer'd, did immerse
The sound within the silentness of things.
Lights—meteors—mystic messengers, with wings,
Wands, trumpets, crowns—silently came and went
In the profound, but lucid, element
Of that divine abysm. Befitting form
Each Spirit shaped itself from calm, or storm,

Snow, fire, rain, thunder, and sea-thrilling wind:
All creatures of the All-creative Mind,
That makes each moment, and each moment mars,
Its own imaginings: thoughts, many as stars,
Or birds innumerable upon the wing:
Some, with congenial chance incarnating
Their restless essence, and so, brightening: some,
As soon as born, dissolved within the dome
Of that deep-lighted distance.   Underneath,
The dim world, wrapt in mist of mortal breath,
Low glimmering, sea and land.   And all about
The belted orb, close-coiling in and out,
Like a sleek snake with vary-colour'd back,
Glitter'd the constellated zodiac.
But, over tented camp, and temple wall
Or gated court, in tower'd cities tall,
Serenely slided down the silent sky,
Bearing disaster, bearing victory,
With benedictions these, as those with ills,
The viewless heralds of the Heavenly Wills,
Unmindful of the murmuring of mankind.

v.

All vague as vapour shapen by the wind
To mimic mountain, cape, or continent,
That every moment changes, came and went,
With wondrous modulation manifold,
The vision of that marvellous movement, roll'd
Around the zonèd orb of Circumstance,
Revolving in the marginless expanse
Whereon the serene doors and porches all
Of that sublime god-builded Banquet Hall
Opening, let in and out Eternity.

VI.

There, midmost of his kindred godheads, high
In contemplative glory, and calm as morn
On lone Olympus (where no foot hath worn
Heaven's white snow from the summit of the world)
Sat Father Jove.   From whose crown'd temples curl'd
The locks that, shaken, shake the woody tops
Of scornful hills, and o'er the full-ear'd crops
Roll blighting thunders, in storms, white or blue,
Of hail and rain.   Broad-brow'd, broad-bearded too,
In meditative mood, with slack right hand
The cypress sceptre of his vast command
He, leaning forward, lightly held.   All bare
The god's broad chest and ample shoulders were :
For gods, in company with gods, forego
Disguises meant for men : but all below
His spacious waist, in floods of massy fold,
From his large knees the lilied vesture roll'd :
Lest mortal eyes should, even in Heaven, espy
Aught save the robe that wraps the Deity.

VII.

At the right hand of her great spouse, the Queen,
Of scorn majestic, with man-quelling mien,
And regnant eyes, whose large looks everywhere
Were felt in Heaven, gazed from her blazing chair ;
Whereon, to left and right, from either side,
Four crested peacocks droop'd their Argus-eyed
Junonian trains.   Behind, above her head
The attendant Iris, her handmaiden, spread
Her bright bow, woven from the azure grain
Of the midsummer silver-threaded rain.

That eloquent spirit of the woodland air,
Men call the cuckoo (which, being bodiless there,
Needs not, and builds not, any nest on earth),
Sat on her stately sceptre.

VIII.

       Solemn mirth,
Like sempiternal summer, fill'd the hall
Where, round that Twain, the lesser godheads all,
At ease reclining by the ambrosial board,
In rosy circle ranged. Save one: Hell's lord,
The black-brow'd Pluto. Thro' Heaven's cloudy gaps,
Loom'd his dim realm,—one vague, drear, vast Perhaps.
There, dubious in the light by Hecate brew'd
For ghastly uses, a vast multitude
Of shapes—all shadows of the lives of men—
Continually coming, sought the den
Man's fear digs in his conscience for his crimes:
The outcasts of all ages, from all climes,
Doom'd by all creeds: Religion's shipwreck'd crew,
Barbarian, Roman, Christian, Greek, and Jew:
Who, in the glare of that disastrous light,
Gazed on each other's faces (dismal sight!)
And knew themselves, at last, for kinsmen drear,
The common offspring of one parent, Fear.
For, tho' man change his gods full many times,
Yet changed gods change not man, nor he his crimes:
Still from the knowledge of himself he breeds
Fears that make Hell the helpmate of all creeds,
Or old or new. And, even already, all
The brazen bound of that Tartarean wall,
Which not the gods themselves can overleap,
In windy circuit o'er the sulphurous deep,

Half-Gothic towers, by monkish masons built,
Put dimly forth.   Nought but the shame and guilt
Seem'd real in the ghostly flux below
Of swimming change, that surged from woe to woe :
So, flexile as man's ever-moving mind,
Whose masonry all monstrous forms combined
In one immense metropolis of Pain,
Tho' moor'd by Fear upon a midnight main,
Yet pace with time Hell's fluent structures kept,
From each new architectural adept
Fresh grimness winning.

IX.

　　　　　　　But all this was seen
In fluctuation indistinct between
The gaps of Heaven, thro' filmy distances
Of darkness, wild as wicked fancy is :
Nor marr'd the mirth of that Olympian feast
More than spots floating on the sun's bright breast
Darken his glory.

X.

　　　　　　Only, in the first
Amazing moment, when the vision burst
On him that saw it, Hebe, filling up
With nectarous œnomel a glorious cup,
Paused, as she pour'd, and stared, with open eyes
And open mouth, in half-displeased surprise,
Upon the wondering mortal.   For he had,
To her, the over-insolently-glad,
In the great human sadness of his face,
The aspect of a creature out of place :

As tho' into her golden cup had dropp'd
A sudden spider.   Ganymede, too, stopp'd
Teasing Jove's Eagle : who, with a great cry,
Rose, rough'd his feathers, seem'd about to fly,
But, seeing Jove so quiet, droop'd his wing,
And waited watchful of his keen-eyed king.
Venus with glance disdainful turn'd to scan
The old man's face : then, seeing that the man
Was chopp'd with battle, sun-bronzed, seam'd with scars,
She, whose white arm was round the throat of Mars,
Pointed a rosy finger, veiling half
In her soft eyes a little mirthful laugh
Under delicious lids dark-lash'd.   But he
Look'd on his worshipper remorsefully,
As some grave chieftain, when the strife is done,
Safe and unhurt himself, might gaze upon
His wounded battle-horse about to die.
Amor, that, trifling with his bow hard by,
Noticed not this new comer of the earth
(He having both eyes bandaged from his birth),
Guess'd with that instinct arch to children given
For mischievous occasion (since, thro' Heaven,
The babble of the mighty banquet hall
Suddenly ceased, a moment's space) that all
The attention of the gods was occupied :
And furtively, by Dian unespied,
From her chaste quiver stole the arrows keen,
And, in their places, with mock-serious mien,
Did his own little wanton darts dispose.

V.   D

PART IV.

THE PAST.

I.

But great Apollo in all his glory uprose.
And, even as when, what time strong mountains swoon,
And tremble, in a sumptuous summer noon,
And all the under air is still, so still
That no leaf stirs, o'er some etherial hill
Round which heaven's highest influences range
Invisibly, a cloud, with solemn change,
Begins to move; drooping his globèd glory
Slowly adown that inland promontory;
So down Olympus moved the Lyric God,
Majestic.   All his serious visage glow'd
With inner light; and music, mixt with fire,
Stream'd from the strings of his Mercurial lyre,
Preluding prophecy.

II.

    Severe, he stood
Above the Roman, resting in a flood
Of radiance clear, and thus stern speech began:

" Ill-counsell'd, and rash-spirited old man!
Learn to revere the all-wise Necessity,
That to the unceasing wheel of Time, whereby
Earth takes the shape by Heaven design'd, holds fast
Man's ductile clay; and, with the solid Past
Fusing the fluid Present's ardours, doth
The bright fantastic Future form from both.

Deem'st thou that, at thy summons, shall return
To earth the Powers whose parting footsteps spurn
Shrines where forever, since his course began,
The Names man worships are belied by man?
I will unfold the full mind of the gods,
From men obscured by Time's dull periods.
For man was on the earth ere we, that are
Not his first teachers, nor his last, were 'ware
Of his unblest condition: who, being born
Above the brutes, is but the more forlorn,
If missing consciousness of aught above
Himself, for him, in turn, to serve and love.
We, therefore, then, with gentle visitings,
To earth descended; and, from lonesome springs,
And hollow woods, lending to mountain winds,
And forest leaves, our language, with men's minds
Held commune. Wisdom, out of whisperous trees,
More sweet than whitest honey by wild bees
Suck'd from Midsummer's veins, to shepherd-priests
We pour'd in oracles; and at men's feasts
Sat down familiar, hail'd with dance and song.
Brutish we found man's life, the brutes among;
Beauteous we strove to make it . . . strove in vain!
Since man's low nature, failing to attain
The life of gods, but filch'd from gods their names
To deify what most degrades, most shames,
The life of man. Ill thank'd was all our toil!
To glorify earth's clay, oh, not to soil
Heaven's azure! came we from the kindly skies,
Kindling immortal fire in mortal eyes.
We gave men Beauty. But our gift, misused,
Hath wrong'd the givers. Have not men abused
Our very names, invoking them amiss

To deify ill deeds?   Was it for this
Dian is chaste? 'Mars brave? and Venus fair?
And Jove just-minded?   Wherefore, howsoe'er
Henceforth man's worship may be named by man,
Not ours shall be the names it mocks.   Nor can
Man's offerings shame our altars any more.
Not unto us, henceforth, your priests shall pour
The blushing wine, nor blood of victims shed.
Nor yet to us shall praise be sung, prayer said,
Whenever men henceforth have injured men.
Why should we bide on earth, and be again
Dishonour'd in the deeds whereby mankind
Profess to honour Heaven?   Yet shall they find,
Who yet may seek, us.   Not where we have been,
By thrones, on altars, seen, and vainly seen,
Thro' purchased incense clouding shrines profaned!
But I, that from of old this power attain'd,—
Having foreseen the Future,—to make fast
What in the Future man desires—the Past,—
Have wrought for man, by means of mighty Song,
A mystic world, which neither change can wrong,
Nor time can trouble.   And, therein, man yet
May gaze on gods, and fashion from Regret
Fair forms resembling Hope.   Wherefore, do thou
Cease to avoid the Inevitable.   Know
That we, the gods, who minister no more
To man's ambition, fairer than of yore
Thy fathers found us, since henceforth set free
From all that mixt us with mortality,
Range undisturb'd, beyond all reach of change,
In regions where immortal memories range,
Unvext by mortal hopes : responsible
For mortal wrongs no longer.

" Deem not ill
For man whatever betters aught man deems,
Or hath deem'd, beautiful, tho' but in dreams.
Not by shrines shatter'd, not by statues spurn'd,
Temples deserted, altars overturn'd,
And incense stinted, are the gods disgraced;
But by base homage of a herd debased,
By Faith in service to a fraudful Force,
And wrongful deed by righteous name made worse.
Time, that returns not, errs not. Be content,
Knowing thus much: nor toil against the event
Whereto Time tends."

III.

Thus, frowning, Phœbus said.
And Jove, from High Olympus, bow'd his head.

PART V.

THE PRESENT.

I.

There is a stillness of the upper air,
Foreboding change; when mighty winds prepare
In secret sudden war upon the world.
And when that stillness breaks, forests are hurl'd
Asunder, and sea-sceptring navies drown'd.
There is another stillness, more profound,
Worse change foreboding; of the inmost soul,
In that dread moment when, from the controul

Of life's long acquiescence in whate'er
Life's faith has been, revolted thoughts prepare
War on man's nature.   When that stillness breaks,
A heart breaks with it, in the shock that shakes
Deep-planted custom, and roots up the hold
Of long-grown habit, and observance old.

From such a stillness in himself, at last,
Licinius raised his voice.   The spasm, that pass'd
Across the quivering features of the man,
Smit by stern speech from lips Olympian,
Vext, as it rose, the staggering voice, down-weigh'd
With heavy meanings hard to express.

II.

He said :
" Immortal gods, by Rome revered ! to me,
A mortal man, revering Rome, did she
This creed bequeath : that to all sons she bears
There is but One Necessity (made theirs
In Rome's requital for a Roman's name)
—Living, or dying, never to know shame :
Never to shrink from pain : never recant
Recorded faith : never be suppliant
For life less noble than 'tis man's to make
Death in the cause which, even tho' gods forsake,
Honour, retain'd, keeps sacred to the last.
This, also, in the records of Rome's Past
My life read once : and read long since, indeed,
Too far to new-live now a new-learn'd creed :
—That, when to all the creatures under heaven
Their severally allotted tasks were given,

On man—man only—the injunction fell,
To do, by daring, the impossible :
That he who doth, tho' dying, dauntless still,
Plant the pale standard of unbaffled Will
On Fate's breach'd battlements, and to the end,
Defeating thus defeat itself, contend
Tenacious in the teeth of tenfold odds,
Uplifts the life he loses to the gods.

"Lies! lies! all lies!   Since gods live careless lives,
Concern'd in nought for which man's being strives.
Justice? men deem'd the image of the mind
Of gods—a mere invention of mankind!
Love?—some blind blood-beat in the veins of youth!
Belief?—man's substitute for knowledge !   Truth ?
—Unknown in Heaven ! Why man, whom you despise,
O'erweening gods, for getting all these lies
By heart in vain, seems nobler after all,
More god-like, than yourselves.
                              " Nor yet, so small,
So slight, so all unworthy, first appear'd
Man's race, but what you gods have interfered
Too much with man's condition to assume
This late indifference to your work—his doom.
Since one thing have you been at pains to do,
—To cheat the chosen fools that trusted you,
False gods, and filch thanksgiving, foully gain'd,
For all whereto the woeful end ordain'd
Was but betrayal.
                         " What ! then, all meant nought ?
All, all, that Delos told and Delphi taught,
Tho' a god spake it ?   All your oracles,
Your priests, your bards, your sacred woods and wells?

Liars of lies! all pledged to cheat man's hope
In gods too careless, or too weak, to cope
With aught man suffers!

                    " Well can I believe
How man's imperfect progress might deceive,
And fail, as 'twere (man's prowess, at the best,
Crippled by means inadequate confess'd!)
The august hopes, by some bright periods
Of his brave promise, in the minds of gods
Inspired. But I, a man, no way can find,
Among the many wanderings of my mind,
To imagine even how gods (whose godheads are
Glorious with power, each perfect as a star)
Should at the last fall short of hopes by them
In man's mind once awaken'd.

                    " Gods, condemn,
Punish man, plague him . . . but forsake him? No!
Not for your own sakes! Lest your godhoods grow,
From long disuse of godlike attributes,
Less lovely even than the life of brutes,
Not being so helpful.

                    " Yet, howe'er that be,
I, at the least, have loved ye, trusted ye,
So long that, tho' for me you fight no more,
Still must I fight for you. 'Twill soon be o'er:
Or one way, or another. Soonest, best,
I think: nor greatly care to know the rest.
One thing's to gain yet—death. No room to range
From what I am! The gods may change, Fate change,
I cannot. Not each casual tomb will fit
The fame a Roman's death consigns to it.
And I for this too-long-continued life
Must find fit end: hew out, with gods at strife,

Tho' sword break, heart break, all break, in the attempt,
Memorial—mournful, but, at least, exempt .
From all incongruous contradiction vile.
Nor is life left me to lament, meanwhile,
Life's failure—frustrate faith, and fruitless deed!
One life, wherewith to fail, or to succeed,
Is man's. One only. I, at my life's end,
Cannot go back to the beginning—mend
What it hath made me—unlove what I loved—
Love what I loathed—condemn what I approved—
New-self myself, to suit occasion new.
The arrow, sped, must still its flight pursue
As first the bowman aim'd it, tho' since then
The bowman shift his ground. Life speeds with men
Even thus. And few can chuse, none change, what's
  done.
A man hath but one mother: and but one
Childhood: one past: one future: but one hearth:
One heart—to give or keep: one heaven: one earth:
And one religion.
    "Yet thus much, tho' spent
His force, and spoil'd his whole life's element,
A man may do: and this, at least, will I!
Ere, quench'd, the fires that shall consume me, die,
I will collect their scatter'd heats, push all
Life's ashes, even while yet the embers fall,
Into a heap, and send the dying flame
Full in Heaven's face!
    "O worthy of thy name,
Loxian Apollo! Boots it to me to know
That men may see thee, as I see thee now,
Far from the life thy beauty doth but wrong,
Calm on the golden summits of Old Song?

No singer I! but a dull soldier: fit
Simply to love a thing, and fight for it,
Or hate a thing, and fight against it.   Vent
My soul in song, I cannot, I! content
To do, at least, what merits to be sung:
Hold fast, when old, the faith I pledged when young:
Live up to it: die for it, if needs be.
What comfort, O Apollo, dwells for me,
Or what for any man, in leave to praise
The life of gods whose life his own betrays?
Their loves, that love him not? their power, that is
The mockery of the weakness they leave his?
Sing no more songs, Apollo, in men's ears!
Leave us, ye gods, in silence to the tears
You understand not!   Spare this much-vext earth
Distracting visions of Heaven's unshared mirth!
This, also, ere I die " . . . . .

III.

                    But there, his heart
Brake the thought in it, sharply; as a dart
Breaks in the effort of a wounded man
To pluck it from the wound.
                    O'er Heaven's face ran
A tremble of white anger: like the light
Of wind-blown stars when, on a winter night,
The howling earth-born gust, that devastates
His own dark birthplace, having burst the grates
Of some grim-pillar'd forest (whose black bars
Release him, groaning) strives against the stars;
Their icy brilliance only kindling thus
To a keener glory.   Eyes contemptuous,

Eyes cruel with calm scorn of all that pain
Which scorch'd his own, burn'd on him. The disdain
Of brows divine, in phalanx infinite
And formidable of transcendent light,
Glow'd from Heaven's depths against him. But all these
Luminous and severe solemnities
He noticed not. For, when the wretched man
First to accuse the assembled gods began,
Love, from the midmost rosy Heaven, where he
Was sporting, stole a-tiptoe, curiously,
Closer at each word, and with listening ear
And troubled countenance, paused, wistful, near
Whence came that voice (among their bright abodes
Anbrosial, then first heard by those glad gods)
Of Human Pain denouncing Heavenly Joy.
And, on the blind face of the beauteous boy
The man's look lightening, as he lifted it
Defiant of whatever it might meet
In Heaven, was caught, and fasten'd where it fell,
By new incentive irresistible
To special indignation. Even as when
In the throng'd circus, from the swarm of men
That hem and hurt him, some wild beast selects
One man, whom suddenly his wrath detects
As most obnoxious, and, in mid assault
On all the others, swiftly swerves, makes halt,
And flies at him that's nearest ; so the man,
From all that hostile cirque Olympian
Selecting Love, cried to him :

IV.

        " Thou immature
And mindless god ! whose smiling sinecure

Is but a blindfold childhood never grown!
Comest thou to mock at what thou hast not known
—Man's full-grown misery at the end of all
The strivings of a life, spent past recall,
Used out, in urging, on its destined way
To dissolution, force that went astray
By struggling upwards?   Such a vapour streams
From altars vainly lit; which, tho' it seems
To go up to the gods, goes nowhere—is
Made nothing, merged in that wide nothingness
Men take for Heaven!   Thou purblind lord of all
Purblindest instincts! thee, not Love I call,
But Lust.   For man's loss, Love must needs be sad:
Lust, with no eyes to see man's loss, is glad,
As thou art.   Yet, since men misname thee Love,
Loose, if thou canst, what, pent in me, doth move
Importunate, as some dumb creature curst
With such a secret as at length must burst
Its heart, endeavouring to be understood.
O Love, if thou be Love, pluck off that hood
That hides thine eyes from human grief.   Revere
Love's last result on earth—a wretch's tear!
Break silence, Love!

           "My spirit whispers me,
That Love, divinest of the gods must be.
Some other Love than thou—whose only joy
Is incapacity of pain, blind boy.
His face I seek among your faces all,
Olympians; and, not finding it, I call
Earth's woe to witness that you do not well,
Being gods, to leave man godless . . . You! that tell,
Smiling the while, as you depart serene,
Me that have loved you, me whose life hath been

Yours, tho' in vain, yours past recovery, here
At that life's cheated end, to now revere
What love of you hath bid me loathe . . . .

                  " Depart,

Fair Forms, forgiven by the injured heart
You have deceived! Apollo, load some star
With liquid music far from earth! Far, far
From eyes worn out with weeping wasted love,
O Venus, guide whatever golden dove
Delights to draw thy lucid wheels!

                " But we?

The men that loved you, and are left ?

                  " Ah me,

What goal to us remains, whose course some Fate
Impels unwilling where no prize can wait
The weary runner?

           " He, that late is come
To rule from your abandon'd thrones the scum
And sewage of that rough-hewn rabble world
Wrought from the ruins of Rome's pride down-hurl'd,
Why comes He now, who comes so late ? He too,
Hath He not all too long connived with you
At man's disaster ? If he love to be
Beloved of men, why so long linger'd He,—
Letting men grow familiar, age by age,
With gods not destined to endure ; engage,
Unwarn'd, to you the homage He now claims
And you resign ; while men, that got your names
By heart, have now no heart left to unlearn
The faith which, sued for ages, given, you spurn ?
Is nothing sure ! Must man's existence be
Barter'd and bandied thus eternally
From god to god ? By each new master made

Pull down in haste what each last master bade
The o'ertask'd drudge build up with toil intense?
Oh, for some voice Love's sanction to dispense
To Life's endeavour! oh for one, but one,
Of all you gods, whose forms I gaze upon
With grief left godless, to assure at last
This else-wrong'd spirit, that, in despite the Past,
Which fail'd in power, the Present, by despair
Darken'd, the Future, desolate and bare,
It did not ill to trust an instinct, wrong'd
Not seldom, oft rebuked, but yet prolong'd
Thro' strangling hinderance and confounding chance;
Which, fronting Heaven with constant countenance,
Would whisper, ' I am love, and love is there,
And love to love is kindred everywhere!'
But which of all the gods can do this?"

PART VI

THE FUTURE. ,

I.

"I!"

Love answer'd; and sprang forth with such a cry
As paled, beneath their golden porches, all
The rosy lords of that Ambrosial Hall.
Olympus groan'd aghast beneath the sound,
Whereto the throbbing universe all round
Responded with a million echoes wild
Of awful joy.

II.

For lo! the glorious child,
By one transcendent moment's mighty throe,

Full-statured sprang into the new-born glow
Of his superlative godhead. His right hand
Wrench'd from his lustrous orbs the blinding band
That had for ages held their lordly light
From flooding heaven and earth with infinite
And all-transforming splendour. Faint and wan
Wax'd all the lesser lights Olympian
In the sunrise of that surpassing gaze :
Like their own orbs. Mars, with diminisht rays,
Reddening receded to what seem'd at last
A single spot of angry fire in fast
Increasing distance. Like a happy tear
About to fall, Venus, a trembling sphere
All pale in rosy air, descended slow.
Of Phœbus rested nothing but a glow
Of solemn gladness on heaven's serene face.
Even Jove himself, in that expanding space
Love's ever-greatening glory lit, became
No brighter than his own broad star, whose flame
Burns lone on night's far frontier.

III.

In amaze,
Beneath the Face whereon he dared not gaze
The man, prostrated, fell. In whose thrill'd ears
A voice rang, musical as moving spheres :
" The sound of Human Sorrow heard in Heaven
Immortal love to mortal life hath given :
Whereby in grief of life is growth of love.
Arise ! On Earth below, in Heaven above,
Part of all creeds, and every creed surviving,
The Ever-loving is the Ever-living.

Heavenly and Human both : which, thro' man's eyes
Forever gazing upward, to Heaven cries,
'Behold me, Father!' and from Heaven anon
Down gazing cries to Earth 'Behold me, Son!'
Arise, and follow where Love leads."

IV.

                                        The man
Arose : and, guided by the Voice, began
To ascend that solemn mountain.   Changed was all
Its aspect.   Gone the Olympian Festival!
Gone all the rosy revellers!   Rough the road
With raunce and bramble, where once breathed and
      glow'd
The clear-cupp'd cistus and bright asphodel.
And lo, where last each golden goblet fell,
A grinning skull!   On the sharp summit seem'd,
Where late Olympian Jove's bright throne had beam'd,
Some dim stupendous image, looming thro'
Red morn's dull mist, and lurid in the dew,
Till at its foot the god-led mortal stood :
Then on his brow fell drops of human blood
From a great Cross, wide-arm'd, that o'er him spread.

V.

He shrank, indignant.
                        Music o'er his head,
Like a light bird, came fluttering.   And again,
To that light music lured, in mistlike train,
From rosiest air's remotest inmost deep,
Troop'd—dim and beautiful, as dreams that creep

Under the sweet lids of a sleeping child,
On whose wet lashes tears, tho' reconciled
With trouble soon dismiss'd, are trembling new—
The old Olympians. Wreaths of every hue,
Fresh-pluckt from bowers of never-fading Thought
In Memory's dewiest meadow-deeps, they brought;
Wherewith to deck that darkling Cross. Whereon
The Past's pale blossom-bearers every one,
Each as he came, fresh garlands hung. Till, lo!
The Cross in flowers—the flowers themselves—the flow
Of flower-bearers—all, began to fade
In ever-deepening light.

VI.

Love, only, staid.
Yet Love's self changed. Whose form, expanding, seem'd,
To him on whose awed gaze its glory beam'd,
To absorb into itself all things that were.
Heaven's farthest stars were glittering in His hair:
All winds of heaven His breathing loosed or bound:
His voice became an ever-murmuring sound,
The sound of generations of mankind:
Shut in His hand, the nations humm'd: Time twined
About His feet its creeping growths; which took
From Him the life-sap of the leaves that shook
Light shadows from His glory.

VII.

Mute with awe,
And lost in light, Licinius mused. He saw
v.   E

His own life, suddenly, as when, thro' rain
And streaming tempest, on a blasted plain
An instantaneous sunbeam strikes.

VIII.

                 Even then,
Even while the vision broaden'd on his ken,
A sudden trumpet sounded as in scorn
From the dark camps.   .

          It was the battle morn.

GENSERIC.

GENSERIC, King of the Vandals, who, having laid waste
    seven lands,
From Tripolis far as Tangier, from the sea to the Great
    Desert sands,
Was lord of the Moor and the African,—thirsting anon
    for new slaughter,
Sail'd out of Carthage, and sailed o'er the Mediter-
    ranean water ;
Plunder'd Palermo, seized Sicily, sack'd the Lucanian
    coast,
And paused, and said, laughing, " Where next ? "
                Then there came to the Vandal a Ghost
From the Shadowy Land that lies hid and unknown in
    the Darkness Below.
And answer'd, " To Rome ! "
                Said the King to the Ghost,
  " And whose envoy art thou ?
Whence comest thou ? and name me his name that hath
    sent thee : and say what is thine."
" From far : and His name that hath sent me is God,"
    the Ghost answer'd, " and mine
Was Hannibal once, ere thou wast : and the name that
    I now have is Fate.
But arise, and be swift, and return. For God waits,
    and the moment is late."

And " I go," said the Vandal.   And went.

         When at last to the gates he was come,
Loud he knock'd with his fierce iron fist.   And full
    drowsily answer'd him Rome.
" Who is it that knocketh so loud ?   Get thee hence.
    Let me be.   For 'tis late."
" Thou art wanted," cried Genseric.   " Open ! His
    name that hath sent me is Fate.
And mine, who knock late, Retribution."

         Rome gave him her glorious things :
The keys she had conquer'd from kingdoms: the
    crowns she had wrested from kings :
And Genseric bore them away into Carthage, avenged
    thus on Rome,
And paused, and said, laughing, " Where next ?"

        And again the Ghost answer'd him, " Home !
For now God doth need thee no longer."

        " Where leadest thou me by the hand ?"
Cried the King to the Ghost. And the Ghost answer'd,
    " Into the Shadowy Land."

IRENE.

"Ye have done it unto me."
Matt. xxv. 40.

I.

THE moonlight lay like hoar frost on the earth
Outside.   But, all within, the marble hearth
Made from its dropping logs of scented wood
A rosy dimness of warm light, to flood
With fervid interchange of gloom and gleam
That gorgeous chamber,—from the mad moonbeam
Curtain'd secure.   No other light was there.
The outer halls were silent everywhere.
Midnight.   And in the bed where he was born,
I' the Porphyry Chamber at Byzance, outworn
By seventeen years of pleasure without joy,
Not yet a man, albeit no more a boy,
His flusht check heavy on the fragrant sheet,
Slept Constantine the Porphyrogenete ;
When glided in his mother leonine,
Irene.

II.

She, reluctant to resign
To her own whelp that prey beneath her paw,
The bloody Empire, stealthily 'gan draw

The crimson curtain ; with keen ear down-bent
To count the breathings, thick and indolent,
Of her recaptured cub : who, sleeping, smiled,
By visions lewd of folly and lust beguiled.
Anon, she beckon'd to the unshut door :
Whence, crafty-footed, down the glassy floor
Crept to her side (with wither'd features white
Bow'd o'er a trembling lamp) her parasite,
Storax, the lean-lipp'd, low-brow'd Logothete.

III.

" Set the lamp down," the mother mutter'd.   " Sweet
Must be his dreams.   My son is smiling . . . see !
Wake him not, Storax ! "   Then, while softly she
Let fall the curtain, he from out its sheath
Slided his dagger, pusht the flame beneath
The weapon's point, and watch'd with moody eye
The heated metal reddening.
                              O'er the high
Bed-head (to safeguard sleeping Cæsars, slung
Slant from the golden sculptured cornice) hung
On dismal ebon cross limbs, carven keen
In livid ivory, of a stretch'd-out, lean,
And ever-dying Christ.

IV.

                         . . . His white lips set
Fast with a formidable will, while yet
Storax, who turn'd and turn'd it slowly, scann'd
The reddening steel, Irene's rapid hand,
With restless finger o'er her pucker'd brow
Flitting, made airy crosses in a row.

Her eyes had settled sullenly upon
The superimpending image of God's Son :
And Habit,—that hard mock-bird of the mind,
Whose tongue, to chance-got utterance confined,
Memories by chance recaptured out of place
Set talking out of season,—to the Face
Mechanic response making, "*If thine eye
Offend thee, pluck it out,*" she mutter'd. "Ay,
That is sound Gospel," Storax in her ear
Whisper'd. "The thing is white-hot now . . . See
    here!"
"And I am Empress" . . . hiss'd Irene . . . "Smite!"

v.

The arm'd Armenian on the guard that night
About the palace precincts somnolent,
Where, like a weary beetle, came and went
Across the flinty platform,—else dead-dumb—
The slumbrous city's desultory hum,
Heard, pacing drowsy-cold (his watch nigh done)
Beneath the stars, thro' shrivelling silence run
A sudden scream, fierce, devilish, agonized,
Of quintessential pain ; and all surprised,
Started upon the watch,—waiting what sound
Should follow. But that dreadful cry, soon drown'd
In dreadful silence, response none uproused,
Save of an owlish echo half unhoused
Among the moody towers, that down again
With churlish mumblings in her mason'd den
Settled to slumber.
        Then the soldier said,
Laughing at the discovery he had made

Of what, to *him* at least, that sound meant, "So!
To-morrow, and the amphoræ shall flow.
Increase of pay to all the Armenian Guard!"
Whereat he turn'd, and (while i' the east, black-barr'd
With lazy clouds, slow-oozed a watery light)
Waited, well pleased, the trump of dawn.

VI.

                                    . That night,
In league with Hell, ere morning streak'd the skies,
Left all its darkness in the misused eyes
Of Constantine the Porphyrogenete:
—The shadow of a shadow, forced to fleet
Out of the glare that gave him in men's sight
The semblance of a substance once.

VII.

                                    That night,
Irene, ere the Porphyry Chamber (pale
With strife wherein to triumph is to fail)
She left triumphant, glancing back,—her glance
Fell casual on the conscious countenance
Of that white Christ upon the black cross spread,
Whose eyes, into the now-close-curtain'd bed
Erewhile down-gazing, had beheld why those
Tight draperies round it had been twitch'd so close.
And lo! where late those witnesses had been,
Instead of eyes, two gory sockets, seen
Thro' the red firelight, stopp'd her, stagger'd her,
And to a Fear, wherefrom she dared not stir,
Fasten'd and froze her.
                        For a while she stood
As one that, traversing a solitude

Where nothing dwells but Danger (all in haste
To reach the end, and, after peril faced
And pass'd, proclaim "The deed I dared is done!")
Turns, by ill chance, midway, to gaze upon
Some hideous gulf in safety cross'd; and so,
Seeing how deep the death that yawns below,
By unanticipated terror, just
In the fresh moment of achievement, thrust
Into the suddenly-suggested jaws
Of an imaginary failure, draws
Breath faint and fainter; forced to keep in sight
His own success, which, seen, defeats him quite.
But, soon return'd, the exasperated will,
Still strong to scourge the rebel senses, still
Defiant tho' dismay'd, with effort fierce
Pluck'd up the keen-cold Fear that seem'd to pierce
Her feet, and fix them to the floor, beneath
That eyeless gaze.   And at the sculptured wreath
Above the unblest bed wherefrom It hung
She, like a wounded cat o' the mountain, sprung,
And caught, and gripp'd, and tugg'd, and tore away,
And crouch'd with glaring face above, her prey,
—God's Image.
                    Still that dreadful dearth of eyes
In the dread Face!
                    With fierce and bitter cries
She dasht It sharp against the marble floor,
And bruised It with wild feet.
                    Still as before
The Eyeless Face implied . . . "Do what thou wilt
Henceforth, and hug thy gain, or hide thy guilt,
Never shalt thou behold God's eyes."
                    She snatch'd

And hurl'd It on the smouldering hearth : and watch'd
The embers quicken round It : heap'd up wood,
And made the blaze leap high : and all night stood
Feeding the flame : till all was burn'd away
To ashes.
         And ere this was done, the day
Began to dawn.

VIII.

         Afterwards, she became
One of the world's chief rulers.   Her fair name
Was praised in all the churches.   God's priests pray'd
God to safeguard the mighty throne she made
Illustrious.
         Three times,—in the hippodrome
Once, in the palace once, once 'neath the dome
O' the high cathedral,—the Estates took oath
After this fashion . . . " Witness Christ ! we both
Swear, on the Gospels Four, to guard the throne
Of our Liege Lady, Thine anointed one,
Irene, and swear also, bearing leal
Allegiance to her person, for her weal
And in her service, ever to oppose
Our lives against the persons of her foes."
This on the wood of the True Cross they swore.
And their recorded oath, with many more,
Among the relics of the Saintly Dead,
On the main altar was deposited
In St. Sophia.
         Four Patricians, proud
So to be seen of the applausive crowd,
Held in their hands the golden reins of four
White horses, pacing in high pomp before

Her festive chariot, when Irene pass'd
Along the loud streets, greeted by the vast
Vociferation of a land's applause.

IX.

To all the Roman world she set wise laws.
Men praised her wisdom.   Wealth was hers immense.
Men praised her splendour and munificence.
Alms to the poor her hand distributed.
Men praised her bounty.   High she held her head
Amid the tempests of a turbulent time.
Men praised her courage.   Cruelty and crime
She scourged with scorpions.   Men her justice praised.
Gifts to the Church she gave, and altars raised.
Men praised her piety.   She in the West
Treaties proposed and embassies addrest
To Charlemagne.   She in the East maintain'd
On equal terms alliance undisdain'd
With great Haroun Alraschid.   " For," said she,
" We understand each other's worth, We Three."
The world, when speaking of her, said, " The Great."

X.

At last her fortune changed.
                              For 'twas her fate
To win a worthier title.   So, one night,
The eunuchs of her palace,—slaves whose spite
Her power had scorn'd,—conspiring its downfall,
Pluck'd the throne from her : seized her treasures all :
And drave her forth from power and wealth, to be
An exile and a pauper.
                        Meekly she

Surrender'd what she had so proudly worn,
Rome's Purple.   And, retiring from men's scorn
To Mitylene, lived there, lone and poor:
A careworn woman at the cottage door
Spinning for bread.
                    The world was sad to see
What it had done, then.   Men remorsefully
Remember'd, not her many evil deeds,
But her few good ones.   For who counts the weeds
In any garden where, tho' desolate,
One rose remains?   And, much admiring fate
So bitter borne so blameless of complaint,
The world, when speaking of her, said, "The Saint."

XI.

And after all these things, at the late end
Of a long life, she died.

XII.

                    Then priests to send
Pilgrims to deck her tomb made haste.   They came
Bare-footed, chanting hymns unto her name,
And made a noise of praise above her bones,
Which waked her spirit in the grave.

XIII.

                    Old tones
Of some glad tune, first heard long years ago,
When to their music life went gladly too,
If heard once more when life, after long years,
Goes not at all, but rests, in him that hears

Awaken thus the wild unwonted spasm
Of life's long-buried old enthusiasm.
Earth under earth, the earthly instinct, raised
By earthly praises in the corpse thus praised,
Return'd to life.
     She rose i' the tomb, and said,
"Open! and let me forth. I am not dead.
For men yet praise me, and their praises give
My joy thereat assurance that I live."
And the tomb answer'd, in its own dumb way,
"I neither know the living, nor obey
Their voice."
    The pious pilgrims above ground,
Their rites perform'd, departing now,—the sound
Of human praise about that tomb wax'd faint,
Then silent.
    "Ay," she mused, "a Saint? . . . a Saint
Should seek, not men, but God." She stood before
The creviced hinge of the tomb's granite door
And struck it with dead hands, and said again,
"Door of the Tomb, since I have done with men,
Show me the way to God."
     The sullen door
Answer'd, "I am the Door o' the Tomb. No more.
Find thou the way."

XIV.

    Even then, an awful light,
Not of this world, thro' chink and crevice (bright.
With brightness as of burning fire that turns
Whatever thing the burning of it burns
Into its sifted elemental worth:
Substance to spirit, ashes unto earth)
Smote all the inner darkness where she stood.

XV.

Whereby she saw, outstretch'd upon the rood
The Image of the Christ (by Human Faith
Placed there in token of life's trust in death),
And on her soul the sudden memory came
Like hope . . . "I am The Way!"

      Who said the same
Was There i' the Tomb.

     To Whom she, kneeling, said,
"Teach me, O Christ (if I, indeed, be dead)
The way . . . Thou seest . . . ."

     A Voice replied, "To Me
Woman, give back mine eyes that I may see!"
She dared not answer : dared not gaze upon
The Face Above.

XVI.

    That moment's light was gone
Even as it came.   Darkness return'd.

       The rest,
Hid in that darkness, never shall be guess'd.

THE SIEGE OF CONSTANTINOPLE.

A CHRONICLE OF THE FALL OF THE GREEK EMPIRE.

IN FOUR PARTS.

" 'Ει δε πεπόνθατε δεινά δι 'ὑμετερὴν κακότητα,
Μή τι Θεδῖς τούτῳν μδιραν ἐπαμφέρετε.
Αυτοὶ γὰρ τόυτους ηὐξησατε ῥυσια δοντες,
Καὶ διὰ ταῦτα κακὴν ἔσχετε δουλοσύνην."

Nicetas.

PART I.

" La vint al Comte, si comme dit
Vn Danziaus, ki ioenes estoit
A qui toute Gresse appendoit,
Par son Oncle ies deseritès
Et de chastiaus & de citès.
  Alexis ot nom, mult fu biaus,
Bien enseniés iere le Danziaus:

*   *   *   *   *

Conté li a tot son afaire,
Et li Quens ki bien li vot faire,
Li fist jurer le sairement,
Kil en iroit tout voirement
A quan qu'il poroit outremer
Auec lui s'il puet recouurer
Sa tierre, & tant faire li sache
Que couronne porter li face."

PHILIPPES MOUSKES.

I.

THE EMPEROR ISAAC

In gold Byzantium, girt with purple seas,
Isaac is Emperor, and reigns at ease.[1]
For, if he smiles, a swarm of gilded slaves
Smiles also, grateful for the grace that saves

Their fortunes one day longer : if he frowns,
Spears sparkle on the walls of frighten'd towns,
And half the East is darken'd : if he sleeps,
The soul of Music o'er his slumber keeps
Melodious vigil, and, down lucid floors
Of marble chambers vast, at sighing doors
Dusk faces watch, while long-hair'd large-eyed girls
Crouch at his pillow fringed with dropping pearls.
Proud to up-prop his throne, four lions—four
Large bulks of blazing gold—crook evermore
Their wrinked backs.   For him the murex dies
In Tyrrhene nets.   For him, 'neath golden skies,
In gorgeous cluster, all those glittering isles
That circle Delos, where the sun first smiles,
Broider the sea's blue breast with beauty rare.
For him, thro' valleys cool'd with shadowy air,
The Phrygian shepherd leads his numerous flocks.
His are the towers on Hellespontine rocks,
And his the hill-built citadels that crown
Morean bays, by many a mountain town.
For him, from antique Thessaly's witch-lands
Sweet sorceries breathe.   For him, the hardy bands
Of snowy Thrace, a multitude of spears,
March with the Macedonian mountaineers.
From strong Durazzo's battlemented steep
To sultry Tarsus, and Malmistra, sweep
His glowing realms ; and to his sway respond
All Anatolia's tribes, from Trebizond
Far as the Syrian Gates.   His standards float
And flash athwart Pamphylian shores remote,
Throng all Meander's many-winding stream,
And in blue Asian weather blaze supreme
From ancient cities, proud and populous,

O'ertopping temples white in Ephesus,
Sardes, and Smyrna, and among the groves
The swarthy-faced Laödicean loves,
Or where, in Philadelphia's teeming squares,
The turban'd trader spreads his silken wares.
The glories of old Rome, by all the line
Of Latin Cæsars left to Constantine,
Blaze in his eyes, to make him glad and great.
Red Asia doth green Europe emulate
Which with most lavish hand shall treasures heap
Within his palace gates.   All sails, that sweep
The waters of the world and every shore,
Meet in his harbours.   Princely Pages pour
For him the Chian and the Lesbian wine
In agate cups and vases crystalline,[2]
Wrought first in Rome, when thro' the Triumph Gate
Pompeïus came from the conquering Mithridate.
For him, on gems and jasper stones is writ
The Arab wisdom, and the Persic wit.
For him, Greek Monks, in Thracian convents cold,
Guard Homer's songs on parchments graved with gold.
To nourish this one man a million starve.:
And on his tables kingborn butlers carve
The quadripartite globe : earth, sea, and air,
Are devastated for his daily fare.
To serve him, twice ten thousand eunuchs stand,
Who start, if he but nod, or wave his hand.
Daily, his Prophet, whom for smiling views
He pays with Patriarchal revenues,
Prophesies to him of ease, pleasantness,
And length of days, glory, and great success,
And realms extended from Euphrates far[3]
As where the Lebanonian cedars are.

v.   F

The grandeur of the East and of the West
Glows in his galleries.   He is potent, blest,
Supreme.   He hath two bloodhounds in a leash,
Terror, and Force : two slaves that serve his wish,
Pleasure, and Pomp.

II.

IS SAD;

Yet, in despite of all,
The Emperor Isaac sits in his vast hall
An undelighted man.   To him all meat
Is tasteless, and all sweetnesses unsweet :
To him all beauty is unbeautiful,
All pleasures without pleasantness, and dull
Each day's delights.   His women and his wine
Nauseate the sense they sate not.   His lamps shine
In cedarn chambers, ceil'd with gold, as gleam
Corpse-lights in charnels.   Music's strenuous stream
Of pining sounds makes passionatest pain
About his joyless heart, and jaded brain.
So harsh an echo in the hollowness
Within him dwells, that echo to suppress
He, if he could, would make the whole world mute.
He curses both the fluteplayer and the flute :
He strikes both lyre and lyrist to the ground :
The silence is less tolerable than sound.
For men's praise undeserved, the pain assign'd
To this praised man is scorn of all mankind.
To please him, Age its reverend form foregoes,
And wrinkled panders for his public shows
Invent new vices.   At his least of looks
Manhood forsakes his manliness, and crooks

Beneath a truculent foot a slavish neck.
White-fronted Womanhood, if he but beck,
Wallows in shame, unshamed; while Youth, to charm
His fancy, all the Virtues doth disarm,
Disgracing all the Graces. And, for this,
He hates Man, Woman, Youth, and Age. No bliss
In youthfulness, no dignity in years,
Men to this man, by man adored, endears:
Because his greatness, being of a kind
That grows from all men's littleness combined,
Dwells self-condemn'd among the multitude
Of voices lifted to proclaim it good,
And tongues that lick the dust, and knees that fall,
And backs that cringe before its pedestal.
Him all these immense means to make him glad,
Misused immensely, make immensely sad.

III.

AND SO IS HIS BROTHER ALEXIUS: WHO PROPOSES

Beside the Emperor sits the Emperor's brother:
Companions, one as joyless as the other,
And soul-distemper'd both:—the first, with what
He hath; the second, that he hath it not.
So, turning to Alexius, with dull eyes
By dull eyes met, Isaac the Emperor sighs,
" How things desired, and had, desire destroy!
How hard it is, enjoyment to enjoy!
Advise us, Brother, how may Pleasure borrow
Some new disguise to fool the querulous Morrow
From his foreseen reproval of To-day?"
Whereto Alexius:

" I have oft heard say

That more wild beasts than men be left in Thrace.
Wherefore " . . .

      " The chase ! " the Emperor cries, " the chase ? "
A happy thought !   Such sleep as nightly flies
The silken couch where Ease, uneasy, lies,
Perchance kind Nature charitably drops
On wearied limbs from perilous mountain tops.
And ancient poets say that pure Content
Was never yet in crowded city pent.
She, with young Health, her hardy child, they say
After the shadows of the clouds doth stray,
Or near the nibbling flocks by grassy dells,
And, bee-like, feeds at eve in myrtle bells
On little drops of dew, deliciously
As the fair Queen of Fays.   I know not, I,
If that be true : but this I know full well,
That not in any palace where I dwell,
—Neither beneath Blachernæ's sculptured roofs,
Nor in Boucoleon, where my horses' hoofs,
Shod with red gold, strike echoes musical
From porphyry pavements in a silver stall,—
This Phantom hath her haunt.   We'll try the woods,
Wild-water'd glens, and savage solitudes ;
And, if she hide with Echo in her cave,
We'll rouse her ; if with Naiads in the wave,
We'll plunge to find her ; tho' black Death should leap
From out the lair whence she may chance to peep.
The chase to-morrow morn ! "

VI.

A PARTY OF PLEASURE,

                The morrow morn
At sunrise, to the sound of fife and horn,

Byzantium's spacious marble wharves, from stair
To stair, with broider'd cloths, and carpets rare
Of crimson seam'd and rivell'd rough with gold,
A train of swarthy servants spread and fold,
For the proud treading of Imperial feet,
Down to the granite pedestals ; where meet
Thick myrtle boughs, and oleanders flush
The green-lit lymph.   There, little galleys push
Their golden prows beneath the glossy dark
Of laurel leaves ; and many a pleasure-bark
Lolls in the sun, with streaming bandrol bright,
And gorgeous canopies, that shut soft light
Under soft shadow.   Suddenly, shrill sounds
The brazen music, and the baying hounds
Drag sideways at the hunter's hand.   The drums
Throb to the screaming trumpet.

        And forth comes
The Emperor.
      Then his courtiers : then his slaves.

At sunset, to the wilds beyond the waves
They came : light revellers arm'd with bow and spear,
Cinct for the chase, and gay with hunting gear.
With silk pavilions gleam the lonely glens,
Glad of their unaccustom'd denizens
That shout across dark tracts of starry weather.
To grassy tufts young grooms, light-laughing, tether
Sleek-coated steeds.   And, where the bubbled brooks
Leap under rushy brinks, white-turban'd cooks
In silver vessels plunge the purple wine.
Within the tents, the lucid tables shine
(Under soft lamps from burning odours lit)
With sumptuous viands ; and young wassailers sit,

With heated faces femininely fair,
And holiday arms thick-sheathed with jewels rare,
Babbling of battles.   Round the mountain lawn
The sportive court leans, propp'd on skins of fawn,
And quilts thick-velveted of foreign fur,
Marten, and zibeline, and miniver,[5]
Brought by the barbarous fair-hair'd folk that come
Blithe from the north star, where they have their home
Among the basalt rocks, and starry caves
Stalactical, and walk upon the waves
Sandall'd with steel.   Low-sounding angelots
Sprinkle light music in among the knots
Of laughing boys that tinkle cups of gold
Round heaps of grapes, and rough-globed melons cold,
And purple figs.   There, down the glimmering green,
Half-naked dance, with tossing tambourine,
Greek girls, whose flusht and panting limbs flash bare
Across the purple glooms.
                              At dawn, they dare
The distant crags, and storm the savage woods.
Then, all day long, thro' slumbrous solitudes,
Flit the sweet ghosts of glad and healthful sounds
Scatter'd from fairy horns, and flying hounds :
And, in and out, among the thickets lone
The dazzling tumult darts; as, one by one,
Thro' bosk and brake, gay-gilded dragon-flies
Flash, and are gone.   When mellow daylight dies,
Well-pleased, they bear their shaggy burthen back
To the silken camp, adown the mountain track,
And roast the bristly boar; and quaff and laugh,
And sing, and ring the goblets gay ; till, half
Drowsed, and half roused again by rosy wine,
They drink, and wink, and sink at last supine

On the fresh herbage by their watchfires red;
While the wind wakes the gloomy woods o'erhead
Unnoticed, and unnoticed, now and then,
Some distant roarings from the rocky glen.
So pass the days, the nights : so pass the weeks,
The months.

v.

WHICH ENDS UNPLEASANTLY.

At length, the Emperor upbreaks
His wandering camp.   Of wood and mountain tired,
Town-life he deems once more to be desired.
Aye, from illusion to illusion tost,
Men seek new things, to prize things old the most.
Life wastes itself by wishing to be more,
And turns to froth and scum whilst bubbling o'er.
Thus, having all things, save the joy they give,
The Imperial pauper still is fain to live
For means of life (which nothing known supplies)
Dependent on the charity of surprise.
Sick as he went, he to Byzance returns,
There, from the warders on the walls he learns
That his bold brother, whom (while he the chase
Pursued) himself had charged to hold his place,
Is pleased to keep it ; which the soldiery, bought,
Are pleased to sanction ; and the people, taught
That Power in Place is Power where it should be,
Pleased, or displeased, obedient bow the knee.
'Tis idle knocking at your own house-door
When your own house-dog knows your voice no more.
Fly, or be bitten !

Flying all alone,

(Friendless, being powerless) into Macedon,
—A fugitive from his own guards, the scorn
Of his tame creatures, turn'd on, hunted, torn
By his own bandogs, Isaac—yesterday
Lord paramount of half a world, great, gay,
Glorious, and strong,—to-day, a something less
Than all earth's common kinds of wretchedness,—
Fled from the refuse of himself; but, caught,
And back a prisoner to Byzantium brought,
They dropp'd him down a dungeon.

VI.

OUT OF THE LIGHT, INTO THE DARK.

Four wet walls:
Round which the newt, his sickly housemate, crawls
To criticise, and, being abhorr'd, abhor
What men had crown'd, and surnamed Emperor,
And tremblingly admired. A mouldy crust,
Some muddy water, once a day downthrust
Into this putrid pit, still keep aware
The nameless human thing forgotten there
That it is wretched, and alive in spite
Of wretchedness. In nothingness and night
This nothing lives; cast out of Life, flung back
By Death, unpitied. And, to make more black
The blackness that is there to blot it out,
The new-made Emperor beckon'd from the rout
Of smiling and of crawling creatures,—things
That do ill-make, and are ill-made by, kings,
Feeders of infamy, and fed by it,—
One that most smiled, and lowest crawl'd, to fit
His master's humour: unto whom he said

"Our Brother hath two eyes yet in his head,⁶
Worth nothing now to him, worth much to me.
Get them away from him, and thou shalt be
The gainer by his loss."
                        This deed was done.
They left him in the dark.

VII.

ALEXIUS THE YOUNGER FLIES FROM ALEXIUS THE ELDER,

                        He hath a son,
This miserable remnant of man's being
That lives and hath no life,—unseen, unseeing!
God gave him both a brother and a son,
And both men name Alexius.   And the one
Is Emperor now, and reigns, where he once reign'd,
In bright Byzance; and drains, as he once drain'd,
In agate cups, from vases crystalline,
Careless, the Chian and the Lesbian wine,
By princes pour'd; for him, the murex dies
In Tyrrhene nets: for him, green Europe vies
With tawny Asia, to extol his state:
For him those twice ten thousand eunuchs wait
In whisperous halls: for him, the Thracian spears
March with the Macedonian mountaineers:
And him men praise.
            .   Meanwhile, the other flees,⁷
'Scaped from his clutch, across the great salt seas,
And thanks kind heaven's rough winds that blow so
        rude
Upon his cheek.   Among the multitude,
In seaman's garb, he, gliding secret, found
A Venice galley for Sicilia bound:

And, thence, thro' many lands, for many years,
Wandering in search of succour from his peers,
The exiled Prince draws far in foreign climes
The breath of life; and broods upon the times.

VIII.

AND TRIES HIS FORTUNES AND HIS FRIENDS.

But Greatness, God keeps fast upon its throne,
Is ever prompt full greatly to disown
Greatness by God struck down.
      The Pope is wise,
Humane, and just.
     The Pope the Prince first plies [8]
With the sad story of his sire's distress.
And "*Pax vobiscum!*" sighs His Holiness.
"*Leonem, Optime, mox conculcabis*"
Urges the Prince, "*me quoque liberabis
De laqueo venantium.*"
      Whereunto
The Pontiff:
   "*Cælum dedit Domino,
Hominum autem terram filiis.*
Schismatics, also, are ye Greeks, I wis."
And still the Prince:
     "O Holy Father, stay!
The Greek shall to the Latin rite give way,
If Latin arms the Grecian throne recover."

"Another time, my son, we'll talk this over.
Festina lente. Vale!" sighs the Pope,
And waives him off.
    He nurses yet his hope

And flees to Germany.

> In Germany
> Philip is Kaiser; and by craft holds high
> A brow serene above the brawling crowd,
> —Fine-balanced on Fate's pinnacle, and proud.
> And Kaiser Philip hath, in summers fled,
> Irene, sister to Alexius, wed: [9]
> And Kaiser Philip doth with deep concern
> The fallen fortunes of his kinsman learn:
> Concern'd the more, that he just now can spare
> Nor men, nor money; since his rival there,
> The lynx-eyed Otho, lurking for a spring,
> Crouches hard by, and troubles everything.
> The times are wild.

> Meanwhile, the Red Cross Lords [10]
> (Five hundred sail, and thrice ten thousand swords)
> In Zara halt, the new Crusade to plan.
> And thither wends the Prince.

IX.

A GREAT MAN

> Venetian [11]
> Dandolo, Doge elect, and Amiral,
> And Captain, sits in solemn council hall.
> His long beard, lustrous with the spotless snows
> Of more than fourscore winters, amply flows
> To hide the angry jewel, clasp'd with gold,
> That firmly doth his heavy mantle hold.
> Cover'd he sits. Above his blind bald brow
> The Ducal bonnet (Tintoret shows ye how)

Glows like a sunset glory on the scalp
Of some sublime and thunder-scathèd alp.
And the furr'd velvets o'er his breastplate fall
In folded masses, as majestical
As honours on the manhood of the man.
Soon may ye tell, if ye his posture scan,
By the grand careless calmness of the way
His mantle laps and hangs, that in the play
Of this world's business he hath ever been
Chief actor, chosen for each foreground scene;
Whence, living is to him a stately thing
Made easy by long wont of governing.
Those deep blind eyes for Venice' sake burn'd out!
Since he, whom Venice fear'd, most fear'd, no doubt,
Those eyes. The firm fine features of that face,
In strength so delicate, so strong in grace!
All those augustest opposites that mix
In some superlative character, to fix
With one strong soul, and grace with one fit frame,
Man's evanescent elements, became
Associate ministers to this man's will.
—The symbols of the valley and the hill:
The storm, the eagle, and the cataract,—
Passions, and powers that passionately act;
The streamlet, and the vineleaf in the sun,—
Graces that gracious influence acts upon;
Meet in the aspect of that bended head.
And the great Lion of St. Mark doth spread
His mighty wings above the baldachin
That decks the throne; mute 'mid the trumpet's din,
Claiming his own.
            The smooth and spacious floors
Are open-porch'd. Thro' airy corridors

You mark the marshall'd heralds, station'd calm
About the broad stone platform, bathed in balm
Of blissful weather, and the warm noon-light.
Down the sloped hill, the streeted city white
Hums populous.   The sea-breeze, blowing in,
Flutters gay flags in harbours Zaratin ;
Heaving on balustraded ramparts wide,
And at high casements, throng'd and balconied,
Thick streams of many-colour'd silken scarves,
And, all about the warmèd quays and wharves,
The sea is strown with snowy sails, by swarms
Of high-deck'd galleys, from whose prows the arms
Of heroes hang, and low-hull'd palanders.[12]

X.

AND SOME NOTABLE MEN.[13]

Meanwhile, among his council-keeping Sers,
The great Doge greets from his unenvied throne
The Barons, striding inwards, one by one,
From that bright background, and the golden noon,
Like banded forms on Byzant frescoes.   Soon
The hall is cramm'd.   Below the high daïs sit
Peers, princes, prelates, paladins ;
                                        To wit :—
The conqueror of Asti, Boniface,
Marquis of Montferrat ; who with his mace
Can brain a bull.   When Theöbald, their chief,
Count of Champagne, left Christendom in grief,
Dying untimely, and dispute arose
About the headship, him the Barons chose
(Favour'd by fame, tho' foreign to the Franks)
As Dux and Daysman of the Red Cross ranks.

Baldwin ; whose dreams are of a diadem,
Since last the Turks have tugg'd Jerusalem
From Lusignan ; content to wait meanwhile
As Count of Flanders, till his fortunes smile :
Him, also, Hainault's hardy race respect,
Scion of Charlemagne by line direct,
And cousin to the Royalty of France.
Beside him, having broken his last lance
At Bruges, in that great tourney, when the twain
First cross'd their shields, Count Henry, with his train
Of Flanders knights.   Sir Guy, the Gascon ; grim,
Grey, gaunt, as on the Pyrenæan rim
His own three cloudy border castles are,
Held fast for his White Heiress of Navarre,
Daughter of good King Sance, surnamed The Wise,
Blanche with the golden hair and holy eyes,
Whose husband, Theöbald, last year expired
In the fond arms of Friar Fulk, admired
By weeping Barons ; but bewail'd the most
By that stout servant of the Red Cross host,
Geoffroy of Ville-Hardouïn, Lord of Bar
And Arcis, and the hill-side country far
As Troyes, and both the blossom-bearing banks
Of Aube ; Ambassador of all the Franks,
And Marshal of Champagne.   Miles, Lord of Brie.
Geoffroy de Joinville.   And those Gautiers three
Of Vignory, Montbeliard, and Brienne.
Roger de Marche.   Bernard de Somerghen.
William, surnamed The Red ; Lord Advocate
Of Arras, Seigneur of Bethune ; whose straight
Strong amber locks, like haum, in heaps half smother
His heavy brow.   And Conon, his boy-brother.
Renier de Trit.   And Jaen, the Castelain

Of Bruges.   And Dreux, the Seigneur of Beaurain.
Baldwin of Beauvoir.   Anseau de Kaieu.
Huges de Belines.   Eustache de Cantelieu.
With shields slung frontwise o'er chain habergeons,[14]
Gautier de Stombe, and Renier de Monz.
Grey Gervais and young Heruë of Castèl,
Jakes of Avesnnes, Bernard of Monstrüel,
Robert of Malvoisin.   And Nicolas
De Mailli.   Guy de Coucy, he that was
The son of Adela.   Those brothers two,
Stephen and Jeffry, offspring of Rotroù,
And Counts of Perche.   St. Pol, to prove whose power
His daughter Elzabet had brought in dower
To Chatillon two counties.   Mathieu, Lord
Of Montmorency.   Trifling with the sword
He leans on, Piere, the new-made Cardinal
Of Capua; who was the first of all
To take the cross.   And he of Trainel, learn'd
Bishop of Troyes, Garniers; who back return'd
Anon from spoil'd Byzance, "with nothing less"
(Quoth Alberic) "to grace his diocese
Than the true scull, from Grecian monks reclaim'd,
Of Philip the Apostle."   Near him (named
By Gunther *magnæ sanctitatis vir*)
Neuelon; "on whom the Pope was pleased confer
Thessalonica's new archbishopric
Some few years afterwards," writes Alberic;
Bishop, meanwhile, of Soissons; whose grandsire,
Gerard, the Frankish chroniclers admire
As "Castelain of Laon, and noble prince;"
Return'd from Rome, well pleased, a fortnight since
With absolution won from Innocent ˉ
For Zara captured, to the discontent

Of those that sought to break the Red Cross ranks,
This prelate sits, requited by the thanks
Of pious souls, in comfortable chat
With those of Bethlehem and Halberstadt,
Receiving praise of Fulk himself; the Monk
Of Neuilly; who, when English Richard shrunk,
And Frankish Philip, from his fierce appeal,
Stirr'd up their Barons to a proper zeal:
The Boänerges of the new crusade;
A lean sharp-faced enthusiast, with shorn head
And starry eyes,—no hawk's, from Norway brought,
More vivid, or more vigilant,—his thought
So flashes thro' them 'neath his cowl's grey serge.
De Montfort; whom the Pope proclaims " God's
    scourge,"
Tho' styled " Hell's Hangman " by the Albigeois,
And "Bloody Simon." Louis, Count of Blois
And Chartre; the crownless kinsman of the kings
Of France and England, whose high humour springs
From blood twice royal. Peter of Courtenày;
Whose sires upon the sons of kings, men say,
Imposed their name and arms, " *three torteaux, or*,"
Which Godfrey, Bouillon's famous chieftain, bore
In Christ's first battle for His sepulchre.

Not the least warlike of these warriors were
Those Bishops four, of Soissons, Bethlehem,
And Halberstadt. In conference with them
That strong-limb'd Legate, loved by Innocent,
And (thanks to skill in arms with learning blent)
Acre's Elect Archbishop, sits beside
Loces' stout Abbot. Ugo, the one-eyed.
The Lord of Forli, leaning on his spear

And whispering to the grey Gonfalonier
O' the Holy See.   Pons of Sienna, lord
Of empty coffers and a hungry sword
At all men's service, trusting from the sack
Of pagan towns to take good fortune back.·
John of Brienne ; whose daughter Frederic
Made Queen of Naples later ; Almeric,
His wife's grandfather, gave him from the grave
Jerusalem, still later ; grey-hair'd, brave,
And, tho' untitled, honour'd, him men call
The noblest Christian warrior of them all.
Guy, Abbot of Sernay and Val ; anon
Made by the Pope Bishop of Carcasson ;
Suspected leader of the malcontents.
Henry of Orm ; whose Brabant shield presents
Argent, three chevrons, gules.   Roger de Cuick,
Lord only of a little bailiwick.
Garnier of Borland ; whose assaults, when Hell [15]
Stirr'd him against the Church, a miracle
Defeated ; for the blood of God His Son,
To warn him back, did on the rood down-run,
Seen at St. Goar, of Treves, upon the Rhein ;
Sister to Godfried, that of Eppestein
Was Baron (and good Bishop Siegfried's brother),
His mother was ; his sister, too, was mother
O' the other Siegfried that of Ratisbon
Was Bishop.   Ogier de Sancheron.
Jaen de Friaise.   Gautier de Gadonville.
Guillaume de Sains, and Oris of the Isle,
With grey Menasses : and stout-limb'd Machaire
St. Menehould's Lord : and Renaud de Dampière.
Mathieu of Valincourt : and Eudes of Ham :
And Piere of Amiens, call'd The Wolf ; whose dam

v.   G

Was nameless Madge.[16]   Haimon of Pesmes, and Guy;
Eupes of Champlite, and Hugues of Cormory.
Eustache le Marchis, with his helmet on,
And, undisguised, his quilted gamboison,[17]
Fret by no hauberk, half-way to his knee.
Villers, and Aimory of Villerey,
Peter of Braiquel, Eudo of the Vale,
Rochfort, and Ardelliers, and Montmirail.

Pietro Alberti; who, as simple Ser
Of Venice, boasts his power to confer
Titles, he deems less grand because his sire
Help'd Dominic, the Doge, to get back Tyre
(That famous town Agenor built, say some)
From those two former foes of Christendom,
The Egyptian Kailif, and that Soldan damn'd
Who in Damascus kept his dungeons cramm'd
With Christian souls: he fingers his gold chain,
And, with a smile of careless gay disdain,
Folds his patrician robe across his knees.
Less grave, and chatting too much at his ease,
Pataleone Barbo; whose renown,
Scarce older than his senatorial gown,
Folks yet dispute.   Francesco Contarini:
And that famed Ser, Thomaso Morosoni:
Lorenzo Gradenigo: Giammaría
Francesco Gritti, famed in Apulía:
Daniele Gozzi: Jacopo Pisani:
And Giambattista Ercole Grimani;
Noble Venetians.

                    Side by side they sit,
Grey faces in grave circle.   Could I fit

This rough-edged rhyme-work into finer frames
For their smooth-vowell'd, voluble, sweet names,
No wrong done, no wrench to them, bruise or wound
—As when the torturer to his engine bound
The melting-limb'd deliciousness of some
Dear lady, doom'd to luckless martyrdom,—
Friends, you should know their noblenesses all
Henceforth for ever, and to mind recall
By special name each serious face of them,
 Pale, 'mid its pomp of purple robe and gem,
Forth peering over every fur-trimm'd vest.
Search ye the Golden Volume for the rest,
You whom fate favours, whosoe'er ye be,
With leave, once lavish'd, long denied to me,
To walk, a living man, in Venice' streets,
Where ghost meets ghost, and spirit spirit greets,
Among the doves and bells, and bounteous things
Strewn 'twixt the sky that clings, the sea that clings
To the sweet city,—'twixt gloom, glory, 'twixt
Life, death, in maze inextricably mixt
Of gorgeous labyrinth.

                    Leaning by the wall,
Near the great doorway, fair-hair'd, blue-eyed, tall
Behind St. Pol (who tunes, to pass the time,
Humming unheard, an amorous Norman rhyme
To the slow music of a Latin hymn)
Bussy d'Herboise, the frank French knight, whose
    trim [18]
And sober surcoat, of no special hue,
Attracts, by seeming to evade, the view.
Ulric of Thun: and Charles of Aquitaine:
Eberhard, count of Traun, and castelain

Of the Imperial fortress of Pavìa:
Giàn the Unnamed; for whom his mother Pia
Forgot to choose a father ere she died,
Being embarrass'd by a choice too wide:
Martin the fighting Abbot; whose priest's gown
Scarce hides the corselet which in Basel town
He bought last month, to join the northern knights
From windy burgs sea-beat on Baltic heights,
Fair-meadow'd manors, and grey castles cold,
'Mid blue Bohemian woods, on windy wold   .
In the dark Hartz, or Salzburg's mountains bleak.
Henry of Ofterdingen, who the week [19]
Before, came bringing, for his part, indeed,
Only his lute, his lance, his squire, his steed.
Ludwig the Ironhead, of Falkenstein:
Ulric the Hawk; whose mother Adeline
Priests say the Pope will canonize next year:
And Ottoker, men call the Blear-eyed Bear:
The Duke of Styria, leaning on his shield,
—A milk-white panther-rampant, on a field [20]
Vert: Witikind, Carinthia's Duke, some say
The bastard son of Bilstein's Countess gay,
Who, help'd by some sleek nameless Levantine,
Contrives to keep alive the ducal line.

Only the constellations and the suns
Are call'd by kingly names: the millions
Of lesser lights, in charts celestial,
Are noticed merely by a numeral.
These, but the special stars that strongest flame
In foremost firmament. No need to name
The many more, less noble, or less known,
All known, all noble; all content to own

A greater than their greatest in that great
Grey-headed, blind old man, who sits sedate
And serious in their midst; the central soul
Of this brute power which he doth all control,
Shaping the many-minded multitude
To oneness; both the worthless and the good,
The weak, the strong.   For he is born of those
High seldom spirits that of all earth's shows
Suck out the substance, and make all men's wills
The agents of their own.

XI.

LE VALET DE CONSTANTINOPLE.[21]

The trumpet shrills
Thrice in the outer porch, with brazen din,
Thrice in the vestibule, and thrice within
The vaulted aisles.
Then, thro' the clanging arch,
The gaunt, red-cross'd, steel-shirted heralds march.
Then silence.
Then, a humming, and a sound
Of metal clink'd upon the marble ground,
And, in between those six that, either side
The column'd entry, gleam in tabards pied,
Bare-headed, with no blazon on his breast,
Comes the discrownèd Heir of all the East,
Alexius Angelus, the last in line
Of those Greek heirs to Christian Constantine,
The Byzant Emperors.

Who seeks for aid
Must show how service sought can be repaid.

Therefore the Prince, as soon as on bent knee
He gave the Doge the Kaiser's letter,—free
To plead his cause before the assembled knights
Of Christendom, and urge his wrongs and rights,
—Pledges himself to pay, upon his crown,
Two hundred thousand marks of silver down :
To join the Egyptian Pilgrims : and make cease
The long-aged schism dividing Rome and Greece :
To find and furnish at his proper cost,
For Christendom, and to the Red Cross host
For one whole year, ten thousand mounted men,
Soldier and horse : and, ever after then,
A company of fifty knights,—a Band
Vow'd to the service of the Holy Land.—
"*Le Valet de Constantinople*," states
The Frankish Chronicler, whose pen relates
What his eye witness'd, since himself was there,
"*Li cuers des genz esmeut, mainte lerme amere
Moult durement plorant.*" Thus, with filial tears,
Comment and argument, to lay their fears
And lift their valours,—now, with pour'd appeal
To sacred Justice and the Public Weal,
Now, hinting novel outlets to be won
To teeming Trade,—until the set of sun,
Full passionately pleading, spake the Prince.

XII.

A BLIND MAN SEES FAR.

And all this time, Doge Dandolo,—for, since
His sight was saved from surfaces and shows
That grossly intercept the sight of those
Who, seeing many things, see nothing thro',
He with serene, unvext, internal view

Beheld all naked causes and effects
In that clear glass whereon the soul reflects,
Unshaked by Time's distraught and shifting glare,
Events and acts,—while passionately there
The Prince stood pleading, saw, as in a trance,
Constructed out of golden circumstance,
The stedfast image of a far off thing
Glorious, and full of wonder . . . .

                        Clear upspring
Into the deep blue sky the golden spires
That top the milkwhite towers, like windless fires:
O'er garden'd slopes, slant shafts of plumy palm
Lean seaward from hot hillsides breathing balm:
Green, azure, and vermilion, fret with gold,
Blaze the domed roofs in many a globèd fold
Of splendour, set with silver studs and discs:
And, underneath, the solemn obelisks
And sombre cypress stripe with blackest shade
Sea-terraces, by Summer overlaid
With such a lavish sunlight as o'erflows
And drops between thick clusters of wild rose
And clambering spurweed, down the sleepy walls
To the broad base of granite pedestals
That prop the gated ramparts, round about
The wave-girt city; whence flow in and out
The wealth and wonder of the Orient World:
And, high o'er all this populous pomp, unfurl'd
In the sublime dominions of the sun,
And fann'd by floating Bosphorus breezes, won
To waft to Venice each triumphant bark,
The wing'd and warrior Lion of St. Mark!
All this he saw beforehand: so foreknew

What last great deed God kept for him to do :
Which, being apprehended, was half done
In his deep soul, though yet divined by none.
So when the Prince had ended, and the Hall
Began to buzz, and those flusht faces all
To turn their glances on the Doge (because
He was the inventor of their wills) no pause
For further thought they needed : but smooth'd down
Across his knee one crease of his calm gown,
And answer'd, very quietly, "It is good,"
And rose.

XIII.

QUOT HOMINES TOT SENTENTIÆ.

But then began that multitude
To murmur.   And some said, "The thing is wild,
And not to be endeavour'd."   Others smiled,
Play'd silent with the pommels of their swords,
And sided with the loudest.   Many lords
And many princes drew themselves aside,
And, blaming all the rest, with ruffled pride,
Took ship and so departed home again,
Gnawing their beards and hinting high disdain.
So was there great division of men's minds,
And tempest worse than of the waves and winds
When tides are equinoctial.   It appears
The priests first took each other by the ears,
Arguing if war be lawful, waged as well
On Christian sinner, as on infidel,
Bid text trip text, and learning learning trample.
The unlearnèd laics follow'd their example.
Those Abbots stout of Loces and of Val
With Latin curses evangelical

Denounced each other.   Borland then took sail,[22]
And left the camp, followed by Montmirail.
Froieville, and Belmont, and Vidame as well,
And with them the boy Henry of Castèl,
Went, swearing on the Holy Gospels Four
To come again, but never came they more;[23]
Nor spared God's wrath the recreant fugitives,
Of whom five hundred Barons lost their lives,[24]
Sunk in one ship, and hundreds more beside,
Slaughter'd by peasants in Sclavonia, died.
And daily still, some brawling baron went,
Clinking his arms and clamouring discontent
Whereon he in his burgs and towers would brood.

The Doge said very quietly, " It is good."

Now, of the remnant of the Red Cross ranks
The most part were Venetians, the rest Franks.

PART II.

"Li bruis fu mult granz par le dedenz, et le message s'en
tornent, & vienent à la porte, et montent sur les chevaux.
Quant ils furent de fors la porte, ni ot celui ne fust mult liez
et ne fu mie granz mervoille, qui il erent mult di grant peril
escampé : que mult se tint à pou, que il ne furent tuit mort, &
pris."—GEOFFROY DE VILLE-HARDOUIN, c. 113, p. 86.

I.

THE EMPEROR MAKES A PROCLAMATION,

On all the walls and gateways of the town
Of great Byzantium, passing up and down,
Men read this placard:

"IN THE EMPEROR'S NAME.

Great, gracious, just, and clement! let his fame
Endure, whom may God bless and keep!   Amen.
People!

         It is notorious to all men
That one Alexius, son of Isaac (late
Emperor of the East; whom, by just fate
And the high hand of Heaven dethroned, our grace
And clemency, ill-merited, did place
In safety, suffering him to live) hath stirr'd
By treasonable act and trait'rous word
Against our state a barbarous armament
Of Latins, chiefly out of Venice sent
And France; pretexting in the misused name
Of Christendom, by them deceived, the same
High cause which our own arms have heretofore
Not slightly served, in famous fields of yore.
Now therefore, having called about our throne
Our loyal liegemen, we to all make known
That we have set our price upon the head
(Six, if alive, three thousand, byzants, dead)
Of this Alexius Angelus, self-styled
Prince and Augustus, falsely, since exiled
And forfeit of his life, and titles all.
         By order of our Lord Imperial
            and Paramount, his servant,
                  MUZUFER."

And after this, the city was astir
With rumours; and, from ramparts, wharves, and streets
Wild whisperers watched the coming of the fleets.

II.

AND RECEIVES THE AMBASSADORS.

When the Ambassadors of Venice, France,[25]
And the Allied Crusade, bearing the lance
And lion of St. Mark, the gonfalon
O' the Holy See, the sword, and habergeon,
And mace of Charlemagne, with heralds came
Before the Emperor, and the amber flame
Of the great Oriental sunlight flow'd
Thro' the long-galleried hall, and hotly glow'd
About the pillar'd walls with purple bright,
They were at first as men whom too much light
Staggers, and blinds ; so much the inopinate
Magnificence and splendour of his state
Amazed them.
              At the Emperor's right hand,
Tracing upon the floor with snaky wand
Strange shapes, was standing his astrologer
And mystic, Ishmael the son of Shur,
A swarthy, lean, and melancholy man,
With eyes in caverns, an Arabian,
Who seem'd to notice nothing, save his own
Strange writing on the floor before the throne.
At the Emperor's feet, half-naked, and half-robed
With rivulets of emeroldes, that throbb'd
Green fire as her rich breathings billow'd all
Their thrill'd and glittering drops, crouch'd Jezraäl,
The fair Egyptian, with strange-colour'd eyes
Full of fierce change and somnolent surprise.
She, with upslanted shoulder leaning couch'd
On one smooth elbow, sphynx-like, calm, and crouch'd,
Tho' motionless, yet seem'd to move,—its slim

Fine slope so glidingly each glossy limb
Curved on the marble, melting out and in
Her gemmy tunic, downward to her thin
Clear ankles, ankleted with dull pale gold.
Thick gushing thro' a jewell'd hoop, down roll'd,
All round her, rivers of dark slumbrous hair,
Sweeping her burnisht breast, sharp-slanted, bare,
And sallow shoulder.   This was the last slave
The Emperor loved.   No sea-nymph in a cave
Ever more indolently dreaming lay,
Lull'd by low surges on a summer's day.
The midnight theft of some Bohemian witch,'
Stolen from a Moslem mother, when the rich
Turk camps in Carmel fled before the cross
That lured the remnant left by Barbaross
To Suabia's Duke, was Jezraäl.   Four black dwarves
Like toads, green-turban'd, and in scarlet scarves,
The four familiars of the fair witch-queen,
With fans of ostrich feathers, dipt in sheen
Arabian dyes and redden'd at the rims,
Stood round her, winnowing cool her coilèd limbs.
And, behind those, on either side the throne,
Stand two tame jackals to Apollyon:
One, in his right, across his shoulder props
An axe, and from his left a loose cord drops,
And he is nameless, and his trade is death.
The other, whose silk vest flows loose beneath
The small enamell'd dagger at his hip,
Smiles, with a restless finger at the lip;
Sleek, subtle, beauteous, bloodless minister
Of evil; and men call him Muzufer;
And when he smiles the people are afraid,
And hide themselves.   And smiling is his trade.

The Ambassadors of the Red-cross'd Allies
Spake to the Emperor upon this wise,
" The supreme Pontiff of the Holy See
Of Rome, in concert with the sovereign, free
Republic of St. Mark, the Chevisance,
And gentlemen of Germany and France
In arms,—by us, Charles, Count of Aquitaine,
Eberhard, lord of Traun, and Castelain
Of the Imperial fortress of Pavìa,
Lorenzo Gradenigo, Giammarìa
Francesco Gritti, Jacopo Pisani,
And Giambattista Ercole Grimani,
Noble Venetians,—to Alexius, styled
And titled, falsely, Emperor, who despoil'd
His brother of the purple and high place
Of power, to him allotted by God's grace :
—Render to Cæsar what is Cæsar's own,[26]
And unto God good deeds : restore the throne,
By thee usurp'd with sacrilegious sword,
To Isaac, thine hereditary lord
And master : and so live, forgiven of men
And God.   But if thou dost not this, know then
Thou art accurst, and anathematized."
The Egyptian lifted her large eyes, surprised,
And laugh'd.   The scarlet-clad huge-handed man
That stood behind, with axe and cord, began,
Under a snarling lip, to gnash white teeth.
The other monster, half out of its sheath
Lifted his dagger, with the self-same smile
Wherewith he had been listening all this while.
The Emperor glanced at Jezraäl, and said,
" Yon young French Envoy hath a comely head.
Answer him, girl."

                    The glittering witch leap'd up
With a shrill laugh, and seized a golden cup,
And shook her sparkling tunic to green flame,
And, hand on haunch, made answer

                              " In the name
Of Satan, and the Powers that be ! Who saith
To Life, ' Live not; give up thy place to Death ? '
Who calleth to the Sun, ' Come down : make way
For Darkness ? '   Who demandeth of the Day
To give his golden palace to the Night ?
Life answers ' Fool ! I live.'   And, saith the Light,
' Thou fool ! I shine.'   Who cannot keep his throne
May lose it : while he hath it, 'tis his own.
And, were I Emperor, I would answer ' Lo !
Upon all hills that rise, all waves that flow,
And on the lives and souls of men, is cast
The shadow of my purple.   Heaven is vast,
And Hell is deep.   And God, if God there be,
Doth hide Himself, to leave this world to me.
Mankind is my tame dog; and, knowing it,
Fawns on me; on whose collar there is writ
Sum Cæsaris.   The world is but a wheel
That draws my chariot.   I hold fast my heel
Upon the neck of my cringed vassal, Time.
Fear is my slave : my household creature, Crime.
The Lords of Hell are my retainers.   When
I frown or smile, all valour dies in men,
Virtue in women : men and women are mine,
Body and soul; their blood is in my wine.
The lion croucheth on my palace floors :
And Life and Death are suppliants in my doors.
The bolted thunder hangeth on my walls,

And, lo ye, when I nod the thunder falls!'"

"The thunder hangeth in the hand of God,"
Lorenzo cried; "and falleth at His nod.
See ye, from yonder golden pole, that props
The baldachin his burnisht barb o'ertops,
The many-coloured silken streamers fall?
The same hand, from the same silk, fashion'd all,
Nor hath the stuff with purple tinct imprest
Essential value more than all the rest.
Great Cæsar with his fortunes to admit
Death opes his doors no wider by a whit,
Than for the beggar buried in a ditch.
The dust is brother to the dust.   Seeing which,
And that alone the actions of the just
Are lords forever, and defy the dust,
Repent! spread sackcloth on thy former sin.
For, by the Living Lord that listeneth in
The everlasting silences on high,
I swear—beneath the patience of the sky,
Beneath yon gorgeous canopy, beneath
Yon golden roof, tho' incensed by the breath
Of prostituted slaves like this, and throned
In pomp, and girt with power, and crown'd, and zoned
With the imperial purple of the East,
Alexius is a miscreant, and a beast.
And God shall say to him, as to that other
Whom he resembles, ' Cain, where is thy brother?'
But thou, dread degradation of the form
Of woman,—what art thou, strange glittering worm?
What public mother, to what sire unknown,
Spawn'd thee, shamed creature of a shameless throne,
That dost with insult answer Christendom?"

The Egyptian sprang, then stood death-white.   A
    hum
As of a hornet's nest, all round the hall,
Responded to her gesture, augural
Of wrath.   She stood, a sorceress brewing storm:
The jewels crackled on her stiffening form:
Her wild unholy eyes flash'd hate: the breath,
Drawn sharply in, hiss'd thro' her sparkling teeth
Close clench'd.   But her rude lord, with laughter rough,
Waved to her a careless hand, and call'd "Enough!
Crouch."   And she crouch'd: then, like a beaten child,
Whimper'd upon the marble.   Drily smiled
The Emperor; and to Muzufer he said,
" The old Venice Envoy hath a reverend head,
Answer thou him."   But he, " Great Lord, I have
Not any knowledge nor experience, save
(What much, I doubt, delights not these grave Sers)
A little, of the various characters
Of wines and women.   Nor indeed have I
Enough of latinized theology
To answer, text for text, this reverend man."

The Emperor laugh'd.   "Speak thou, Arabian,
That knowest all things."   Then the Arab said:

" Nebuchadnezzar reign'd: and he is dead.
When Babylon was mistress of the world,
He was the lord of Babylon.   Death furl'd
His face in dark: and him the world forgot.
Greek Alexander reign'd: his bones do rot.
This little earth was smaller than his state,
He held it in his hand.   Men call'd him Great.
At last God blew his life out like a spark,
And he became a darkness in the dark.

To Alaric the eagle gave his wing,
His claw the lion, and the snake her sting.
His clarions, blown upon the seven hill tops,
Shook the round globe.   Grasses the wild goat crops
Grow over him.   A little sickness made
Of all he was nothing but dust and shade.
Attila reign'd.   The strong Huns worshipp'd him.
All mankind fear'd him.   He was great and grim.
Rome grovell'd at his feet.   One night he ceased.
The worms upon his flesh have held high feast.
Behind the host of suns and stars, behind
The rushing of the chariots of the wind,
Behind all noises and all shapes of things,
, And men, and deeds, behind the blaze of kings,
Princes and paladins and potentates,
An immense solitary Spectre waits.
It has no shape : it has no sound : it has
No place : it has no time : it is, and was,
And will be : it is never more, nor less,
Nor glad, nor sad.   Its name is Nothingness.
Power walketh high : and Misery doth crawl :
And the clepsydra drips : and the sands fall
Down in the hourglass : and the shadows sweep
Around the dial : and men wake, and sleep,
Live, strive, regret, forget, and love, and hate,
And know it not.   This spectre saith, ' I wait.'
And at the last it beckons, and they pass.
And still the red sands fall within the glass :
And still the shades around the dial sweep :
And still the water-clock doth drip and weep :
And this is all."

          " Yea,". said the Emperor, " then

If thus it fare with the world's mighty men,
And there be no more greatness in the dust,
How fares it with the men the world calls just,
Who lived not for the body but the mind,
Augustin, Plato, Socrates?"

                      " Behind
The mingled multitude of mortal deeds
Call'd good or ill, behind all codes and creeds,
All terrors, all desires, all hopes, all fears,
Behind all laughter, and behind all tears,"
The Arabian said, " this shapeless Spectre waits.
And no man knoweth what it meditates."

Frowning, he turn'd, and fashion'd as before,
With snaky wand, upon the porphyry floor
Strange figures, cube, and pentagram, and sphere.
The Emperor mused ; then murmur'd in the ear
Of Muzufer some word, whereto replied
That minister, " Let your Majesty decide.
Yet I have heard what Emperors decree
Heaven doth approve ; whereby it seems to me
This maxim may be broadly understood,
That for the good o' the state all means are good."

Thereat the Emperor rose ; and from his face
Suddenly all its smiling ceased,—gave place
Forthwith to hate too deadly for disguise ;
As when thro' sultry seeming-empty skies
Suddenly rushes, wrapt in glare and gloom,
The blood-red darkness of the strong simoom.
With lips that labour'd 'neath the weight and strain
Of wrath, he cried,
                " You—Sir of Acquitaine,

You—Sir of Traun—whose title we ignore,
Whose master styles himself an Emperor,
And is . . . . a puny Suabian Duke! You,—all,
Of Venice—whose nobility we call,
Like its new banner and filch'd patron both,
Of doubtful origin, and upstart growth!
This is our answer to your host, and you :
—Come ye as peaceful pilgrims, to pursue [27]
A pious journey to Jerusalem?
Then, nor your course we check, nor zeal condemn ;
Then, market free, and passage fair, expect ;
Our wealth shall aid you, and our power protect.
But come ye here, in hostile arms array'd,
The sanctuary of Empire to invade?
Then,—mark me! as I live . . . as I that speak
An Emperor both of Roman and of Greek,
(Mark me!) I swear—and swear it by the line
Of God-like Cæsars all since Constantine,
—Your myriads, were they ten times what they
        be,
Our scorn shall sweep from land, and sweep from sea,
As easily as yon light fan could sweep
A swarm of midges from the unvext sleep
Of our dark-eyelash'd leman. And, in pledge
Of power to smite,—not less than we allege,—
Our answer prompt to your barbarian crew [28]
Shall be your heads . . . the head of each of you!
Yours—Sir of Acquitaine! yours—Sir of Traun!
Fresh trophies for each gate of yonder town!
And yours—Venetian! . . . yours! and yours! and
        yours!
Ho, in the gallery, there! Bar all the doors.
No foot budge hence till we be satisfied!"

"Disloyal lord! . . . Enough!" Lorenzo cried.
"For us,—our response shall, in thunder-falls,
Be heard anon round yonder doomèd walls,
And rain'd in blood—less innocent than ours,
Ay, and less pure !—round yonder trait'rous towers.
For thee,—mock emperor, true barbarian !
Whose image, stamp'd in the alloy of man,
Sullies the wealth that buys obedience base
To Treason trembling on a throne,—disgrace
Would be grace wasted.   But hark . . . ye, his
          slaves !
Who falls on us must fall on iron staves.
'Ware, the first traitor here, that lifts his hand !
Christ and His cause about this banner stand.
For every hair upon our heads, a host
In arms, for Justice wrong'd, shall claim the cost.
'Ware, the first slave that stands across our path
To yonder door !   This wingèd lion hath
—(For God, the giver of all strength to men,
Shall smite the smiter now, Who smote him then)
The self-same strength between the wings, of him
That once, between the wingèd Cherubim,
In Ashdod smote usurping Dagon down,
And shatter'd in the dust his idol crown,
Before the captived but triumphant Ark.
Now,—God defend the Right, and good St. Mark!"

Forthwith outfurl'd, in resonant circle shone
Round those eight knights the rustling gonfalon.
And, thro' a hundred hands with hired swords
To murder purchased, march'd the Red Cross Lords
Majestic, unmolested, down the hall,
Strode thro' the startled Guards Imperial,

And from the treacherous threshold pass'd in scorn.
Alexius, with white lips, and garment torn,
Scream'd, "Cowards! slaves! Is Cæsar disobey'd?
Traitors? a hundred byzants for each head
Of those eight churls! Up, bloodhounds! or the whip
Shall mend the mongrel valour that lets slip
An Emperor's quarry!"
                     But the Eight meanwhile,
Spurring full speed, had pass'd the embattled pile
Of the great gate. Foil'd, as they forward sprang,
Down in the gap the shrill portcullis rang.

PART III.

"ὧν μὲν γὰρ χεῖρας ἀπέτεμεν, ὧν δὲ δακτύλους ὡς ἀμπέλων
περιέκειρε κλάδους, τινῶν δὲ πόδας ἀφῆρηκε, πολλοὶ δέ χειρῶν καὶ
ὀφθαλμῶν ὑπέστησαν στερήσιν. ἦσαν δ'οἳ καὶ ὀφθαλμὸν δεξιὸν καὶ
πόδα εὐώνυμον ἐζημίωντο, καὶ αἱ τοὐνάντιον ἐπιπόνθεισαν ἕτεροι."—
Nicetas Chon. de And. Comn. lib. i. 374.

I.

HOW THE EMPEROR PICKED UP WHAT THE DEVIL LET FALL,

Thereafter, met for mischief and debate
Morose, within a certain intricate
Small chamber, plann'd for plotting, with slant glooms
In glooms, beyond a maze of banquet rooms,
Muzufer and his liege lord up and down
Were pacing leopard-like. Meanwhile, the town
Mutter'd outside the porphyry porches all
Like souls perturb'd in Purgatorial
Abysses paced by lamentable throngs;
As to and fro i' the streets with surly songs

Among his myrmidons the headsman strode,
Beckoning in turn from each condemn'd abode
(So to appease the Emperor's discontent
Of his own creatures for that morn's event)
Some terror-stricken wretch, whose mangled limb,
—Lopp'd foot or hand,—must serve ere dark to trim
Arch, column, obelisk, and cornice, where
Already sallow-visaged slaves prepare
The midnight banquet board in galleries bright.
For 'mid his Court the Emperor sups to-night.
And in that chamber dim where these debate,
O'er the low bronzen door elaborate,
Some old Greek sculptor (dead an age ago
Ere Pisa yet brought forth her wondrous Two,
For Florence' sake, and all the world's, to impart
New sweetness to his barbarous Christian art)
Had wrought in monstrous imagery, bold,
Uncouth, and drear despite of paint and gold,
Christ tempted of the Devil upon the Mount:
Varying the tale the Evangelists recount
After the manner of the artist's mind.
Colossal forms! the Saviour of mankind,
And Tempter,—not alluring he, but grim
As the grim Middle Age imagined him;
Satan; that ancient hodman of the souls
That God forgets; in corners, dens, and holes
Where'er Sin squats, taking what he can find,
He rakes earth's offal for that hod behind
His hateful back; God's scavenger is he;
Who here, with obscene gesture coarse and free,
Hell's twy-prong in his claw-bunch-fingers clutch'd,
Picks from the rubbish at his shoulder hutch'd,
And proffers to the Son of Man, a crown.

Now, while these two were pacing up and down
In moody talk, and Muzufer began
To praise and pity much that day's marr'd plan,
As being shrewdly plotted,—righteous, too,
If rightly looked at . . . . "For, Sir Emperor, who
Disputes the right of Christian Emperors
To slay the infidel ambassadors
Of Moslem monarchs, that by nature stand
Outside the law of every Christian land?
Yet Christians that, unchristianly, oppose
Your Christian Majesty, are, certes, foes
More formidable, therefore worse by far,
Than merely Ottoman and Moslem are.
Meanwhile, they have escaped us. We have fail'd.
Which is a pity. Fifty slaves impaled
Will poorly, poorly at the best, replace
Those eight Frank heads which we had hoped should
    grace
This evening's banquet. For altho' we preach
Thereby a wholesome homily to each
Incipient traitor, and altho', indeed,
These cravens merit death, methinks you feed
On your own limbs thus—prey on your own power,
Devour'd the more, the more that you devour."
—He speaking thus, against the bronzen door
Alexius struck his fist fierce-clench'd, and swore
An angry oath that neither Heaven nor Hell
Should mar that evening's merriment.

                                    Then there fell
With clink and clatter, by that blow shaked down,
Out of the Devil's claw the Devil's crown
Striking the Emperor's foot.

                     The two stood still,
And stared upon each other.
                       " Omen ill ! "
Mused Muzufer.   " Hell's Monarch's clutch is not
So sure but it lets go what it has got."
Alexius, laughing, answer'd quick, " Not so.
Nor is it the first time I have stoop'd as low
To get—nor, gotten, thank'd the Devil for—
This glittering hoop."   And " Ay, Sir Emperor ! "
With mimic mirth laugh'd Muzufer.   Within
His dusky niche a sympathetic grin
The wrinkled visage of the Father Fiend
Emitted, till his coarse brow seem'd thick-vein'd,
And dull eye seem'd to wink with dismal glee.
So altogether laugh'd that Wicked Three,
While Day, to reach the West's red innermost
With lurid foot the lucid pavement crost.
Then at the casement Muzufer cried, " Hark !
The butchery has begun before 'tis dark.
One . . . two . . . three . . . four . . . five wretches ?
    how they twist
On those spiked staves !   Sure, that's a woman's
    wrist
And hand there, with the fluttering fingers ?   Phew !
We must not sup to windward of this stew,
Or you will find the hippocras smell strong.
Burn, burn benzoin !   How heavily hums along
Yon beetle, caring nothing for it all,
—Fool, and it sets me talking ! "

                     " The shades fall
Fast," cried Alexius.   " Come ! the Banquet waits."

II.

AND HOW HE AFTERWARDS GAVE AWAY WHAT HE NO LONGER POSSESSED.

And while spake he, Byzantium's golden gates
From silver clarions to the setting sun
Breathed farewells musical; and, Day being done,
Night enter'd swift to meet the Sons of Night.

Not black however, but in blaze of light
Luxurious.
        Gardens.   Galleries.   Walls o'erlaid
With marvellous, many-colour'd marbles, made
By multitudes of fragrant flames, that pant
From flashing silver lampads, fulgurant:
Cornelian, agate, jasper, Istrian stone
And Carian mix'd, to shame the glories gone
From Roman streets since first Mamurra had
His own housewalls with milkwhite marble clad.
And down deep lengths of glowing colonades
The dim lamps twinkle soft thro' slumbrous shades
Around rich-foliaged frieze, and capitals
Of columns opening into halls and halls
Warm with sweet air, and wondrous colour roll'd
From rare mosaics—azure dasht with gold;
'Neath domes of purple populous with star
On star of silver, coved o'er circular
Vermiculated pavements interlaid
With wreaths of flowers and intricatest braid
Of delicate device, about the base
Of granite basins broad, which all the race
Of sea-gods and sea-horses linger round,
In love for ever with the long cool sound

Of lucent waters that low-laughing fall
And fall from pedestal to pedestal
Among those curling nymphs and tritons bold
That bridle restive dolphins rein'd with gold.
Beyond, 'twixt pillar'd range and statued plinth,
The lustrous maze of marble labyrinth
Unfolds; and, disentangling from itself
Its luminous spaces, spreads into a shelf
Of shining floorage carpeted with deep
Thick-tufted crimsons, soft as summer sleep
Under the footsteps of delicious dreams,
O'er which, thro' dark arcades, steal airy gleams
And sumptuous odours, and mellifluous waves
Of music that with swimming languor laves
Dim gardens green and deep, and flowery plots
Where minstrels strike their golden angelots,
And sing—now, Cæsar's splendour, Cæsar's state,
That doth Olympian glories emulate,
—And now, lascivious songs, the wanton loves
Of Mars and Venus,—till the lemon groves
Are loud with lyric rapture.

                    Piled and built
On glowing tables, garlanded and gilt,
Of Mauritanian tree, the Banquet shines,
—Bright-beaming vessels brimm'd with costly wines,
And savorous fruits on golden salvers heap'd,
And smoking meats in misty spices steep'd—
All round the terraced porch. In plenitude
Of power, here, midmost of his multitude
Of Greek Patricians, robed in purple pomp
Alexius sits. Meanwhile the bronzen tromp,
Blown from dim-gaping galleries far behind,

Strives, with the clang of sudden cymbals join'd,
To crush all feebler sound out of each dull
Low wail, or intense shriek, that in the lull
Of that loud music ever and anon
Some wind, from outer darkness pour'd upon
The palace thresholds, pulsing passionate,
Contrives to filter thro' the golden grate.

Along a brilliant frieze of burnish'd wall
That beams behind the throne Imperial,
In rangèd groups emboss'd and painted, blaze
Byzantine sculptures that perpetuate praise
Of Trajan's Justice, and the Sages Seven
Of Antique Greece : between whose tablets driven
Great cedarn beams, that prop the deep pavilion,
Drop cataracts down of silken streams vermilion.
Beneath, in bronze, Alcides with his club,
And that she-wolf that had for sucking cub
Rome's founder. But before the Emperor gleam
High argent censers, whence thick odours stream
From left to right in vast voluptuous clouds
Of incense that with floating mist enshrouds
His glory like a God's. And by his side,
At his left hand, dark-hair'd delicious-eyed
Egyptian Jesraäl leans. Around her twine
The curling odours, and the fragrant wine
Is lucent on her humid lip : and he,
Beneath the loaded board, with amorous knee
Frets her lascivious tunic's light-spun folds,
And in hot palm her languid finger holds.
Anon, with heated eyes, turning from her
(All glitter and all glare) to Muzufer
(All gravity, all gloom), that sits meanwhile

On his lord's right,—forgetting even to smile,
So much his mind is busy at the task
Of plotting how to slip from life's main masque,
Silently, unperceived, by some side-way
Into safe darkness, ere God's Judgment lay
Pride's revel all in ruins . . . for he read
Strange writing on the walls,—Alexius said,
" What wise and weighty matter is astir
Behind those knitted brows ? "

                           Then Muzufer,
Like one surprised without his armour on,
Caught up his smile in haste, and answer'd, " None,
Great Master, weigh more anxiously than I
The mighty interests of Your Majesty ;
Whose greatness needs must oft oppress the brain
Compell'd its utmost faculty to strain
In contemplating the august extent
Of power that doth, as doth heaven's firmament,
Invest the world with glory.   Who oppose
Your Majesty, oppose mankind, which owes
From realms unnumber'd homage to your rule.
Who doubts this is a miscreant and a fool :
Whoe'er Your Majesty's most sacred, high,
And solemn rights dare question or deny
Is a vile traitor and an arrant knave :
But they that now in arms presume to brave
Your power supreme are sinners more accurst
Than any, save (if such there be) that worst
Of wicked men that, being Grecian born,
This barbarous rabble doth not loathe and scorn
More than Turk, Jew, or Saracenic scum
Of nameless nations scorn'd by Christendom.

If such there be, were he my father's son,
Myself would hold, to hang that caitiff on,
No gibbet high enough.   My thoughts are these."

"Paul's body!" quoth Alexius, "well they please
Our passing humour.   Wherefore we assign
Hereby, from this time forth to thee and thine
In title principal, and lordship free,
Our palace of Chalcedon by the Sea."
And while he spake thus, echoed by the shout
"Long live Alexius!" from the gates without
Hoarse hubbub stream'd, and up the revelling hall,
Bearing the banner'd bird imperial,
A legionary captain, pale with fear,
Made way towards the throne.

                    To whom "What cheer?"
With husky wine-quench'd voice the Emperor cried;
And to the Emperor, rueful, he replied,
"Ill cheer, Sir Emperor!   The Latin Host
Hath fall'n upon Chalcedon.   We have lost
Many brave men, and one fair palace you."
"Pish!" cried the Emperor.   "The Franks are few.
What's lost to-night may be to-morrow won,
Palaces be there many a fairer one
For us to feast in, you to fight for, still.
Begone!"

III.

WHAT WAS SHOWN TO THEOCRITE, THE MONK.

So feasted they.   No bird of ill
With boding note around the rooftree croak'd,
Nor bearded star the mason'd turrets stroked,

Nor howl'd the hoarse wolf near the revelling town.
Only, that night a marvellous thing was shown
To Theocrite the Monk, when he in prayer,
After long fast went forth to breathe the air
What time the air was stillest.   For to him
Appear'd in heaven, above the city dim,
The helmeted Arch-Angel of high God,
That in his right hand held a measuring rod,
Stretch'd over all the East.   To whom God gave
Command to measure out a mighty grave
Wherein to bury and hide from human eye
The body of a world about to die.
This thing in vision at the mid of night,
'Twixt heaven and earth, was shown to Theocrite.

PART IV.

"Ὦ πόλις πόλις, πόλεων πασῶν ὀφθαλμέ, ἄκουσμα παγκόσμιον, θέαμα ὑπερκόσμιον, ἐκκλησιῶν γαλουχέ, πίστεως ἀρχηγέ, ὀρθοδοξίας ποδηγέ, λόγων μέλημα, καλοῦ παντὸς ἐνδιαίτημα! ὦ ἡ ἐκ χειρὸς κυρίου τὸ τοῦ θυμοῦ πιοῦσα ποτήριον, ὦ ἡ γενομένη πυρὸς μερὶς πολλῷ δραστικωτέρου τοῦ καταιβασίου καλαι πυρὸς πενταπόλεως, τι μαρτυρήσω σοι."—*Nicetas*, Alexius Ducas, p. 763, c. 5.

———

I.

JUSTICE

"*Te lucis ante terminum*" . . . and lo,
One half of heaven is wrapt in rosy glow!
"*Rerum creator poscimus*" . . . the hymn
Sweet-heaving swells o'er solemn air and dim.
Sunset.   A few large stars.   The sea-wind vents
Among the narrow-streeted silken tents.

From Chalcedonian palace chambers calm,
The lofty, pure, sonorous Latin psalm
Forth-pour'd by sworded priests athwart the tramp
And hoarse buzz humming deep from camp to camp
Of those six battles, ranged and banner'd all
Under the Counts of Flanders, of St. Paul,
Of Montmorency, of Blois, and Montferrat,
Who, with his Lombards, holds the rear, stretch'd flat
Behind the city, lengthening many a mile
Into the midnight toward St. Stephen's pile.—
And all athwart this rustling region far
Buzz'd over by the sounding wings of War
(That frets and flutters, bound in brazen chain,
And breasts his iron cage) from brain to brain
One passionate purpose seethes.

                              For now those eight
Ambassadors, return'd, with wrath relate
In clamorous conclave their scorn'd embassage :
Whose high compeers consult how best to wage
Now-imminent conflict with self-confident Crime,
And wield the weighty instrument of Time,
Ready to smite.

              So, after lowly prayer,
Each Knight upon his naked sword doth swear
A solemn oath to see dread justice done,
And rouse the slumbering war at rise of sun.
Therefore, all night, the humming tents about,
By twos and threes conversing, in and out
'Twixt mighty mangonel, and wheelèd tower
Arm'd with spring-shoulder'd arbalists of power,
The great chiefs stride indignant.

II.

ARMED

                                        At sunrise
The six-times-folded Battle, serpent-wise,
Slid past Blachernæ, and with steely fold
At sunset wrapt grey Boemond's castle hold.
There, by long labouring in the dark, was made
All round the camps deep trench and palisade;
'Gainst which the war for many a night and day
Flared, rock'd, and roar'd.
                                Full hard it were to say
What multitudes of mighty deeds were done,
Since first Lascaris by the Bourgignon
Was captived, till the Danish curtle axe
Dropp'd on the walls, before those fierce attacks
Which, all unarm'd, Eustache Le Marchis led,
Only an iron cap upon his head.

III.

BY SEA AND LAND,[29]

Meanwhile, at sea, the white Fleet, following,
Hover'd hard by; and crept with cautious wing
Under the wave-girt city; planting there
A formidable grove.

                        Not anywhere
Thro' seas and skies were ever sail'd or row'd
Ships huge as these.   The Paradiso proud,
Like a broad mountain, monarch of the morn,
By the mad clutch of tumbling Titans torn
Down from the windy ruins of the sky,
With Jove's chain'd thunders throbbing silently

In his strong pines, adown the displaced deep
Shoulders the Pelegrino,—half asleep,
With wavy fins each side a scarlet breast
Slanted. Hard by, more huge than all the rest,
—Air's highest, water's deepest, denizen,
A citadel of ocean, throng'd with men
That tramp in silk and steel round battlements
Of windy wooden streets, mid terraced tents
And turrets, under shoals of sails unfurl'd,
—That vaunting monster, Venice calls " The World."
And now is pass'd each purple promontory
Of Sestos and Abydos, famed in story, ·
And now all round the deep blue bay uprise
Into the deep blue air, o'er galleries
Of marble, marble galleries ; and lids
O'er lids of shining streets ; dusk pyramids
O'er pyramids ; and temple walls o'er walls
Of glowing gardens, whence white sunlight falls
From sleepy palm to palm ; and palace tops
O'ertopp'd by palaces. Nought ever stops
The struggling Glory, from the time he leaves
His myrtle-muffled base, and higher heaves
His mountain march from golden-grated bower
To bronzen-gated wall,—and on, from tower
To tower,—until at last deliciously
All melts in azure summer and sweet sky.
Then, after anthem sung, sonorous all
The bronzen trumpets to the trumpets call ;
Sounding across the sea from bark to bark,
Where floats the wingèd Lion of St. Mark,
The mighty signal for assault.
                              A shout
Shakes heaven. And swift from underneath upspout

V.   I

Thick showers of hissing arrows that down-rain
Their rattling drops upon the walls, and stain
The blood-streak'd bay.   The floating forest groans,
And creaks, and reels, and cracks.   The rampart-stones
Clatter and shriek beneath the driven darts.
And on the shores, and at the gates, upstarts,
One after one, each misshaped monster fell
Of creaking ram, and cumbrous mangonel.
Great stones, down-jumping, chop, and split, and crush
The rocking towers; wherefrom the spearmen rush.
The morning star of battle, marshalling all
That movement massive and majestical,
Gay through the tumult which it guides doth go
The grand grey head of gallant Dandolo.
With what a full heart following that fine head,
—Thine noble Venice by thy noblest led!
In his blithe-dancing turret o'er the sea,
Glad as the grey sea-eagle, hovers he
Thro' sails in flocks and masts in avenues.

Elsewhere, the inland battle, broken, strews
With flying horse the hollows; while but ill
The heavy-harness'd Frankish Knighthood still
Strains, staggering as each Flanders stallion falls,
In the rear region, round the city walls,
Against those silken turms and squadrons light,
That follow and fly, scatter and reunite,
Tormenting their full-bulk'd too-cumbrous foe;
Like swarms of golden bees that come and go
About the bear whose paw is on their hive
Patient and pertinacious, tho' they drive
Their stings into his eyes, settle and swarm,
Disperse and close again, to do him harm,

Unharm'd.   For there in splendour eminent
Is pitch'd the purple-topt Imperial tent,
And domes of crimson glow i' the azure sky,
Girt by Byzantium's gorgeous chivalry.

So to the kindling of the Even Star
The groaning-hearted battle greatens.

IV.

IS TRIUMPHANT.

                                    Far
And near the strong siege tugs by sea and land
The storm-struck city,—hugg'd on either hand
By heavy ruin,—till from mast to wall,
From sea to shore, the high drawbridges fall,
And in mid-air the arm'd men march, and drop
On battlemented roof and turret top.
The deadly Greek fire dips, and drips, and crawls,
And twists, and runs about the ruining walls,
And all is blaze and blackness, glare and gloom.
Pietro Alberti, the Venetian, whom
His sword lights, shining naked 'twixt his teeth
Sharp gripp'd, thro' rushing arrows, wrapt with death,
Leaps from his ship into the waves : now stands
On the soak'd shore : now climbs with bleeding hands
And knees the wall : now left, now right, swift, bright,
Wild weapons round him whirl and sing : now right,
Now left, he smites, fights, shakes, breaks, all things
        down.

The Standard of St. Mark is on the town !

André d'Herboise, the gallant gay French knight,
Fast following him, hath gain'd the other height.

Prompt as a plunging meteor, that strikes straight
And instantaneous thro' the intricate
Thick-crowded stars its keen aim, flitting thro'
The choked breach, flashes dauntless Dandalo.
In rush the rest.   In clattering cataract
The invading host rolls down. Disrupt, distract,
The invaded break and fly. The great church bells
Toll madly and the battering mangonels
Bellow. The priests in long procession plant
The cross before them, passing suppliant
To meet the marching conquest. With fierce cries
Against the throne the rabble people rise,
And slaves cast off their fetters, and set free
Their hidden hates. For aye the craven knee
That meekest crooks, adoring present power,
Before the little idol of the hour,
Is cousin to the craven hand that smites
Most fiercely down the image it delights
To insult and shame when greater gods wax wroth.

V.

SICUT FUMUS.

Now, therefore, when Alexius saw that both
The creatures and destroyers of his power
Were on him, to his soul he said, " The Hour
Is mine no more. Soul, we have lived our day."
Then, waiting for the night, he fled away
Into the night. Night took him by the hand
And led him silently into the land
Of darkness. Darkness o'er his forehead cast
Her mighty mantle, murmuring, " Mine, at last!"

In the great audience chamber at Byzance
A Latin soldier, leaning on his lance
Fatigued with slaughter, on the marble ground
Blood-bathed an empty purple garment found.
And then, for the first time, immersed in thought,
The Latin soldier mutter'd, " I have fought
Against an Emperor ! "
                               Jewels in her head
And serpents in her hand,—smiling, and dead,
And beautiful in death,—each glorious globe
(Loosed from the glittering murrey satin robe)
Of her upturn'd defiant bosom, bare
Save for the few locks of delicious hair
That swept them—saved by scornful death from
       scorn—
Only the beauty left of her—at morn
They found the Egyptian Jezraäl.

                               So fades
Star after star along the cypress glades,
Face after face from the rose bowers : so song
After song dies the lonesome lawns along.
Each to his time ! The revel and the rout,
Lamp after lamp, mask after mask go out ;
Still for new singers the old songs to sing
In the same place to the same lute-playing :
Still for new dancers, to new tunes the same
Dance dancing ever, to take up the game
All lose in turn.
                 Another time begins.
New passions, and new pleasures, and new sins,
For ever the old failure in new forms ;
To fashion a metropolis for worms

And write in dust man's moral!

                Meanwhile, where
Hides Muzufer? what doth he? how doth fare?
How fares the small sunshiny insect thing
That feeds on death and in the beam doth sing,
When quench'd the beam, and stopp'd the moment's
    play?
Nature both brings to birth and sweeps away
Myriads of minims such: whose souls minute
For loss or gain doth Heaven or Hell compute?
Please they, or tease they, how shall Fate devise
Fit retribution for dead butterflies?

Then, Power being changed, the changeful people
    went,
And from the noisome pit where he was pent
Drew forth blind Isaac.

                Seven black years of night
Clung to him, and kept him cold in the sun's light.
For he had grown to hold familiar talk
With newts and creeping things,—long wont to walk
About him in the silent dark down there,
Which he would miss henceforth. He was aware
Of little else. And it was hard to him
To understand (so very faint and dim
To his dull memory were the former times)
Why the great world, intent upon its crimes
And pleasures, was at pains to take him back
Unto itself from that oblivion black,
Where he, the loveless man of long ago,
Had learn'd to love, what men abhor—the slow
Soft-footed dwellers of the dark. He had
So lost the habitude of being glad,

And all the strength of it, that, tho' thrice o'er
New friends explain'd to him his joy, no more
Than one born deaf and dumb he seem'd to find
A meaning to the matter in his mind.
So, passively, he yielded to the crowd
That robed him, crown'd him, and proclaim'd aloud
Him only the true Cæsar.

VI.

TWO BLIND MEN.

　　　　　　　Now once more
Proud to up-prop all Power, those lions four,
Subservient, their broad blazing backs upon
The bright floor crouch, beneath the throne whereon
Blind Isaac sits; with fumbling hand, in dull
Delaying doubt, to fix the golden bull
And great sign manual, by the Barons claim'd,
To that high treaty with Alexius framed
In Zara.

　　　　　　Which to place in those weak hands,
Blind Dandolo before blind Isaac stands.
Two grey old men, and sightless each.　The one
Sits robed in royal state on sumptuous throne,
Distinguisht by the imperial diadem
And purple mantle proud with many a gem;
And sees them not: but, in himself, doth gaze
On darkness, gloomy death, and guilty days.
The other, by long noble labours marr'd,
With august brows by battle thunder scarr'd,
Stands,—mark'd to sight by honourable soils
Of his yet recent self-regardless toils;

And sees them not : but, in himself, doth see
The bright beginnings of great days to be,
And glory never dying.

VII.

THE DOGE IS OBSTINATE.

After this,
In the Cathedral (as old custom is)
On battle shield, in purple buskins, borne,
And vermeil robe, by new-made Cæsars worn,
The young Alexius, in full pomp and state
Of sovran power, supreme beneath the great
Imperial ensign's eagle wings unfurl'd,
Receives high homage of one half a world.

Which things accomplisht ; and a month or more
Of pageant and carousal being o'er
(Whose swiftly-sliding and soft-footed hours
Slipp'd unsuspected by, mid myrtle bowers,
From porphyry palaces) the Red Cross lords,
Yawning, with listless looks down their long swords,
As banquet after banquet pall'd on them,
Cry . . . " Now for Joppa and Jerusalem ! "

The new-made Emperor still their presence prays
And added aid, with promised guerdon : says
Need yet remains to heal by wholesome arts
The much-hurt empire,—all the popular parts
Bind up in single, and compact the state ;
Which tasks more time : hints vaguely hindrance
    great ;

Claims to appease, and scruples nice to weigh;
Funds hard to find; grave causes for delay;
With promise fair of further profit still,
Thereby implied.
         "The Treaty, sign'd, fulfil
First, Emperor of the East," said Dandolo.

VIII.

VERTIGO.

Alas, that in this world 'tis ever so!
For men might be as gods if it were not
That greed of power goes mad from power got.
Who stands upon the pinnacle, as 'twere,
Of Greatness,—seeing, hearing, everywhere
About himself the dazzling orb spin round,
Turns dizzy at the sight and at the sound,
And tumbles from the top to the abyss.
Of all high places this the danger is :—
—That those who stand there needs must gaze beneath,
Till they wax desperate; being woo'd to death
By depth; from whose black clutch some point of sight
Above them seen, if such there were,—some height
Higher than theirs,—whereon to fix their eyes,
Might haply save them.   But this Heaven denies.
And, seeing that, of Emperors and Kings,
The Scribe of Judgment (who plucks out his wings
To write their histories o'er and o'er again,
Leaving meanwhile the lives of meaner men
To kind oblivion) doth record to us
So many monsters, so few virtuous,
What wonder if some weary souls suppose
That 'tis perchance *the thing itself* (who knows?)

Time cannot cure : the nature of the *thing*,
Not of the *man* : the *kingship*, not the *king* ?

Howe'er that be, Alexius, now made strong
By rights restored, forthwith wax'd weak by wrong
Renew'd : and palter'd both with his allies
And with his people ; teasing each with lies,
And fronting both ways with a double face.
Thus, since, with reason shrewd, the populace
Look'd coldly, and askance, on power restored
By foreign arms, the frighten'd Prince ignored
Those foreign friends to whom he owed his throne :
Carp'd at their claims, and did his oath disown.
For heedless Hope in misery oft is fain
To mortgage more of gratitude for gain
Than, in possession, frugal Memory yields
Her clamorous claimant, from full harvest fields.
But since, withal, he fear'd the people too,
He plotted still, and still desired (untrue
To all alike), by foreign arms kept still,
Still, too, to keep in check the people's will.
Till foes, thus finding friends in friends turn'd foes,
Said, " Power is powerless."

IX.

A DARK DEED.

Then one night uprose
Myrtillus, the one-eyebrow'd,[30] in the dark
(Mark'd out for mischief by the devil's mark
Across his squinting double-minded eyes)
And seized on the Boy-Emperor by surprise

And treason foul, in unsuspecting sleep ;
Whom, having plunged him down a dungeon deep,
Six times with hell-brew'd hebanon he tried
To poison.   But the Prince, because he died
That way too slowly, being young and hard
Of life, 'tis said, was strangled afterward.
No need to strangle Isaac.   Soon as told
Of what was done, he did his mantle fold
Across his brows, and said, " This was to be
Because of my great sins that follow me."
And that same night he died.
                              The morrow morn,
On battle shield, in purple buskins, borne,
Myrtillus men crown'd Emperor.

X.

THE FULNESS OF TIME.

Dandolo

Said then . . . . " The time is come, which long ago
I saw in Zara.   Who eschew the good
Must choose the evil.   Drunk with brawl and blood,
This Empire reels upon her downward road ;
Corrupt at home, contemptible abroad.
Devilish, she would be godlike without God :
Godless, would rule, who needs, herself, the rod :
And deems, not being good, she can be great :
—Great, without one great man, i' the face of Fate !
The singular tyrant breeds the general slave,
And shameless citizens shamed cities have.
The time is now, and ours the hands, O friends,
To sweep this rubbish hence, and make amends

To earth, too long encumber'd with the same.
—To arms, for all men's sake, and in God's name!''

So, down before the iron Occident
The guilty golden-crownèd Orient went.

Because those Powers that make, and break, and keep,
And cast away—Spirits that in the deep
And toilful stithy of that underground
Grey miner, Nature, with unheeded sound
Monotonously hammer, heave, and beat,
And bend with blow on blow, and heat on heat,
The pliant world to every shape it wears,
Upon the stubborn anvils of the years—
—Said to each other, " Break we up this Past!"
And suddenly one half a world was cast
Into the furnace, to be forged anew.

XI.

THE HORSES OF LYSIPPUS.

At midnight, in the murtherous streets, the dew
Was blood-red, and the heavens were hurt with sound
Of shriek and wail the ransack'd region round.
So that men heard not, in the Hippodrome,
Those Four Bronze Horses, that had come from Rome,
In conference, talking each to each.

One said,
" Our purple-mantled master, Power, is fled.
And how shall We Four fare?   Let us away
Thro' the thick night!   For ever since the day
We follow'd that great Western Cæsar home
To grace the glories of Augustine Rome,

We Four have felt no hand upon our manes
Less great than theirs, who grasp the golden reins
Of Empire; they, behind whose chariot wheel
Yet-burning ruts their fervid course reveal,
Who rode the rolling world.   We also, when
Power pass'd from Rome, his car drew here again,
And carried Conquest in his course divine
From West to East, to dwell with Constantine.
But now is Power departed, who knows where?
Out of the East!"
                 So spake that voice in air.
The others answer'd, "Whither shall we go?
Our master being gone?   For who doth know
Where we may find him?"

XII.

AND THE LION OF ST. MARK.

                 Listening in the dark,
To these replied the Lion of St. Mark.
"Power rideth on my wings.   Come also ye
Whither I go, across the vassal sea.
And let us bear with us, to please him well,
Beauty, the spouse of Power.   And we will dwell
Together."
            Then they answer'd " Even so,
Lion! and where thou goest, we will go."

So those Five Beasts went forth.   And took with them
Power, and Beauty.   For whose diadem
They also brought great store of precious things,
And gather'd graven gems in golden rings,

And carved and colour'd stones, to be the dower
Of Beauty and the heritage of Power:
Clear agate cups and vases crystalline,
Porphyry, and syenite, and serpentine,
Obsidian, alabaster: statues fair
Of lucid gods: garments of richness rare:
And gold, and bronze, and silver: turkis blue
As Venus' veins: and rubies red in hue
As Adon's lips: and jasper, onyx, opal.

In this way Venice took Constantinople.

NOTES

TO

THE SIEGE OF CONSTANTINOPLE.

[1] P. 63. *Isaac is Emperor, and reigns at ease, etc.*

"ἦν οὖν τὰ περὶ δίαιταν ὁ βασιλεὺς οὗτος πολυτελέστατος καὶ διαδοτικὸς βρωμάτων τοῖς παρεστῶσιν. εἶχεν οὖν ἀτεχνῶς τὴν τράπεζαν Σολομώντειον, καὶ τὰς ἐσθῆτας ὡς ἐκεῖνος καινοφαντεῖς περιέκειτο, βουνίζων μὲν τοὺς ἄρτους, λόχμην δὲ κνωδάλων ἰχθυών τε διάπλευσιν καὶ πόντον οἴνοπα δεικνὺς τὴν ἑστίασιν. ναὶ μὴν ἑτερημέροις ἐνηυπάθει λουτροῖς, ὠσφραίνετό τε μυρεψουμένων εὐώδιῶν, καὶ ταῖς στακταῖς ἐρραντίζετο, ὡς ὁμοίωμά τε ναοῦ στολαῖς ἐξάλλοις ἐκέκαστο βοστρυχιζόμενος· ἐπιδεικτικός τε ἦν ὡς ταὼς ὁ φιλόκοσμος καὶ μὴ δὶς τὸν αὐτὸν χιτῶνα ἐνδιδυσκόμενος ὥσπερ ἐκ παστοῦ νυμφίος καὶ ὡς ἐκλίμνης περικαλλοῦς ἥλιος προῄει καθ' ἑκάστην τῶν ἀνακτόρων· χαίρων δὲ ταῖς εὐτραπελίαις καὶ τοῖς ἐκ τῆς ἁπαλῆς Μούσης ᾄσμασιν ἁλισκόμενος, ἐγερσιγέλωσί τε ἀνθρωπίσκοις συμπαραθύρων, οὐκ ἐπεζύγου Κέρκωψί τε καὶ μίμοις καὶ παρασίτοις καὶ ἀοιδοῖς τὰ βασίλεια." κ. τ. λ.

.Nicetæ Choniatæ, de Isaaco Angelo, lib. iii. p. 592. 2.
(The Bonn edition, edited by Bekker.)

[2] P. 65. *In agate cups, and vases crystalline, etc.*

" Vasi d'oro, d'argento, d'agata, sorprendenti per la loro grandezza, i quali erano stati portati in trionfo da Gneo Pompeo dopo la sua vittoria su i re Tigrane o Mitridate."
Origine delle Feste Veneziane, di Giustina Renier Michiel.
Venice, 1817. Vol. ii. p. 163.

[3] P. 65. *And realms extended from Euphrates far, etc.*

See Nicet. Chon. de Isaac. Ang. lib. iii. pp. 565-6.

[4] *P. 68.   "The chase!" the Emperor cries, "the chase!" etc.*

See Nicet. Chon. de Isaac. Ang. lib. iii. p. 593.

[5] *P. 70.   Marten, and zibeline, and miniver, etc.*

"De samiz, et de dras de soie, & de robes Vaires, and Grises, & Hermines, and toz les chiers auoirs qui onques furent trouué en terre."

Ville-Hardouin, p. 102, cap. 132.   Paris, 1557, folio.

[6] *P. 73.   Our Brother hath two eyes yet in his head, etc.*

See Nicet. Chon. de Isaac. Ang. lib. iii. p. 595. 3.   This punishment was special to the usage of the Greeks of the Lower Empire, and adopted from them by other nations. There were two ways of inflicting it.   The first, by means of a bull's pizzle so applied as to force, by extreme pressure, the eyeballs out of their sockets: the second, and least painful, by pouring boiling vinegar into the eyes.   See *Procopius Hist. Arcana.*   There is also a curious account (which is probably false) in Egantius, *lib. ix. c. 12, de exempl. illustr. Viror. Venet. Civit.*, of the manner in which (according to this writer) the eyes of Henry Dandolo were destroyed by the Emperor Manuel, —"*candente laminâ æreâ ejus oculis objectâ, quam ille intueri continuo cogeretur.*"

[7] P. 73.   *Meanwhile, the other flees, etc.*

"Et ejus filium Alexium interfici jusserat; sed per quemdam Senescaldum manus ejus evadens Alexius, ad Suevorum ducem Philippum regem Alemaniæ confugit."

Alberic. Ann. MCCII.

[8] P. 74.   *The Pope the Prince first plies, etc.*

See Gest. Innocent. III. pp. 71–72.

[9] P. 75.   *Irene, sister to Alexius, wed, etc.*

She was widow of Roger, King of Sicily (the son of Tancred) and espoused Philip, the Suabian Kaiser, after the death of her first husband.   In Germany she seems to have been best

known under the name of Maria. Witness her epitaph in the
monastery of Lorch:—

> " Nobilis atque pia hic cineratur graeca Maria
>   Philippi regis conjux. Hanc atria regis
>   fac intrare pia semita virgo Maria."

[10] P. 75.   *Meanwhile, the Red-Cross Lords, etc.*

> " Et li Quens & tous ses Barnés
>   S'en fu droit à Gadres alés,
>   V li Duc de Venise l'ot
>   Menet, car el faire n'en pot."

Philippes Mouskes.

[11] P. 75.   *Venetian Dandolo, etc.*

He was eighty years old when elected to the Dukedom, and
died thirteen years afterwards at Constantinople, where his
tomb in S. Sophia (*see Ville-Hardouin*) existed till that city
was taken by the Turks (*see Rhamusius*).   Most authors
attribute the loss of the Doge's eyesight to Manuel Comnenus;
and in the present poem I have adopted this supposition,
although I think the truth of it extremely doubtful. Godefroy,
a monk of S. Pantaleone, writes of him that " *ad expugnandam
quandam civitatem Regis Vngariæ nomine Sadram cæcatus fuit;* "
and Philippes Mouskes also asserts that the Doge lost his sight
at the siege of Zara.   This is obviously a mistake, or perhaps
even a wilful misstatement, designed to imply a divine judgment on an undertaking condemned by the Pope. But it is
highly probable that his blindness was from accidental or
natural causes. Sabellicus, indeed, avers that the Doge was
not entirely blind, and this opinion is supported by a passage
in Sanutus.

[12] P. 77.   *From whose prows the arms
         Of heroes hang, and low-hull'd palanders.*

Ville-Hardouin (c. 14) makes the Doge say in his reply to
the embassy from the Barons, " *Nos ferons Vuissiers à passer
quatre milles cinq cens chevaux, et neuf mille Escuyers.*" This
indicates clearly enough the character of these vessels, which
were built flat for carrying horses. The etymology of the

word itself also (Huissiers—*Galies Huissieres*—from *huis*, or
doors) implies that they were made with doors to open and
shut for the entry and issue of the horses,—probably much
after the same fashion as the flying bridges now common in
Germany and America.   Huges Count of S. Pol, in an
epistle describing the first siege of Constantinople, calls
them *naves usariæ*, and the Greeks, *Hippegi*, *Hippagogi*,
Hippagones, etc.   The Sire de Joinville (Hist. of S. Louis) describes the usage of them very distinctly : " *Nous entrasmes
au mois d'Aoust celuy an en la nef à la Roche de Mar-
seille, & fut ouuerte la porte de la nef pour faire entrer nos che-
uaux, ceux que deuions mener outremer.   Et quant tous furent
entrez, la porte fut reclouse, & estouppée, ainsi comme l'on voudrait
faire un tonnel de vin : parce que quand la nef est en la grant
mer, toute la porte est en eau.*"

It was the custom of this time for the knights to hang their
shields over and along the decks of the galleys, so as to form
a sort of shelter from the arrows of the enemy.   This was also
done for show in naval parade.   Guillaume Guiart sings of the
naval armament under Grimaldi—

> " *Où tant ot bannieres inclines
> Dras enarmés à euures fines,
> Enuiron les bors espandus,
> Lances droites, escus pandus,
> Blans haubers,*" etc.

And again,   " *Et au desous des creneleures
> De riches dras à enarmures,
> Atachiés comme à bastonceaus,
> Targes, banieres, penonceaus,*" etc.

[13] P. 77.   *And some notable men.*

In Ville-Hardouin ([12]) the Doge says to the embassy from
the Barons, " *Vostres Seignors sont li plus hauts homes qui
soient sans corone.*"   Some few of these names will be familiar
to every reader, but the greater number of them is unnoticed
by either Gibbon or Voltaire, or any modern historian that I
know of.   They will be found, however, in Ville-Hardouin,

Alberic, and other of the early chroniclers. The reader can, of course, if he pleases, skip the list of these Notables, which, following the fashion of the old rhymers, I have furnished for the satisfaction of a curiosity which is not likely to be felt by many.

[14] P. 79. *With shields slung frontwise o'er chain habergeons.*

These shields or scutcheons were blazoned with the arms of those who wore them, and usually slung under the neck. "Is scutum simul colloque pependit." Abbo de Bel. Par. lib. II. So, also, the Sire de Joinville, "et s'en alla à eux l'escu au coul," p. 61.

[15] P. 81. *Garnier of Borland, whose assaults when Hell, etc.*

"*Eodem anno contigit in Diœcesi Treverensi supra Renum apud S. Goaris oppidum, cùm Garnerus de Borlande, qui erat in parte Regis de Suevia, obsideret Ecclesiam in ipso castro sitam et munitam Clericis deintus Crucifixum locantibus in fenestra, unus de forinsecus diabolico spiritu repletus querelam repente traxit contra Crucifixum, et ecce de Crucifixo infixo sanguis fluxit largissimè, cunctis et foris et intus qui aderant cernentibus, et ipse Garnerus territus obsidionem dimisit, et ab eo loco aufugit.*"
Alberic, Ann. 1201.

[16] P. 82.   *Whose dam*
      Was nameless Madge.

The surname and family of Marguerite, his mother, is not known. His father was Dreux of Amiens.

[17] P. 82.   *. . . his quilted gamboison.*

"*Tot ferri sua membra plicis, tot quisque patenis*
    Pectora tot coriis, tot Gambesonibus armat."
Guillaume le Breton, lib. XI. Philipp.

So also the Sire de Joinville in his History of S. Louis, "*Je trouué illec près un Gaubisson d'estouppes,*" etc., and Guillaume de Guigneville, in the Soul's Pilgrimage :—

        "*Car dessous va la Gamboison*
        Qui le veut armer par raison."

It was a quilted garment of thick stuff, which went under the hauberk and reached over the thighs. That it was sometimes worn in war without armour of any kind would appear from a passage in Ville-Hardouin, as well as from the following, in which Nicetas, speaking of Conrad of Montferrat, describes his gamboison ... "αὐτὸς μεντοι ἄνευ θυρεοῦ τηνικαῦτα διηγωνίζετο ἐκ δὲ λίνου πεποιημένον ὕφασμα οἴνῳ αὐστηρῷ ἱκανῶς ἠλισμένῳ διάβροχον πολλάκις περιπτυχθὲν δίκην θώρακος ἐνεδύετο· ἐς τοσοῦτον δ'ἦν ἀντιτυπὲς ἁλσὶ καὶ οἴνῳ συμπιληθὲν ὡς παὶ βέλους εἶναι παντὸς στεγανώτερον· ἠριθμοῦντο δ'εἰς ὀκτωκαίδεκα καὶ πλείω τὰ τοῦ ὑφάσματος συμπτύγματα." From which it would seem to have been prepared with wine and salt, and doubled eighteen times.

[18] P. 83.　　*Bussy d'Herboise, the frank French knight.*

Brother of André d'Herboise, who distinguished himself (together with Pietro Alberti the Venetian) at Constantinople.

[19] P. 84.　　・ *Henry of Ofterdingen, etc.*
Mythical.

[20] P. 84.　　*A milk-white panther—rampant, on a field Vert.*

"*Panthera alba in campo, ut vocant, viridi splendebat.*"
　　　　　　　Wolfg. Lazü de Gent. migr. p. 223.

[21] P. 85.　　*Le Valet de Constantinople.*

So King Pepin, in the Roman des Loherancs, says of himself—

> "*Iceste guerre commant à maufez vis,*
> *Quant commença Vallez ere & meschins.*"

That is to say, that, when the war began, he was still valet, and young prince. In France, at this time, the Nobility consisted of Three Orders. The First, composed of all who were entitled to carry their own banner in war (hence knights Banaret—the lowest of this order): the Second, Chevaliers (simple) or knights, whose fiefs were not large enough to furnish the contingent entitled to carry a banner, and who therefore fought under the banner of some more powerful chief; these were called Bachelors (Bacheliers—Bas Chevaliers): the Third, Esquires (Escuyers), sons of nobles of all ranks, to whose youth the genius of Chivalry assigned the grace and dignity of a noble servitude (*Ich dien*), and who carried (as a privilege) the shields (*Escus*) of their patrons in war. Camden derives the term Esquire (scutcheon-bearer), from the right to bear arms. But it is more probable that the term represents the "*devoir*" to bear the shield of another—not the right to blazon one's own. To be Chevalier or Baron, it was necessary to have risen as it were from the ranks in the service of chivalry, to have been Valet before being Lord, Soldier before being Captain, Esquire before being Knight. Our playing cards record the tradition, which our usage dishonours. The Valets, although they have become knaves, still retain the noble names of Launcelot du Lac, and Huon of Bordeaux, etc.

[22] P. 89. . . . *Borland then took sail.*

" En cel termine se trauailla tant un halz hom de l'ost qui ére d'Alemaigne Carniers de Borlâde, que el s'en alla en une nef de merchcans."

Ville-Hardouin, 51.

[23] P. 89. . . . *but never came they more.*

" Et li sairemenz que il firent ne furent mie bien tenu, que il ne reparérent pas en l'ost."

Id. id.

[24] P. 89. *Of whom five hundred Barons lost their lives.*

" En une nef s'en emblérent bien cinq cens, si noiérent tuit, & furent perdu. Vne altre compagnie s'en embla par terre, & s'en cuida aller par Esclavonie : & li paisant de la terre les assaillierent, & en occistrent assez."

Id. id.

[25] P. 91. *When the Ambassadors of Venice, France, etc.*

"Giunti nella sala del trono, i loro occhi furono abbagliati dallo splendore dell' oro e delle gemme, solita sostituzione al poter vero, e alla vera virtù."

Origine delle Feste Veneziane, vol. 2, p. 153.

[26] P. 93. *Render to Cæsar what is Cæsar's own, etc.*

" Quar il le tint à tort, & à perchié contre Dieu, & contre raison. Ainz est son neuvu qui çi siet entre nos . . . fil de son frere l'Empereor Sursac. Més s'il voloit à la merci son neuou venir, & li rendoit la corone, & l'empire, nos li proieriens que il li pardonast," etc.

Ville-Hardouin, c. 73, p. 55.

[27] P. 99. *Come ye as peaceful pilgrims, to pursue, etc.*

" Se vos vos i estes poure, ne disetels, il vou donnera volentiers de ses viande & de son auoir, et vos li vindiez sa terre. . . . Car se vos estiez vint tant de gent, ne vos en porroiz vos aller, se il mal vos voloit faire, que vos ne fussiez morz & desconfiz."

Id., c. 72, p. 54.

[28] P. 99. *Our answer prompt to your barbarian crew*
Shall be your heads, etc.

" Prima però di nulla intraprendere si deliberò di spedere Ambasciatori all' usurpatore Alessio, intimandagli di remettere la città e lo scettro a Isaaco ed al giovane Alessio, che n'erano i padroni legitimi. Il tiranno non solo recusè di arrendersi, ma minacciò persin della vita gli stessi Ambasciatori."

Feste Veneziane, vol. 2, p. 152.

This, however, is not true. The Embassage was sent, not by the Barons to Alexius, but by the Emperor to them; and the only menace put forth on that occasion was what I have cited above, from Ville-Hardouin. The author or authoress of the Feste has evidently confounded the event here referred to with what Ville-Hardouin describes as having afterwards taken place between the deputies of the Barons and the younger Alexius, in reference to which that pious chronicler thanks God that the Ambassadors escaped with their lives. Justification for the episode, as I have related it, exists nevertheless in the universal custom of the time to address in the first instance, by embassage, a summons to the sovereign against whom war was to be declared, and the fact, which is sufficiently attested by Ville-Hardouin, that on these occasions the Ambassadors were sometimes placed in no small peril of their lives.

[29] P. 112. *By sea and land.*

For obvious reasons, justifiable, I trust, by the purposes and privileges of art, the principal details of the two Sieges have been thrown together, so as to present only a single picture.

[30] P. 122. *Myrtillus, the one-eyebrowed, etc.*

For the sake of euphony, the Italian orthography of Murzoufle has been adopted. The name, I believe, implies the peculiar feature of its owner's physiognomy. He is said to have had but a single eyebrow, extending over both eyes, without interruption at the nose. Some say that he also squinted.

THE IDEAL WORLD.

AS INTERPRETED BY RABBI BEN ENOCH.

(FROM THE SCROLL AND ITS INTERPRETERS.)

(BEN ENOCH EXPOUNDS.)

        . . . Mark, how of old
Men held what I, alone of moderns, hold:
(Ben Shishak's known philosophy in this
I recognize, and take the gloss for his)
—Namely, that this thrice complicated world,
Whereof Man stands i' the centre, hath enfurl'd,
And superposed as 'twere, three orbs distinct
Of Life.   Each diverse, tho' together linkt
By Life's one law for whatsoever lives,
Whereby of each Earth gains, to each Earth gives,
What helps in turn, the End-all, and the Be-all:
One Animal : one Human : one Ideal :
Three circles of one sphere.   Of these, the least
And lowest, is the kingdom of the beast,
Which man commands : who holds the middle place
Between Earth's lowest, and her highest, race.
But that which is the loftiest of the Three,
Sole region of Ideas, I take to be :
Which man, in truth, subserveth and obeyeth,
As him the brute beneath him.   Whoso sayeth
A man's ideas to a man belong,
Knoweth not what he saith, or argueth wrong.

Far rather, I imagine, doth the Man
Belong to the Idea.   For neither can
The Man command the Idea, nor deny
Submission to its mandate.   Can he fly
From its pursuing ? or its path dictate ?
Or summons, or dismiss, or bid it wait,
Or hasten—here advance, and there stand still—
Now active be, now passive—at his will ?
And, if it live not servile to his whim,
Say, can he slay it ?   Doth it not slay *him*,
Inexorably, with no mercy shown,
As he would slay a beast that is his own,
If his death, rather than his life, promote
That end whereto the Idea doth devote
The Man it uses ?   All as well my mule,
Whose footsteps I by staff and bridle rule,
Might think he rules me,—goeth by the road
His choice, not mine, selects, nor own the goad,
As that, for my part, I should boast to be
The lord of that ideal lord of me
Whose force I follow, and whose burthen bear,
Not as I will, but as I must, where'er
He goads me.   And, if this brute mule of mine
Should lord it o'er his fellow mules, opine
Himself the sage whose way is Wisdom's track,
Because he bears *my* wisdom on his back,
Were not his folly all the worse ?   "What then,"
One asketh, "arguest thou, apart from men,
Ideas can exist ? doth not man's mind
Create the Ideal?"   Nay, friend, for I find
Ideas make men, not men ideas.   They,
The dwellers of the ideal world, I say,
Are independent of mankind so much

As man is of the brutes. No more. For such
As is mankind's requirement of a race
Beneath it, born to serve it,—in like case
Is man. . . . Oh not by any means the lord,
But sturdy servitor, of that dim horde
Of dwellers on his brain; which, truly, need
And freely use,—to bear them, or to feed,—
For pasture, or for burthen, as may be—
Man, for their sakes created. Natheless he
Doth commonly consider and declare
That he is Something Great, because aware
Of Something Great within him. In like way
I dream'd the dial to the beam did say,
" Lo, I am Time ! " A little wind was waked,
Across the sun a little cloudlet shaked,
And the vain index of the heedless hour
Relapsed to nothingness. In many a flower
The moth and grub their dubious egglets hide.
Can the flower choose, or doth the flower decide
What to the summons of the sun shall rise
From her chance treasures to amaze men's eyes?
This launches, sapphrine-mantled, mail'd with gold,
Some warlike wyvern beautiful and bold,
Fit for the Persic fay that rides to woo
His shy queen, gaily, in her globe of dew :
That sends forth, barely fit to browze on burrs,
A monster hateful as the imp that spurs
His sooty flank, and hums a hell-born hymn,
Forth venturing darkly when the air is dim.
I can but laugh, but seldom, in my sleeve
When I look round the world, and there perceive
How men have builded monuments of brass
To others on whose brains the whim it was

Of some Idea, on its sightless way
About the world, to settle, seize, and prey.
Why should the beasts, man scorns, not also raise,
After their fashion, some such baaing praise
About the sure-foot horse man drives, the ox
He ploughs with, or the fatlings of the flocks
Man kills for his best banquet? Now, I deem
That in the purpose of the One Supreme
Man is not, as he holds himself to be,
The highest necessity on Earth. But he,
Born for the service of Ideas alone,
Is for their sake, as they are for their own.
Notice, which most concerns, most occupies,
That Providence whereby man lives and dies:
Men or Ideas? An Idea hath need
Of growth,—full scope to satisfy its greed
Of power, and multiply, and propagate.
To meet which, man is there i' the mass. Now wait.
What happens? mark the issue. Men must perish
Wholesale, it may be, or piecemeal, to cherish,
Enrich, and ratify, the otherwise
Starved and pent life this one Idea tries
To nourish at men's cost; itself or these
Succumbing. Which doth the World's Ruler please
To rescue or confirm? Why, horde on horde
Nature, to serve her supernatural lord,
Of her selectest human children gives.
Little accounts she their mere deaths or lives!
'Tis but a race to ravage, but a realm
To wash away in blood, expunge, o'erwhelm.
Doth Nature shrink from,—Providence impeach,—
The sacrifice required? Men's bodies bleach
On bloody battle-fields uncounted. Men

Born to be used thus: ended there and then,
Their use being over. Dead and done with, they !
Yet not in vain, do after-comers say,
Lived they or died they, since their lives and deaths
(Else vainly born and buried in vain breaths)
Have served to manifest, make eminent,
The Idea for which they lived and died, content.
But to themselves, who doubts these men's lives seem'd
Of all surpassing value ? Each was deem'd
By the dead owner of it something worth
The special cherishing of Mother Earth.
And if to save and foster man's life were
Earth's, or Earth's Arch Disposer's, chiefest care
We must, for those men's sakes (whose life, pour'd
    forth
Like water, seems mere waste of what was worth
Such frustrate forethrift, care so baulk'd of gain,
In the fine fashioning of nerve and brain)
Attribute failure vast, or drear neglect,
To Earth's great Justicer and Architect.
But He,—that wrecks man's life i' the sharp ordeal
Which rescues life's pure essence from the unreal,
The false, the fleeting—heeds not how it fare
With the mere Human, born for death : Whose care
Is for the Ideal that doth never die.
The human swarm swims, in its season, by :
Races on races rise and roll away :
The generations flourish and decay.
What laughing Phantom leads, and mocks, the dance
Of those blind mummers thro' the Masque of Chance ?
Lives on the life that from their lips it drains,
More glorious waxes as their glory wanes,
Brightens its deathless eyes in that fine air

Whose ardent essence man's prolong'd despair
Feeds with the fires that waste it, and doth dwell
On dead men's graves, deathless, impalpable,
Made of immortal element, the pure
Result of man—man's life that doth endure
Above the dust man drops in?   What survives
Save this, the ceaseless dying of men's lives?
Egypt and all her castes—bold Babylon,
Beautiful Hellas—Rome's Republic—gone!
What rests, on earth, the lone result of these?
The airy, but immutable, images
Of their Ideals, in the life that lies,
To light our own, above us.   Starrier eyes
Than ours are on us.   Egypt's Thought, the Grace
Of Hellas,—now no more to render place
To Rome's strong Will,—the stout town-stealer . . .
    There
Behold man's bright pall-bearers—they that bear
On their calm brows, for costliest coronal,
The symbols of the summ'd-up ages all!
    *   *   *   *

THE EYES OF MAHMUD.

Sultàn Mahmùd, son of Sabaktogin,
Swept with his sceptre the hot sands of Zin,
Spread forth his mantle over Palestine,
And made the carpet of his glory shine
From Cufah to Cashmere ; and, in his pride,
Said, " All these lands are mine."

At last he died.

Then his sons laid him with exceeding state
In a deep tomb.   Upon the granite gate
Outside they graved in gold his titles all,
And all the names of kingdoms in his thrall,
And all his glory.   And beside his head
They placed a bag of rice, a loaf of bread,
And water in a pitcher.   This they did
In order that, if God should haply bid
His servant Death to let this sultan go
Because of his surpassing greatness, so
He might not come back hungry.   But he lay
In his high marble coffin night and day
Motionless, without majesty or will.

Darkness sat down beside him, and was still.

Afterwards, when a hundred years had roll'd,
A certain king, desiring to behold
This famous sultan, gave command to unlock
The granite gate of that sepulchral rock,
And, with a lamp, went down into the tomb,
And all his court.

              They in the nether gloom
The pitcher found unemptied, but all green
With mildew.   Something, rats it may have been,
Had eaten all the rice, and all the bread.
Nothing was left upon his marble bed
Of the Great Sultan save a little heap
Of yellow bones, and a dry skull, with deep
Eye-sockets.   But in those eye-sockets, lo !
Two living eyes were rolling to and fro,
Now left, now right, with never any rest.

Then was the king amazed, and smote his breast,
And call'd on God for grace.   But not the less
Those dismal eyes with dreadful restlessness
Continually in their socket-holes
Roll'd right and left, like pain'd and wicked souls.
Then said the king, " Call here an Abid, wise
And righteous, to rebuke those wicked eyes
That will not rest."
           And when the Abid came
The king said, " O mine Abid, in the name
Of the High God that judges quick and dead,
Speak to those eyes."

           The Abid, trembling, said,
" Eyes of Mahmud, why is your rest denied

In death ?　What seek ye here ?"
　　　　　　　　　　　　The eyes replied,
Still rolling in their wither'd sockets there,
"God's curse upon this darkness !　Where, O where
Be my possessions ?　For with fierce endeavour
Ever we seek them, but can find them never."

THE APPLE OF LIFE.

FROM the river Euphrates, the river whose source is
    in Paradise, far
As red Egypt,—sole lord of the land and the sea,
    'twixt the eremite star
Of the orient desert's lone dawn, and the porch of the
    chambers of rest
Where the great sea is girded with fire, and Orion
    returns in the West,
And the ships come and go in grand silence,—King
    Solomon reign'd. And behold,
In that time there was everywhere silver as common
    as stones be, and gold
That for plenty was 'counted as silver, and cedar as
    sycamore trees
That are found in the vale, for abundance. For GOD
    to the King gave all these,
With glory exceeding; moreover all kings of the earth
    to him came,
Because of his wisdom, to hear him. So great was
    King Solomon's fame.
And, for all this, the King's soul was sad. And his
    heart said within him, " Alas,
" For man dies! if his glory abideth, himself from his
    glory shall pass.

And that which remaineth behind him, he seeth it not
    any more :
For how shall he know what comes after, who knoweth
    not what went before ?
I have planted me gardens and vineyards, and gotten
    me silver and gold,
And my hand from whatever my heart hath desired I
    did not withhold :
And what profit have I in the works of my hands
    which I take not away?
I have searchèd out wisdom and knowledge : and what
    do they profit me, they?
As the fool dieth, so doth the wise.   What is gather'd
    is scatter'd again.
As the breath of the beasts, even so is the breath of
    the children of men :
And the same thing befalleth them both.   And not any
    man's soul is his own."

This he thought, as he sat in his garden, and watch'd
    the great sun going down
In the glory thereof; and the earth and the sky, in
    that glory, became
Clothed clear with the gladness of colour, and bathed
    in the beauty of flame.
And, "Behold," said the King, "in a moment the glory
    shall vanish!"   Even then,
While he spake, he was 'ware of a man drawing near
    him, who seem'd to his ken
(By the hair in its blackness like flax that is burn'd in
    the hemp-dresser's shed,
And the brow's smoky hue, and the smouldering eye-
    ball more livid than lead)

As the sons of the land that lies under the sword of
 the Cherub whose wing
Wraps in wrath the shut gateways of Paradise. He,
 being come to the King,
Seven times made obeisance before him. To whom,
 "What art thou," the King cried,
"That thus unannounced to King Solomon comest?"
 The man, spreading wide
The palm of his right hand, show'd in it an apple yet
 bright from the Tree
In whose stem springs the life never-failing which Sin
 lost to Adam, when he,
Tasting knowledge forbidden, found death in the fruit
 of it. . . . So doth the Giver
Evil gifts to the evil apportion. And, "Hail! let the
 King live for ever!"
Bowing down at the feet of the monarch, and
 laughingly, even as one
Whose meaning, in joy or in jest, hovers hid 'twixt the
 word and the tone,
Said the stranger (as lightly the apple he dropp'd
 in the hand of the King),
"For lo ye! from 'twixt the four rivers of Eden, God
 gave me to bring
To his servant King Solomon, even to my lord that on
 Israel's throne
He hath 'stablisht, this fruit from the Tree in whose
 branch Life abideth: for none
Shall taste death, having tasted this apple."
     And therewith he vanish'd.

          Remain'd
In the hand of the King the life-apple: ambrosial of
 breath, golden-grain'd,

Rosy-bright as a star dipt in sunset. The King turn'd
    it o'er, and perused
The fruit, which, alluring his lip, in his hand lay
    untasted.
             He mused,
" Life is good : but not life in itself. Life eternal,
    eternally young,
That were life to be lived, or desired ! Well it were if
    a man could prolong
The manhood that moves in the muscles, the rapture
    that mounts in the brain,
When life at the prime, in the pastime of living, led on
    by the train
Of the jubilant senses, exulting goes forth, brave of
    body and spirit,
To conquer, choose, claim, and enjoy what 'twas born
    to achieve or inherit.
The dance, and the festal procession ! the pride in the
    strenuous play
Of the sinews that, eager for service, the will, tho' it
    wanton, obey !
When, in veins lightly flowing, the fertile and bounti-
    ful impulses beat,
When the dews of the dawn of Desire on the roses of
    Beauty are sweet.
Ay ! sweet to the young that yet know not what life is.
    But life, after Youth,
The gay liar, leaves hold of the bauble, and Age, with
    his terrible truth,
Picks it up, and perceives it is broken, and knows it
    unfit to engage
The care it yet craves. . . . Life eternal, eternally
    wedded to Age !

What gain were in that? Why should any man seek
    what he loathes to prolong?
The twilight that darkens the eyeball: the dull car
    that's deaf to the song,
When the maidens rejoice and the bride to the bride-
    groom, with music, is led:
The palsy that shakes 'neath the blossoms that fall
    from the chill bridal bed.
When the hand saith "*I did*," not "*I will do*," the
    heart saith, "*It was*," not "*'Twill be*,"
Too late in man's life is Forever—too late comes this
    apple to me!"
Then the King rose. And lo, it was evening. And
    leaning, because he was old,
On the sceptre that, curiously sculptured in ivory
    garnish'd with gold,
To others a rod of dominion, to him was a staff for
    support,
Slow paced he the murmurous pathways where
    myrtles, in court up to court,
Mixt with roses in garden on garden, were ranged
    around fountains that fed
With cool music green odorous twilights: and so,
    never lifting his head
To look up from the way he walk'd wearily, he to the
    House of his Pride
Reascended, and enter'd.

    In cluster, high lamps, spices, odours, each side,
Burning inward and onward, from cinnamon ceilings,
    down distances vast
Of voluptuous vistas, illumined deep halls thro' whose
    silentness pass'd

King Solomon sighing; where columns colossal stood,
    gather'd in groves,
As the trees of the forest in Libanus,—there where the
    wind, as it moves,
Whispers,. " I, too, am Solomon's servant ! "—huge
    trunks hid in garlands of gold,
On whose tops the skill'd sculptors of Sidon had
    granted men's gaze to behold
How the phœnix that sits on the cedar's lone summit
    'mid fragrance and fire,
Ever dying and living, hath loaded with splendours her
    funeral pyre ;
How the stork builds her nest on the pine-top; the
    date from the palm-branch depends ;
And the shaft of the blossoming aloe soars crowning
    the life which it ends.
And from hall on to hall, in the doors, mute, mag-
    nificent slaves, watchful-eyed,
Bow'd to earth as King Solomon pass'd them. And,
    passing, King Solomon sigh'd.
And, from hall on to hall pacing feebly, the king
    mused . . . " O fair Shulamite !
Thy beauty is brighter than starlight on Hebron
    when Hebron is bright,
Thy sweetness is sweeter than Carmel. The King
    rules the nations ; but thou,
Thou rulest the King, my Belovèd."

                      So murmur'd King Solomon low
To himself, as he pass'd thro' the portal of porphyry,
    that dripp'd, as he pass'd,
From the myrrh-sprinkled wreaths on the locks and the
    lintels ; and enter'd at last,

Still sighing, the sweet cedarn chamber, contrived for
repose and delight,
Where the beautiful Shulamite slumber'd. And
straightway, to left and to right,
Bowing down as he enter'd, the Spirits in bondage to
Solomon, there
Keeping watch o'er his love, sank their swords, spread
their wings, and evanish'd in air.
The King with a kiss woke the sleeper. And, showing
the fruit in his hand,
"Behold! this was brought me erewhile by one
coming," he said, "from the land
That lies under the sword of the Cherub. 'Twas
pluckt by strange hands from the Tree
Of whose fruit whoso tasteth shall die not. And there-
fore I bring it to thee,
My belovèd. For thou of the daughters of women
art fairest. And lo,
I, the King, I that love thee, whom men of man's
sons have call'd wisest, I know
That in knowledge is sorrow. Much thought is much
care. In the beauty of youth,
Not the wisdom of age, is enjoyment. Nor spring, is
it sweeter, in truth,
Than winter, to roses once wither'd. But thine, O
thou spirit of bliss,
Thine is all that the living desire,—youth, beauty,
love, joy in all this!
Wherefore keep thou the gift I resign. Live for ever,
rejoicing in life!
And of women unborn yet the fairest shall still be
King Solomon's wife."
So he said, and so dropp'd in her bosom the apple.

But when he was gone,
And the beautiful Shulamite, eyeing the gift of the
    King, sat alone
With the thoughts the King's words had awaken'd,
    as ever she turn'd and perused
The fruit that, alluring her lip, in her hand lay un-
    tasted—she mused,
"Life is good; but not life in itself.   So is youth, so
    is beauty.   Mere stuff
Are all these for Love's usance.   To live, it is well;
    but it is not enough.
Well, too, to be fair, to be young; but what good is in
    beauty and youth
If the lovely and young are not surer than they that
    be neither, forsooth,
Young nor lovely, of being beloved?   O my love, if
    thou lovest not me,
Shall I love my own life?   Am I fair, if not fair,
    Azariah, to thee?"
Then she hid in her bosom the apple.   And rose.
And, reversing the ring
That, inscribed with the word that works wonders, and
    sign'd with the seal of the King,
Hath o'er spirits and demons dominion—(for she, for a
    plaything, erewhile
From King Solomon's aweful forefinger, had won it
    away with a smile)—
The beautiful Shulamite folded her veil o'er her fore-
    head and eyes,
And, with footsteps that fleeted as silent and swift as
    a bird's shadow flies,
Unseen from the palace, she pass'd, and pass'd down
    to the city unseen,

Unseen pass'd the green garden wicket, the vineyard,
   the cypresses green,
And stood by the doors of the house of the Prince
   Azariah.   And cried,
In the darkness she cried—"Azariah, awaken! ope,
   ope to me wide!"
Azariah arose.   And unbolted the door to the fair
   Shulamite.
"O my queen, what dear folly is this, that hath led
   thee alone, and by night,
To the house of King Solomon's servant?   For lo you,
   the watchmen awake.
And much for my own, O my queen, must I fear, and
   much more for thy sake.
For at that which is done in the chamber the leek on
   the housetop shall peep:
And the hand of a king it is heavy: the eyes of a king
   never sleep:
But the bird of the air beareth news to the king, and
   the stars of the sky
Are as soldiers by night on the turrets.   I fear, O my
   queen, lest we die."
" Fear thou not, O my love!   Azariah, fear nothing. ·
   For lo, what I bring!
'Tis the fruit of the Tree that in Paradise God hideth
   under the wing
Of the Cherub that chased away Adam.   And whoso
   this apple doth eat
Shall live—live for ever!   And, since unto me my own
   life is less sweet
Than thy love, Azariah (sweet only thy love maketh
   life unto me!),
Therefore eat!   Live, and love, for life's sake, still, the
   love that gives life unto thee!"

Then she held to his lips the life-apple, and kiss'd him.

But soon as alone,
Azariah lean'd out from his lattice, he mutter'd, "Tis
   well! She is gone."
While the fruit in his hand lay untasted. "Such
   visits," he mused, "may cost dear.
In the love of the great is great danger, much trouble,
   and care more than cheer."
Then he laugh'd, and stretch'd forth his strong arms.
   For he heard from the streets of the city
The song of the women that sing in the doors after
   dark their love ditty.
And the clink of the wine-cup, the voice of the wanton,
   the tripping of feet,
And the laughter of youths running after, allured him.
   And "*Life, is it sweet*
While it lasts," sang the women, "*and sweeter the good*
   minute, in that it goes,
For who, if the rose bloom'd for ever, so greatly would
   care for the rose?
Wherefore haste! pluck the time in the blossom." The
   prince mused, "The counsel is well."
And the fruit to his lips he uplifted: yet paused.
   "Who is he that can tell
"What his days shall bring forth? Life for ever . . .
   But what sort of life? Ah, the doubt!"
'Neath his cloak, then, he thrust back the apple. And
   open'd the door and pass'd out
To the house of the harlot Egyptian. And mused, as
   he went, "Life is good:
"But not life in itself. It is well while the wine-cup
   is hot in the blood,

And a man goeth whither he listeth, and feareth no
    snare by the way.
Shall I care to be loved by a queen, if my pride with
    my freedom I pay?
Better far is a handful in quiet than both hands, tho'
    fill'd to o'erflow
With pride, in vexation of spirit. And sweeter the
    roses that blow
From the wild seeds the wind, where he wanders, with
    heedless beneficence flings,
Than those that are guarded by dragons to brighten
    the garden of kings.
Let a man take his chance and be happy. The hart,
    that is chased by the hounds
When the horn of the hunter hath scatter'd the herd
    from the hills where it sounds,
Is more to be envied, tho' Death with his dart follow
    fast to destroy,
Than the tame beast that, pent in the paddock, tastes
    neither the danger nor joy
Of the mountain, and all its surprises. The main
    thing is, not to live *long*,
But to *live*. Better moments of rapture soon ended,
    than ages of wrong.
Life's feast is best spiced by the flavour of death in it.
    Just the one chance
To lose it to-morrow the life that a man lives to-day
    doth enhance.
The may-be for me, not the must-be! Best flourish
    while flourish the flowers,
And fall ere the frost falls. The dead, do they rest, or
    arise with new powers!
Either way, well for them. Mine, meanwhile, be the
    cup of life's fulness to-night.

And to-morrow . . . Well, time to consider" (he felt
   at the fruit). "What delight
Of his birthright had Esau, when hungry? To-day
   with its pottage is sweet.
For a man cannot feed and be full on the faith of
   to-morrow's baked meat.
Open! open, my dark-eyed beguiler of darkness!"

                    Up rose to his knock,
Light of foot, the lascivious Egyptian, and lifted the
   latch from the lock,
And open'd. And led in the prince to her chamber,
   and shook out her hair,
Dark, heavy, and humid with odours; her bosom
   beneath it laid bare,
And sank 'twixt his knees. Like a leopard, anon she
   sprang loose from his clasp,
And whirl'd from the table a flagon of silver twined
   round by an asp
That glitter'd—rough gold and red rubies; and pour'd
   him, and praised him, the wine
Wherewith she first brighten'd the moist lip that
   murmur'd, "Ha, fool! art thou mine?
I am thine. This will last for an hour." Then,
   humming strange words of a song,
Sung by maidens in Memphis the old, when they bore
   the Crown'd Image along,
Apples yellow and red from a basket with vine-leaves
   o'erlaid she 'gan take,
And play'd with, peel'd, tost them, and caught them,
   and bit them, for idleness' sake;
But the rinds on the floor she flung from her, and
   laugh'd at the figures they made,

As her foot pusht them this way and that way together.
    And, " Look, fool," she said,
" It is all sour fruit, this ! But those I fling from me,
    —see here, by the stain !—
Shall carry the mark of my teeth in their flesh. Could
    they feel but the pain,
O my soul, how these teeth should go through them !
    Fool, fool, what good gift dost thou bring ?
For thee have I sweeten'd with cassia my chambers."
    " A gift for a king,"
Azariah laugh'd loud ; and tost to her the apple.
    " This comes from the Tree
Of whose fruit whoso tastes lives for ever. I care not.
    I give it to thee.
Nay, witch ! 'tis worth more than the shekels of gold
    thou hast charm'd from my purse.
Take it. Eat. Life is sweeter than knowledge : and
    Eve, thy sly mother, fared worse,
O thou white-toothèd taster of apples !" " Thou liest,
    fool ? " " Taste, then, and try.
For the truth of the fruit's in the eating. 'Tis thou
    art the serpent, not I."
And the strong man laugh'd loud as he.push'd at her
    lip the life-apple. She caught
And held it away from her, musing ; and mutter'd . . .
    " Go to ! It is nought.
Fool, why dost thou laugh ? " And he answered,
    " Because, witch, it tickles my brain
Intensely to think that all we, that be Something
    while yet we remain,
We, the princes of people—ay, even the King's self—
    shall die in our day,
And thou, that art Nothing, shall sit on our graves,
    with our grandsons, and play."

So he said, and laugh'd louder.

But when, in the grey of the dawn, he was gone,
And the wan light wax'd large in the window, as she
on her bed sat alone,
With the fruit that, alluring her lip, in her hand lay
untasted, perusing,
. Perplext, the gay gift of the Prince, the dark woman
thereat fell a-musing,
And she thought . . . "What is Life without Honour?
And what can the life that I live
Give to me, I shall care to continue, not caring for
aught it can give?
I, despising the fools that despise me—a plaything not
pleasing myself—
Whose life, for the pelf that maintains it, must sell
what is paid not by pelf!
I? . . . the man call'd me Nothing. He said well.
'The great in their glory must go.'
And why should I linger, whose life leadeth nowhere?
—a life which I know.
To name is to shame—struck, unsexed, by the world
from its list of the lives
Of the women whose womanhood, saved, gets them
leave to be mothers and wives.
And the fancies of men change. And bitterly bought
is the bread that I eat;
For, tho' purchased with body and spirit, when
purchased 'tis yet all unsweet."
Her tears fell: they fell on the apple. She sigh'd . . .
" Sour fruit, like the rest!
Let it go with the salt tears upon it. Yet life . . . it
were sweet if possess'd

In the power thereof, and the beauty. 'A gift for a
    king' . . . did he say?
Ay, a king's life is life as it should be—a life like the
    light of the day,
Wherein all that liveth rejoiceth. For is not the King
    as the sun
That shineth in heaven and seemeth both heaven and
    itself all in one?
Then to whom may this fruit, the life-giver, be worthily
    given? Not me.
Nor the fool Azariah that sold it for folly. The King!
    only he,—
Only he hath the life that's worth living for ever.
    Whose life, not alone
Is the life of the King, but the life of the many made
    mighty in one.
To the King will I carry this apple. And he (for the
    hand of a king
Is a fountain of hope) in his handmaid shall honour the
    gift that I bring.
And men for this deed shall esteem me, with Rahab by
    Israel praised,
As first among those who, tho' lowly, their shame into
    honour have raised:
Such honour as lasts when life goes, and, while life
    lasts, shall lift it above
What, if loved by the many I loathe, must be loathed
    by the few I could love."

So she rose, and went forth thro' the city. And with
    her the apple she bore
In her bosom: and stood 'mid the multitude, waiting
    therewith in the door

Of the hall where the King, to give judgment, ascended
    at morning his throne :

And, kneeling there, cried, " Let the King live for
    ever ! Behold, I am one

Whom the vile of themselves count the vilest. But
    great is the grace of my lord.

And now let my lord on his handmaid look down, and
    give ear to her word."

Thereat, in the witness of all, she drew forth, and
    (uplifting her head)

Show'd the Apple of Life, which who eats, cannot die.
    " And this apple," she said,

" Last night was deliver'd to me, that thy servant
    should eat, and not die.

But I said to the soul of thy servant, ' Not so. For
    behold, what am I ?

That the King, in his glory and gladness, should cease
    from the light of the sun,

Whiles I, that am least of his slaves, in my shame and
    abasement live on.'

For not sweet is the life of thy servant, unless to thy
    servant my lord

Stretch his hand, and show favour. For surely the
    frown of a king is a sword,

But the smile of the King is as honey that flows from
    the clefts of the rock,

And his grace is as dew that from Horeb descends on
    the heads of the flock :

In the King is the heart of a host : the King's strength
    is an army of men :

And the wrath of the King is a lion that roareth by
    night from his den :

But as grapes from the vines of En-Gedi are favours
    that fall from his hands,

And as towers on the hill-tops of Shenir the throne of
    King Solomon stands.
And, for this, it were well that for ever the King, who
    is many in one,
Should sit, to be seen thro' all time, on a throne 'twixt
    the moon and the sun!
For how shall one lose what he hath not? Who hath,
    let him keep what he hath.
Wherefore I to the King give this apple."
               Then great was King Solomon's wrath.
And he rose, rent his garment, and cried, " Woman,
    whence came this apple to thee ? "
But when he was 'ware of the truth, then his heart
    was awaken'd. And he
Knew at once that the man who, erewhile, unawares
    coming to him, had brought
That Apple of Life was, indeed, God's good Angel of
    Death. And he thought
" In mercy, I doubt not, when man's eyes were open'd
    and made to see plain
All the wrong in himself, and the wretchedness, God
    sent to close them again,
For man's sake, his last friend upon earth—Death, the
    servant of God, who is just.
Let man's spirit to Him whence it cometh return, and
    his dust to the dust ! "

KING SOLOMON AND THE MOUSE.

I.

King Solomon stood, in his crown of gold,
   Between the pillars before the altar,
In the House of the Lord.   And the King was old,
   And his strength began to falter,
So that he lean'd on his ebony staff,
Seal'd with the seal of the Pantagraph.

II.

All the golden fretted work,
   Without and within so rich and rare,
As high as the nest of the building stork,
   Those pillars of cedar were :—
Wrought up to the brazen chapiters
Of the Sidonian artificers.

III.

And the King stood still as a carven king,
   The carven cedarn beams below,
In his purple robe, with his signet ring,
   And his beard as white as snow,
And his face to the Oracle, where the hymn
Dies under the wings of the Cherubim.

IV.

The wings fold over the Oracle,
　And cover the heart and eyes of God :
The Spouse with pomegranate, lily, and bell,
　Is glorious in her abode ;
For with gold of Ophir, and scent of myrrh,
And purple of Tyre, the King clothed her.

V.

By the soul of each slumbrous instrument
　Drawn soft through the musical misty air,
The stream of the folk that came and went,
　For worship and praise and prayer,
Flow'd to and fro, and up and down,
And round the King in his golden crown.

VI.

And it came pass, as the King stood there,
　And look'd on his house he had built, with pride,
That the Hand of the Lord came unaware,
　And touch'd him ; so that he died,
In his purple robe, with his signet ring,
And the crown wherewith they had crown'd him king.

VII.

And the stream of the folk that came and went
　To worship the Lord with prayer and praise,

Went softly ever, in wonderment,
    For the King stood there always;
And it was solemn and strange to behold
That dead king crown'd with a crown of gold.

VIII.

For he lean'd on his ebony staff upright!
    And over his shoulders the purple robe;
And his hair, and his beard, were both snow-white;
    And the fear of him fill'd the globe;
So that none dared touch him, though he was dead,
He look'd so royal about the head.

IX.

And the moons were changed: and the years roll'd on:
    And the new king reign'd in the old king's stead:
And men were married and buried anon:
    But the King stood, stark and dead;
Leaning upright on his ebony staff;
Preserved by the sign of the Pantagraph.

X.

And the stream of life, as it went and came,
    Ever for worship and praise and prayer,
Was awed by the face, and the fear, and the fame
    Of the Dead King standing there;
For his hair was so white, and his eyes so cold,
That they left him alone with his crown of gold.

XI.

Magnificent, dead, and dread, in the House
    Of the Lord, held there by the Pantagraph!
Until out from a pillar there ran a red mouse,
    And gnaw'd through his ebony staff!
Then, flat on his face, the King fell down:
And they pick'd from the dust a golden crown.

QUEEN GUENEVERE.

*　　　　*　　　　*　　　　*

THENCE, up the sea-green floor, among the stems
Of mighty columns whose unmeasured shades
From aisle to aisle, unheeded in the sun,
Moved without sound, I, following all alone
A strange desire that drew me like a hand,
Came unawares upon the Queen.
　　　　　　　　　　　　　She sat
In a great silence, which her beauty fill'd
Full to the heart of it, on a black chair
Mail'd all about with sullen gems, and crusts
Of sultry blazonry.　Her face was bow'd,
A pause of slumbrous beauty, o'er the light
Of some delicious thought new-risen above
The deeps of passion.　Round her stately head
A single circlet of the red gold fine
Burn'd free, from which, on either side, stream'd down
Twilights of her soft hair, from neck to foot.
Green was her kirtle as the emerolde is,
And stiff from hem to hem with seams of stones
Beyond all value; which, from left to right
Disparting, half reveal'd the snowy gleam
Of a white robe of spotless samyte pure.
And from the soft repression of her zone,
Which, like a light hand on a lutestring, press'd

Harmony from its touch, flow'd warmly back
The bounteous outlines of a glowing grace,
Nor yet outflow'd sweet laws of loveliness.

Then did I feel as one who, much perplext,
Led by strange legends and the light of stars
Over long regions of the midnight sand
Beyond the red tract of the Pyramids,
Is suddenly drawn to look upon the sky
From sense of unfamiliar light, and sees,
Reveal'd against the constellated cope,
The Great Cross of the South.
                                    The chamber round
Was dropt with arras green ; and I could hear,
In courts far off, a minstrel praising May,
Who sang . . . *Si douce, si douce est la Margarite!*
To a faint lute.   Upon the window-sill,
Hard by a latoun bowl that blazed i' the sun,
Perch'd a strange fowl, a Falcon Perigrine ;
With all his feathers puft for pride, and all
His courage glittering outward in his eye ;
For he had flown from far, athwart strange lands,
And o'er the light of many a setting sun,
Lured by his love (such sovereignty of old
Had Beauty in all courts of Christendom !)
To look into the great eyes of the Queen.

THE DEATH OF KING HACON.

I.

It was Odin that whisper'd in Vingolf,
  "Go forth to the heath by the sea;
Find Hacon before the moon rises,
  And bid him to supper with me."

II.

They go forth to choose from the Princes
  Of Yngvon, and summons from fight
A man who must perish in battle,
  And sup where the gods sup to-night.

III.

Leaning over her brazen spear, Gondula
  Thus bespake her companions, "The feast
Of the gods shall, in Vingolf, this evening,
  O ye Daughters of War, be encreast.

IV.

"For Odin hath beckon'd unto me,
  For Odin hath whisper'd me forth,
To bid to his supper King Hacon
  With the half of the hosts of the North."

V.

Their horses gleam'd white through the vapour:
In the moonlight their corselets did shine:
As they waver'd and whisper'd together,
And fashion'd their solemn design.

VI.

Hacon heard them discoursing—"Why hast thou
Thus disposed of the battle so soon?
Oh were we not worthy of conquest?
Lo! we die by the rise of the moon."

VII.

"It is not the moon that is rising,
But the glory which penetrates death,
When heroes to Odin are summon'd:
Rise, Hacon, and stand on the heath!"

VIII.

"It is we," she replied, "that have given
To thy pasture the flower of the fight;
It is we, it is we, that have scatter'd
Thine enemies yonder in flight.

IX.

"Come now, let us push on our horses
Over yonder green worlds in the east,
Where the great gods are gather'd together,
And the tables are piled for the feast.

x.

"Betimes to give notice to Odin,
   Who waits in his sovran abodes,
That the King to his palace is coming
   This evening to visit the gods."

xi.

Odin rose when he heard it, and with him
   Rose the gods, every god to his feet.
He beckon'd Hermoder and Brago :
   They came to him, each from his seat.

xii.

"Go forth, O my sons, to King Hacon,
   And meet him and greet him from all,
A King that we know by his valour
   Is coming to-night to our hall."

xiii.

Then faintly King Hacon approaches,
   Arriving from battle, and sore
With the wounds that yet bleed through his armour,
   Bedabbled and dripping with gore.

xiv.

His visage is pallid and aweful
   With the awe and pallor of death,
Like the moon that at midnight arises
   Where the battle lies strewn on the heath.

XV.

To him spake Hermoder and Brago,
  " We meet thee and greet thee from all,
To the gods thou art known by thy valour,
  And they bid thee a guest to their hall.

XVI.

" Come hither, come hither, King Hacon,
  And join those eight brothers of thine,
Who already, awaiting thy coming,
  With the gods in Walhala recline.

XVII.

" And loosen, O Hacon, thy corselet,
  For thy wounds are yet ghastly to see.
Go, pour ale in the circle of heroes,
  And drink, for the gods drink to thee ! "

XVIII.

But he answer'd, the hero, " I never
  Will part with the armour I wear.
Shall a warrior stand before Odin
  Unshamed, without helmet and spear?"

XIX.

Black Fenris, the wolf, the destroyer,
  Shall arise and break loose from his chain,
Before that a hero like Hacon
  Shall stand in the battle again.

THE EARL'S RETURN.

I.

RAGGED and tall stood the castle wall.
And the squires, at their sport, in the great South
    Court,
Lounged all day long from stable to hall
Laughingly, lazily, one and all.
The land about was barren and blue,
And swept by the wing of the wet sea-mew.
Seven fishermen's huts on a shelly shore:
Sand-heaps behind, and sand-banks before:
And a black champaign streaked white all through
To the great salt pool which the ocean drew,
Suck'd into itself, and disgorged it again
To stagnate and steam on the mineral plain:
Not a tree nor a bush in the circle of sight,
But a bare black thorn which the sea-winds had
    wither'd
With the drifting scum of the surf and blight,
And some patches of gray grass-land to the right,
Where the lean red-hided cattle were tether'd:
A reef of rock wedged the water in twain,
And a stout stone tower stood square to the main.

II.

Here she lived alone, and from year to year
She saw the bleak belt of the ocean appear

At her casement each morn as she rose; and each morn
Her eye fell first on the bare black thorn.
This was all: nothing more: or sometimes on the
    shore
The fisherman sang when the fishing was o'er;
Or the lowing of oxen fell dreamily,
Close on the shut of the glimmering eves,
Through some gusty pause in the moaning sea,
When the pools were splash'd pink by the thirsty
    beeves.
Or sometimes, when the breezy morns drew the tinges
Of the cold sunrise up their amber fringes,
A white sail peer'd o'er the rim of the main,
Look'd all about o'er the empty sea,
Stagger'd back from the fine line of white light again,
And dropp'd down to another world silently.
Then she breath'd freer.   With sickening dread
She had watch'd five pale young moons unfold
From their notchy cavern in light, and spread
To the fuller light, and again grow old,
And dwindle away to a luminous shred.
"He will not come back till the Spring's green and
    gold.
And I would that I with the leaves were dead,
Quiet somewhere, with them, in the moss and the
    mould,
When he and the Summer come this way," she said.

III.

And the snow was lifted into the air
Layer by layer,
And turn'd into vast white clouds that flew

Silent and fleet, by the breezes driven
Over aëry chasms of fathomless blue
In the rainy depth of an April heaven.
From caves and leaves the quivering dew
Sparkled off; and the rich earth, black and bare,
Was starr'd with snowdrops everywhere,
And the crocus upturn'd its flame, and burn'd
Here and there.
" The Summer," she said, "cometh blithe and bold;
And the crocus is lit for her welcoming:
And the days will have garments of purple and gold;
But I would be left by the pale green Spring
With the snowdrops somewhere under the mould;
For I dare not think what the Summer may bring."

IV.

Pale she was as the bramble blooms
That fill the long fields with their faint perfumes,
And her cheek each year was paler and thinner,
And white as the pearl that was hung at her ear,
As her sad heart sicken'd and pined within her,
And fail'd and fainted from year to year.
So that the Seneschal, rough and gray,
Said, as he look'd in her face one day,
" St. Catherine save all good souls I pray,
For the sweetest Christian soul, I ween,
Day by day is dying away
In the saddest eyes were ever seen.
O the Saints," he said, smiling bitter and grim,
" Know she's too fair and too good for him!"

V.

Sometimes she walk'd on the upper leads,
And lean'd on the arm of the weather-worn Warden:
Sometimes she sat 'twixt the mildewy beds
Of the sea-singed flowers in the Pleasaunce Garden;
Till the rotting blooms that lay thick on the walks
Were comb'd by the white sea-gust like a rake,
And the stimulant stream of the leaves and stalks
Made the coilèd Memory, numb and cold,
That slept in her heart like a dreaming snake,
Drowsily lift himself fold by fold,
And gnaw and gnaw hungrily, half-awake.

VI.

Sometimes she look'd from the window below
To the great South Court, and the Squires, at their
    sport,
Loungingly loitering to and fro.
She heard the grooms there as they cursed one another.
She heard the great bowls falling all day long
In the bowling alleys. She heard the song
Of the shock-headed Pages that drank without stint in
The echoing courts, and swore hard at each other.
She saw the red face of the rough wooden Quintin,
And the swinging sand-bag ready to smother
The awkward Squire that miss'd the mark.
And, all day long, between the dull noises
Of the bowls, and the oaths, and the singing voices,
The sea boom'd hoarse till the skies were dark.

VII.

But at last,—and it was at the fall of the day,
When the thought of a fair land far away
And a face she should never behold again
Was filling her heart with a faint dull pain,
There came a trample of horses and men;
And a blowing of horns at the Castle-Gate :
Then a clattering noise; then a pause; and then,
With the sudden jerk of a heavy weight,
The sound of the falling of cable and chain;
And the grey Seneschal bawl'd out in the hall,
"The Earl and the Devil are come back again ! "
High up on the beach were the long black ships :
And the brown sails hung from the masts in strips;
And the surf was whirl'd over and over them,
And swept them dripping from stern to stem.
There was a wringing of horny hands;
And a swearing of oaths; and a great deal of laughter;
The grim Earl growling his hoarse commands
To the Warden that follow'd him growling after;
A lowing of cattle along the wet sands;
And a plashing of hoofs on the slippery rafter,
As the long-tail'd black-maned horses each
Went over the bridge from the grey sea-beach.
Then a babble as tho' of building crows
That came and went in the court below :
And then, as a prisoner counts the blows
Of the death-bell's hammer, heavy and slow,
Crouch'd in her turret, that lady counted
Step after step of her lord, as he mounted
The narrow stair.   Then a pause.   Then the shock
Of an iron glove on the iron lock,

And the door burst open—the Earl burst through it—
But she saw him not.   The window-pane,
Far off, grew large and small again ;
For the staggering light did wax and wane,
As, when through windy mist you view it,
Moonlight mix'd with shadowy rain ;
Till there came a snap of the heavy brain ;
And a slow-subsiding pulse of pain ;
And, the life of her sank into darkness and rest,
As the grim Earl press'd to his unloved breast
The dead face of the woman that he loved best.

VIII.

That night, and the whole of the next sad day,
Like a lion whose paw is upon his prey,
He waited and watch'd by his fair dead wife :
For, " To plague me, in death," they heard him say,
" She is hiding, but cannot escape that way,
And again I shall catch her returning to life."
Not a vassal ventured to speak or stir :
And the castle was fill'd with the silence of her,
And the fear of those two in the turret alone ;
One, because she was dead, and the other one
Because he lived yet, tho' he made no sign.
But, at last, he arose, took bread and wine,
And ate and drank.   And the Seneschal said,
" Good fellows all, hang sable in hall !
For the worst hath fallen that can befall.
Our lord is alive, and our lady is dead."

IX.

Then the Earl, he bade them lift her lightly,
And bury her by the grey sea-shore,

v.   N

Where the winds that blew from her own land nightly
Might wail round her grave through the wild rocks
    hoar.
So they lifted her lightly at dead of night,
And bore her down by the long torch-light—
—Down to the deep-mouth'd bay's black brim,
Where the pale priests, all white-stoled and dim,
Lifted the cross and chaunted the hymn,
That her soul might have peace when her bones were
    dust,
And her name be written among the Just.
There, under that thorn-tree lone and lean
(A blighted life as her own had been),
With mattock and spade a grave was made,
Where they carved the cross, and they wrote her
    name,
And, returning each by the way that he came,
Their task being o'er, in a month or more,
By night in the hall, and by day on the shore,
With never a thought of their buried dame,
And no heart of them sore for the days of yore,
They laugh'd and quaff'd, and quarrell'd and swore,
And all things became again the same
As all things had been before.

X.

And the flowers decay'd in their dismal beds,
And dropp'd off from their lean shanks one by one,
Till nothing was left but the stalks and the heads,
Clump'd into heaps, or ripp'd into shreds,
To steam into salt in the sickly sun.
And the cattle low'd late up the glimmering plain,

Or dipp'd knee-deep, and splash'd themselves
In the pools spat out by the spiteful main,
Wallowing in sandy dykes and delves:
And the blear-eyed filmy sea did bloom
With his old mysterious hungering sound:
And the wet wind wail'd in the chinks of the tomb,
Till the weeds in the surf were drench'd and drown'd.
And the Earl, as years went by, and his life
Grew listless, took him another wife.
But once a stranger came over the wave,
And paused by the pale-faced Lady's grave.

XI.

It was when, just about to set,
A sadness held the sinking sun.
The moon, a mere white mist as yet,
Hover'd faint in the fervid blue:
The Ave-Mary chime was done;
The grey-gown'd priest was passèd through
The chapel porch of grassy stone;
And from the bell-tower lean'd the ringers;
And in the chancel paused the singers,
With lingering looks, and claspèd fingers:
And the day reluctantly turn'd to his rest,
Like some untold life, that leaves exprest
But the half of its hungering love ere it close:
So he went sadly toward his repose
Deep in the heart of the slumbrous waves
Kindled far off in the desolate west.
And the breeze sprang up in the cool sea-caves.
The castle stood with his courts in shade,
And all his toothèd towers imprest

On the sorrowful light that sunset made—
Such a light as sleeps shut up in the breast
Of some pining crimson-hearted rose,
Which, as you gaze at it, grows and grows
And all the warm leaves overflows;
Leaving its sweet source still to be guess'd.

XII.

Ere the moon was abroad, the owl
Made himself heard in the echoing tower
Three times, four times.   The bat with her cowl
Came and went round the lonely Bower
Where dwelt of yore the Earl's lost Lady.
There night after night, for years, in vain
The lingering moon had look'd through the pane,
And miss'd the face she used to find there,
White and wan like some mountain flower
In its rocky nook, as it paled and pined there
Only known to the moon and the wind there.
Lights flitted faint in the halls down lower
From lattice to lattice, and then glow'd steady.

XIII.

The dipping gull: and the long grey pool:
And the reed that shows which way the breeze blows
    cool,
From the wide warm sea to the low black land:
And the wave makes no sound on the soft yellow sand:
But the inland shallows sharp and small
Are swarm'd about with the sultry midge:
And the land is still, and the ocean still:

And into the silent western side
Of the heaven the moon begins to fall.
But is it the seagull's plaintive call
To her wandering mates o'er the twilit tide,
That is answer'd warily, low yet shrill,
From the sand-heapt mound and the rocky ridge?
And now o'er the dark plain so wild and wide
Floats the note of a horn from the old draw-bridge.

XIV.

Who is it that waits at the Castle-Gates?
Call in the minstrel, and fill the bowl.
Bid him loose the great music and let the song roll.
Fill the bowl.
And first, as was due, to the Earl he bow'd:
Next to all the Sea-chieftains, blithe friends of the
    Earl's:
Then advanced through the praise of the murmuring
    crowd,
And sat down, as they bade him, and all his black
    curls
Bow'd over his harp, as in doubt which to choose
From the melodies coil'd at his heart.   For a man
O'er some Beauty asleep for one moment might muse,
Half in love, ere he woke her.   So ere he began,
He paused over his song.   And they brought him, the
    Squires,
A heavy gold cup with the red wine ripe in it.
Then wave over wave of the sweet silver wires
'Gan ripple, and the minstrel took heart to begin it.

XV.

" There is a land far, far away from yours.
And there the stars are thrice as bright as these.
And there the nightingale strange music pours
All day out of the hearts of myrtle trees.
There the voice of the cuckoo sounds never forlorn
As you hear it far off thro' the deep purple valleys.
And the firefly dances by night in the corn.
And the little round owls in the long cypress alleys
Whoop for joy when the moon is born.
There ripen the olive and the tulip tree.
And in the sun broadens the green prickly pear.
And the bright galingales in the grass you may see.
And the vine, with her royal blue globes, dwelleth
    there,
Climbing and hanging deliciously
By every doorway and lone latticed chamber,
Where the damselfly flits, and the heavy brown bee
Hums alone, and the quick lizards rustle and clamber.
And all things, there, live and rejoice together,
From the frail peach-blossom that first appears
When birds are about in the blue summer weather,
To the oak that has lived through his eight hundred
    years.
And the castles are built on the hills, not the plains.
(And the wild windflowers burn about in the courts
    there)
They are white and undrench'd by the grey winter
    rains.
And the swallows, and all things, are blithe at their
    sports there.
O for one moment, at sunset, to stand

Far, far away, in that dear distant land
Whence they bore her—the loveliest lady that ever
Crost the bleak ocean.   Oh nevermore, never,
Shall she stand with her feet in the warm dry grasses
Where the faint balm-heaping breeze heavily passes,
And the white lotus-flower leans lone on the river!"

XVI.

And the minstrel sung, and they praised and listen'd—
Gazed and praised while the minstrel sung.
Flusht was each cheek, and each fixt eye glisten'd,
And husht was each voice to the minstrel's tongue.
But the Earl grew paler more and more
As the song of the singer grew louder and clearer,
And so dumb was the hall, you might hear the roar
Of the sea in its pauses grow nearer and drearer.
And . . . hush! hush! hush!
O was it the wind? or was it the rush
Of the restless waters that tumble and splash
On the wild sea-rocks? or was it the crash
Of stones on the old wet bridge up there?
Or the sound of the tempest come over the main?
—Nay, but just now the night was fair.
Was it the march of the midnight rain
Clattering down in the courts? or the crash
Of armour yonder? . . . Listen again!

XVII.

Can it be lightning?—can it be thunder?
For a light is all round the lurid hall
That reddens and reddens the windows all,

And far away you may hear the fall
As of rafter and boulder splitting asunder.
It is not the thunder, and it is not the lightning,
To which the castle is sounding and brightening,
But something worse than lightning or thunder,
For what is this that is coming yonder?

XVIII.

Which way?   Here!   Where?
Call the men! . . . Is it there?
Call them out!   Ring the bell!
Ring the Fiend back to Hell!
Ring, ring the alarum for mercy! . . . Too late!
It has crawl'd up the walls—it has burst in the gate—
It looks thro' the windows—it creeps near the hall—
Near, more near—red and clear—
It is here!
Now the saints save us all!

XIX.

And little, in truth, boots it ringing the bell.
For the fire is loose on its way one may tell
By the hot simmering whispers and humming up there
In the oak-beams and rafters.   Now one of the Squires
His elbow hath thrust thro' the half-smoulder'd door—
Such a hole as some rat for his brown wife might
    bore—
And straightway in snaky, white, wavering spires
The thin smoke twirls thro', and spreads eddying in
    gyres,

Here and there toucht with vanishing tints from the
  glare
That has swathed in its rose-light the sharp turret
  stair.
Soon the door ruin'd thro': and in tumbled a cloud
Of black vapour. And first 'twas all blackness, and
  then
The quick forkèd fires leapt out from their shroud
In the blackness: and thro' it rush'd in the arm'd men
From the courtyard. And then there was flying and
  fighting,
And praying and cursing—confusion confounded.
Each man, at wild hazard, thro' smoke ramparts
  smiting,
Has struck . . . is it friend? is it foe? Who is
  wounded?

XX.

But the Earl—who last saw him? Who cares? who
  knows?
Some one, no doubt, by the weight of his blows.
And they all, at times, heard his oath—so they swore:—
Such a cry as some spear'd wild beast might give vent
  to,
When the lean dogs are on him, and forth with that
  roar
Of desolate wrath, the life is sent too.
If he die, he will die with the dying about him,
And his red wet sword in his hand, never doubt him:
If he live, perchance he will bear his new bride
Thro' them all, past the bridge, to the wild seaside.

And there, whether he leave, or keep his wife still,
There's the free sea round him, new lands, and new
    life still,
And . . . but ah, thé red light there ! And high up
    and higher
The soft, warm, vivid sparkles crowd kindling, and
    wander
Far away down the breathless blue cone of the night.
Saints ! can it be that the ships are on fire,
Those fierce hot clots of crimson light,
Brightening, whitening in the distance yonder?
Slowly over the slumbrous dark
Up from those fountains of fire spark on spark
(You might count them almost) floats silent : and clear
In the steadfast glow the great cross-beams,
And the sharp and delicate masts, show black ;
While wider and higher the red light streams,
And oozes, and overflows at the back.
Then faint thro' the distance a sound you hear,
And the bare poles totter and disappear.

.

XXI.

Of the Earl, in truth, the Seneschal swore
(And over the ocean this tale he bore)
That when, as he fled on that last wild night,
He had gain'd the other side of the moat,
Dripping, he shook off his wet leathern coat,
And turning round beheld, from basement
To cope, the Castle swathed in light,
And, reveal'd in the glare thro' My Lady's casement,
He saw, or dreamed he saw, this sight—

XXII.

Two forms (and one for the Earl's he knew,
By the long shaggy beard and the broad back too)
Struggling, grappling, like things half human.
The other, he said, he but vaguely distinguish'd,
When a sound like the shriek of an agonized woman
Made him shudder, and lo, all the vision was gone!
Ceiling and floor had fallen thro',
In a glut of vomited flame extinguish'd;
And the still fire rose and broaden'd on.

XXIII.

How fearful a thing is fire!
You might make up your mind to die by water
A slow, cool death—nay, at times, when weary
Of pains that pass not, and pleasures that pall,
When the temples throb, and the heart is dreary,
And life is dried up, you could even desire
Thro' the flat green weeds to fall and fall
Half asleep down the green light, under them all,
As in a dream, while all things seem
Wavering, wavering, to feel the stream
Wind, and gurgle, and sound, and gleam.
And who would very much fear to expire
By steel, in the front of victorious slaughter,
The blithe battle about him, and comrades in call?
But to die by fire!
O that night in the hall!

XXIV.

As for the rest, some died ; some fled
Over the sea, nor ever return'd.
But until to the living return the dead,
And they each shall stand and take their station
Again at the last great conflagration,
Never more will be seen the Earl or the stranger.
No doubt there is much here that's fit to be burn'd.
Christ save us all·in that day from the danger !

RABBI BEN EPHRAIM'S TREASURE.

PERSECUTION OF THE JEWS IN SPAIN.

(FIFTEENTH CENTURY.)

I.

THE days of Rabbi Ben Ephraim
Were two score years and ten, the day
The hangman call'd at last for him,
And he privily fled from Cordova.
Drop by drop, he had watch'd the cup
Of the wine of bitterness fill'd to the brim;
Drop by drop, he had drain'd it up;
And the time was an evil time for him.
An evil time! For Jehovah's face
Was turn'd in wrath from His chosen race,
And the daughter of Judah must mourn,
Whom His anger had left, in evil case,
To be dogg'd by death from place to place,
With garments bloody and torn.
The time of the heavy years, from of old
By the mouth of His servant the Prophet foretold,
In the days of Josiah the king,
When the Lord upon Jacob his load should bring,
And the hand of Heaven, in the day of His ire,
Be heavy and hot upon son and sire,

Till from out of the holes into which they were driven
Their bones should be strown to the host of Heaven
Whose bodies were burn'd in the fire.
Rabbi Ben Ephraim, day by day
(As the hangman, beating up his bounds
Thro' the stifled Ghetto's sinks and stews,
Or the Arch Inquisitor, going his rounds,
Was pleased to pause, and pick, and choose,
—Too sure of his game, which could not stray,
To miss the luxury of delay)
Had mark'd with a moody indignation
The abomination of desolation,
With the world to witness, and none to gainsay,
Set up in the midst of the Holy Nation,
And the havoc, which Heaven refused to stay,
In the course of his horrible curse move on,
Where, sometimes driven in trembling crews,
Sometimes singly one by one,
Israel's elders were beckon'd away
To the place where the Christians burn the Jews:
Till he, because that his wealth was known,
And because the king had debts to pay,
Was left, at the last, almost alone
Of all his people in Cordova,
A living man picked out by fate
To bear, and beware of, the daily jibe,
And add the same to the sum of the hate,
Made his on behalf of a slaughter'd tribe.

II.

In the gloomy Ghetto's gloomiest spot,
A certain patch of putrid ground,

There is a place of tombs : Moors rot,
Rats revel there, and devils abound
By night, no cross being there to keep
The evil things in awe : the dead
That house there, sleep no Christian sleep—
They do not sleep at all, it is said ;
Tho', how they fare, the Fiend best knows,
Who never vouchsafes to them any repose,
For their worm is awake in the narrow bed,
And the fire that will never be quenched is fed
On the night that will never close.
There did Rabbi Ben Ephraim
(When he saw, at length, the appointed measure
Of misery meted out to him)
Bury his books and all his treasure.
He buried them deep that none might mark
—Hid them from sight of the hated race,
Gave them in guard of the Powers of the Dark
And solemnly set his curse on the place.
Then he saddled his mule, and with him took
Zillah his wife, and Rachel his daughter,
And Manassah his son ; and turn'd and shook
The dust from his foot on the place of slaughter,
And cross'd the night, and fled away
(Balking the hangman of his prey)
From out of the city of Cordova.

III.

Rabbi Ben Ephraim never more
Saw Cordova. For the Lord had will'd
That the dust should be dropp'd on his eyes before
The curse upon Israel was fulfill'd.

Therefore he ended the days of his life
In evil times; and by the hand
Of Rachel his daughter, and Zillah his wife,
Was laid to rest in another land.
But, before his face to the wall he turn'd,
As the eyes of the women about his bed
Grew hungry and hard with a hope unfed,
And the misty lamp more misty burn'd,
To Zillah and Rachel the Rabbi said
Where they might find, if fate turn'd kind,
And the fires of Cordova, grown slack,
Should ever suffer their footsteps back,
The tomb where by stealth he had buried his wealth
When he fled from the foe, and the stake, and the
    rack;
And how to open that tomb; and where
To seek within it the wealth hid there,
By means of a spiral, cut down the abyss
To the dead men.

IV.

When he had utter'd this
Rabbi Ben Ephraim turn'd his face,
And slept.

V.

The years went on apace.
Manassah his son, his youngest born,
Trading the isleted sea for corn,
Was wreck'd and pick'd up by the smuggler boat
Of a certain prowling Candiote;

And, being young and hale, was sold
By the Greek a bondsman to the Turk.
Zillah, his wife, wax'd white and old.
Rachel, his daughter, loved not work,
But walk'd by the light of her own dark eyes
In wicked ways for the sake of gain.
Meanwhile, Israel's destinies
Survived the scorching stake, and Spain
At length grew weary of burning men ;
When hunger'd, and haggard, and gaunt, these two
Forlorn Jew women crept again
Into Cordova; because they knew
Where Rabbi Ben Ephraim by stealth,
When he turn'd his back on his own house-door,
Had buried the whole of his wondrous wealth
In the place of tombs ; and they two were poor.

VI.

So poor indeed, they had been constrain'd
To filch from the refuse flung out to the streets
('Mid the rags and onion-peelings rain'd
Where the town's worst gutter's worst filth greets
With his strongest gust and most savoury sweets
Those blots and failures of Human Nature,
Refused a name in her nomenclature,
That spawn themselves toward night, and bend
To finger the husks and shucks heap'd there,)
The wretched, rat-bitten candle-end
Which, found by good luck, they had treasured with
    care
Not a whit less solemn than tho' it were
That famous work of the son of Uri,
The candlestick of candlesticks,

V.   O

—He the long-lost light of Jewry,
Whose almond bowls and scented wicks
Were the boast of the desert, and Salem's glory
Of the knops and flowers, with his branches six !
For this, that once perchance made bright
Round laughing love, and beauty dight
In gem and flower, for dance and song,
Some chamber gay, with arras hung,
Must now, with its hungry half-starved light,
Make bold the shuddering flesh to face
The sepulchre's supernatural night,
And the Powers of the Dark keeping guard on the
    place.

VII.

And, when to the place of tombs they came,
The spotted moon sunk.   Night stood bare
In the waste unlighted air
Wide-arm'd, waiting, and aware,
To horribly hem them in.   The flame
The little candle feebly gave,
As it wink'd and winced from grave to grave,
Went fast to furious waste; the same
As some soul-consuming hope
Doom'd, from grief to grief, to grope
In wavering ways about the world.
The deep enormous night unfurl'd
Her banner'd blackness left and right,
Fold heap'd on fold, to mock such light
With wild defiance; no star pearl'd
The heavy pall, but horror hurl'd
Shadow on shadow; while for spite

The very graves kept out of sight,
And heaven's sworn hatred, winning might
From earth's ill-will, with darkness curl'd
Darkness, all space confounding quite,
So to engender night on night.

VIII.

" Rachel, Rachel, for ye are tall,
Lift the light along the wall."

" Mother, give me the hand, and follow,
Once . . . twice . . . thrice . . . the earth sounds
    hollow ! "

" Rachel, Rachel, ye walk so fast ! "

" Mother, the light will barely last."

" What see ye, Rachel ? "

IX.

                    A square stone cut
With letters.   Thick the moss is driven
Thro' the graver's work now blunt and blurr'd :
There be seven words with letters seven :
A finger-touch on the letter third
Of seven in the seventh word,
And the stone is heaved back: earth yawns and
    gapes :
A cold strikes up the clammy dark,
And clings : a spawn of vaporous shapes

Floats out in films : a sanguine spark
The taper spits : the snaky stair
Gleams, curling down the abyss laid bare,
Where Rabbi Ben Ephraim's treasure is laid.

X.

There, they sat them down awhile,
With that terrible joy which cannot smile
Because the heart of it is staid
And stunn'd, as it were, by a too swift pace.
And the dismal Presence abroad on the place
So took them with awe that they rested afraid
Almost to look into each other's face.
Moreover, the nearness of what should change,
Like a change in a dream, their lives for ever
Into something suddenly bright and strange,
Paused upon them, and made them shiver.
The old woman mumbled at length : " I am old :
I have no sight the treasure to find ;
I have no strength to rake the red gold ;
My hand is palsied, mine eye is blind,
Child of my bosom, I dare not descend
To the horrible pit ! "
                                    And Rachel said :
" I fear the darkness, I fear the dead ;
But the candle is burning fast to the end :
O Mother, we will go, we twain,
Together."
                        The old woman cried again :
" Child of my bosom, I will not descend
To the horrible pit.   Go down, thyself.
Young are ye !   What your beauty brings

Who knows ?   I think ye keep the pelf.
Poverty is the worst of things ! "
Rachel look'd at the dwindling flame,
And frown'd, and mutter'd, " Mother, shame !
I fear the darkness, because there clings
To my heart a thought, I cannot smother,
Of certain things which, whatever the blame,
Thou wottest of, and I will not name ;
For my sins are many and heavy, mother.
Yet because I hunger, and still would save
Some years from sin, and because of my brother
Whom the Greek man sold to be slave to a slave,
(May the Lord requite the lying knave !)
I will go down alone to the pit.
Thou therefore, mother, watch, and sit
In prayer for me, by the mouth of the grave."

XI.

The mother sat by the grave and listen'd.
She waited : she heard the footsteps go
Under the earth, wandering, slow.
She look'd : deep down the taper glisten'd.
Then, the voice of Rachel from below :
" Mother, mother, stoop and hold ! "
And she flung up four ouches of gold.
The old woman counted them, ouches four,
Beaten out of the massy ore.
" Child of my bosom, blessèd art thou !
The hand of the Lord be yet with thee !
As thou art strong in thy spirit now,
Many and pleasant thy days shall be.
As a vine in a garden, fair to behold,

Green in her branches, shalt thou grow,
And so have gladness when thou art old.
Rachel, Rachel, be thou bold!
More gold yet, and still more gold!"

"Mother, mother, the light burns low.
The candle is one inch shorter now,
And I dare not be left in the darkness alone."

"Rachel, Rachel, go on! go on!
Of thee have I said, She shall not shrink!
Thy brother is yet a bondsman—think!
Yet once more,—and he is free,
And whom shall he praise for this but thee?
Rachel, Rachel, be thou bold!
Manassah is groaning over the sea.
More gold yet, and still more gold!"

"Mother, mother, stoop and hold!"

And she flung up from below again
Cups of the carven silver twain.
Solid silver was each great cup.
The old woman caught them as they came up.
"Rachael, Rachael, well hast thou done!
Manassah is free. Go on! go on!
Royal dainties for ever be thine!
Rachel's eyes shall be red with wine,
Rachel's mouth shall with milk be fill'd,
And her bread be fat. I praise thee, my child,
For surely thou hast freed thy brother.
The deed was good, but there resteth another,
And art thou not the child of thy mother?

Thy mother is very poor and old.
More gold yet, and still more gold!"

"Mother, the light is very low.
The candle is well-nigh wasted now,
And I dare not be left in the darkness alone."

"Rachel, Rachel, go on! go on!
Much is done, but there resteth more.
Ye are young, Rachel, shall it be told
That my bones were laid at my children's door?
More gold yet, and still more gold!"

"Mother, mother, stoop and hold!"

The voice came fainter from beneath;
And she flung up a jewell'd sheath.
The sheath was thick with many a gem;
The old woman carefully counted them.

"Rachel, Rachel, thee must I praise,
Who makest pleasant thy mother's days.
Blessèd be thou in all thy ways!
Surely for this must I praise thee, my daughter,
And therefore in fulness shalt thou dwell
As a fruitful fig-tree beside the water
That layeth her green leaves over the well.
More gold, Rachel, yet again!
And we shall have houses and servants in Spain,
And thou shalt walk with the wealthiest ladies,
And fairest, in Cordova, Seville, or Cadiz,
And thou shalt be woo'd as a Queen should be,
And tended upon as the proud are tended,
And the alguazils shall doff to thee,

For thy face shall be brighten'd, thy raiment be
    splendid,
And no man shall call thee an evil name,
And thou shalt no longer remember thy shame,
And thy mother's eyes, as she waxes old,
Shall see the thing she would behold—
More gold yet, and still more gold!"

" Mother, the light is very low—
—Out! out! . . . Ah God, they are on me now!
Mother, mother, they have me, and hold!
Mother, there is a curse on thy gold!
Mother" (the old woman hears with a groan),
" Leave me not here in the darkness alone!"

CATTERINA CORNARO.

(A PICTURE.—A.D. 1470.)

I.

In Cyprus, where live Summer never dies,
Love's native land is.   There the seas, the skies,
Are blue and lucid as the looks, the air
Fervid and fragrant as the breath and hair,
Of Beauty's Queen; whose gracious godship dwells
In that dear island of delicious dells,
'Mid lavish lights and languid glooms divine.
There doth she her sly dainty sceptre twine
With seabank myrtle spray, and roses sweet
And full as, when the lips of lovers meet
The first strange time, their sudden kisses be:
There doth she lightly reign: there holdeth she
Her laughing court in gleam of lemon groves:
The wanton mother of unnumber'd Loves!

What earthly creature hath Dame Venus' grace
Dower'd so divinely sweet of form and face
As that she may, unshamed in Cupid's smile,
Be sovereign lady of this lovely isle?
Sure, Venus, not so blind as some aver
Was thy bold boy, what time, in search of her

Thou bad'st him seek, he roam'd the seas all round,
And barbarous lands beyond; since he hath found
This wonder out; whose perfect sweetness seems
The fair fulfilment of his own fond dreams:
And Kate Cornaro is the Island Queen.

II.

A Queen: a child: fair: happy: scarce nineteen!
In whose white hands her little sceptre lies,
Like a new-gather'd flowret, in surprise
At being there. To keep her what she is,
—A thing too rare for the familiar kiss
Of household loves,—wifehood and motherhood,—
Fit only to be delicately woo'd
With wooings fine and frolicksome as those
Wherewith the sweet West woos a small blush-rose,
Her husband first, and then her babe, away
Slipp'd from her sight, each on a summer day,
Ere she could miss them, into the soft shade
Of flowery graves. She doth not feel afraid
To be alone. Because she hath her toy,
Her pretty kingdom. And it is her joy
To dandle the doll-people, and be kind
And careful to it, as a child. Each wind
O' the world on her smooth eyelids lightly breathes,
As morn upon a lily whence frail wreaths
Of little dew-drops hang, easily troubled,
As such things are. The June sun's joy is doubled,
Shining thro' shadow in her golden hair.
Light-wedded, and light-widow'd, and unaware
Of any sort of sorrow doth she seem;
Albeit the times are stormy, and do teem

With tumult round her tiny throne.   Primrose,
Pert crocus, hardy vetch,—no blossom blows
In March less conscious of a cloudy sky,
More sweet in sullen season.   Days go by
Daintily round her.   If her crown's light weight
Upon her forehead fair and delicate
Leave the least violet stain, when laid away
At close of some great summer holiday,
Her lovers kiss the sweet mark smooth and white
Ere it can pain her.   She hath great delight
In little things : and of great things small care.
The people love her; tho' the nobles are
Wayward and wild.   Yet fears she not, nor shrinks
To show she fears not.   "For in truth," she thinks,
"My Uncle Andrew, and my Uncle Mark,
Have care of me."   And, truly, dawn or dark,
These Uncles Mark and Andrew, busiest two
In Cyprus, find no lack of work to do :
Go up and down the noisy little state
Silent all day : and, when the night is late,
Write letters, which she does not care to read
(The Ten, she knows, will ponder them with heed),
To Venice—not so far from Cyprus' shore,
But what the shadow of St. Mark goes o'er
The narrow sea to touch her island throne.

III.

She is herself a dove from Venice flown
Not so long since but what her snowy breast
Is yet scarce warm within its new-found nest.—
Whence sings she o'er the grave of Giacomo
Songs taught her by St. Mark.

Christofero
(He of the four stone shields which you may spy,
Twice striped, thrice spotted with the mulberry,
In the great sunlight o'er that famous stair
Whose marble white is warm'd with rose hues, where
The crownings were once) wore the ducal horn
In Venice, on that joyous July morn
When all along the liquid streets, paved red
With rich reflections of clear crimson spread,
Or gorgeous orange gay with glowing fringe,
From bustling balconies above, to tinge
The lucid highways with new lustres, best
Befitting that day's pride, the blithe folk press'd
About St. Paul's, beneath the palace door
Of Mark Cornaro ; where the Bucentor
Was waiting with the Doge ; to see Queen Kate
Come smiling in her robes of marriage state
Thro' the cramm'd causeway, glimmering down be-
    tween
The sloped bright-banded poles, beneath the green
Sea-weeded walls ; content to catch quick gleams
Of her robe's tissue stiff with strong gold seams
From throat to foot, or mantle's sweeping shine
Of murrey satin lined with ermine fine.
Flushing the white warmth it encircled glad,
A sparkling karkanet of gems she had
About her fair throat.   Such strong splendours piled
So heavily upon so slight a child
Made Venice proud ; because in little things
Her greatness thus seem'd greatest.

His white wings
The galley put forth from the blue lagoon.

The mellow disk of a mild daylight moon
Was hanging wan in the warm azure air,
When the great clarions all began to blare
Farewell.   And, underneath a cloudless sky
Over a calmèd sea, with minstrelsy,
The Baby Queen to Cyprus sail'd. * * *

JACQUELINE,

COUNTESS OF HOLLAND AND HAINAULT.

(1436.)

Is it the twilight, or my fading sight,
Makes all so dim around me?   No, the night
Is come already.   See! thro' yonder pane,
Alone in the grey air, that star again—
Which shines so wan, I used to call it mine
For its pale face; like Countess Jacqueline
Who reign'd in Brabant once . . . that's years ago.
I call'd so much mine, then: so much seem'd so!
And see, my own!—of all those things, my star
(Because God hung it there, in heaven, so far
Above the reach and want of those hard men)
Is all they have not taken from me.   Then
I call it still My Star.   Why not?   The dust
Hath claim'd the dust: no more.   And moth and rust
May rot the throne, the kingly purple fray:—
What then?   Yon star saw kingdoms roll'd away
Ere mine was taken from me.   It survives.
But think, beloved,—in that high life of lives,
When our souls see the suns themselves burn low
Before that Sun of Righteousness,—and know
What is, and was, before the suns were lit—
How love is all in all . . . Look, look at it,

My Star—God's star—for being God's 'tis mine;
Had it been man's . . . no matter . . . see it shine—
The old wan beam, which I have watch'd ere now
So many a wretched night, when this poor brow
Ached 'neath the sorrows of its thorny crown.
Its crown! . . . ah, droop not, dear, those fond eyes
    down.
No gem in all that shatter'd coronet
Was half so precious as the tear which wet
Just now this pale sick forehead.   O my own,   ·
My husband, need was, that I should have known
Much sorrow,—more than most Queens—all know
    some,—
Ere, dying, I could bless thee for the home
Far dearer than the palace,—call thy tear
The costliest gem that ever sparkled here.

Enfold me, my belovèd.   One more kiss.
Oh, I must go!   'Twas will'd I should not miss
Life's secret, ere I left it.   And now see—
My lips touch thine—thine arm encircles me—
The secret's found—God beckons—I must go.
Earth's best is given.—Heaven's turn is come to show
How much its best earth's best may yet exceed,
Lest earth's should seem the very best indeed.
So we must part a little; but not long.
I seem to see it all.   My lands belong
To Philip still; but thine will be my grave,
(The only strip of land which I could save!)
Not much, but wide enough for some few flowers,
Thou'lt plant there, by and by, in later hours:
Duke Humphry, when they tell him I am dead
(And so young too) will sigh, and shake his head,

And, if his wife should chide, "Poor Jacqueline,"
He'll add, "you know she never could be mine."
And men will say, when some one speaks of me,
"Alas, it was a piteous history,
The life of that poor Countess!"   For the rest
Will never know, my love, how I was blest.
Some few of my poor Zealanders, perchance,
Will keep kind memories of me; and in France
Some minstrel sing my story.   Pitiless John
Will prosper still, no doubt, as he has done,
And still praise God with blood upon the Rood.
Philip will, doubtless, still be call'd "The Good."
And men will curse and kill: and the old game
Will weary out new hands: the love of fame
Will sow new sins: thou wilt not be renown'd:
And I shall lie quite quiet underground.
My life is a torn book.   But at the end
A little page, quite fair, is saved, my friend,
Where thou didst write thy name.   No stain is there,.
No blot,—from marge to marge, all pure—no tear ;—
The last page, saved from all, and writ by thee,
Which I shall take safe up to Heaven with me.
All's not in vain, since this be so.   Dost grieve ?
Belovèd, I beseech thee to believe,
Altho' this be the last page of my life,
It is my heart's first, only one.   Thy wife,
Poor tho' she be, O thou sole wealth of mine,
Is happier than the Countess Jacqueline !

And since my heart owns thine, say—am I not
A Queen, my chosen, tho' by all forgot ?
Tho' all forsake, yet is not this thy hand ?
I, a lone wanderer in a darken'd land,

I, a poor pilgrim with no staff of hope,
I, a late traveller down the sunless slope,
Where any spark, the glow-worm's, by the way,
Had been a light to bless . . . have I, O say,
Not found, belovèd, in thy tender eyes,
A light more sweet than morning's? As there dies
Some day of storm all glorious in its even,
My life grows loveliest as it fades in Heaven.

This earthly house breaks up. This flesh must fade.
So many shocks of grief slow breach have made
In the poor frame. Wrongs, insults, treacheries,
Hopes broken down, and memory which sighs
In, like a night-wind! Life was never meant
To bear so much in such frail tenement.
Why should we seek to patch and plaster o'er
This shatter'd roof, crusht windows, broken door,
The light already shines thro'? Let them break!

Yet would I gladly live for thy dear sake,
O my heart's first and last, if that could be!
In vain! . . . yet grieve not thou. I shall not see
England again, and those white cliffs; nor ever
Again those four grey towers beside the river,
And London's roaring bridges: never more
Those windows with the market-stalls before,
Where the red-kirtled market-girls went by
In the great square, beneath the great grey sky,
In Brussels: nor in Holland, night or day,
Watch those long lines of siege, and fight at bay
Among my broken army, in default
Of Gloucester's failing forces from Hainault:
Nor shall I pace again those gardens green,

v.   P

With their clipt alleys, where they call'd me Queen,
In Brabant once.   For all these things are gone.
But thee I shall behold, my chosen one,
Tho' we should seem whole worlds on worlds apart,
Because thou wilt be ever in my heart.
Nor shall I leave thee wholly.   I shall be
An evening thought,—a morning dream to thee,—
A silence in thy life when, thro' the night,
The bell strikes, or the sun, with sinking light,
Smites all the empty windows.   As there sprout
Daisies, and dimpling tufts of violets, out
Among the grass where some corpse lies asleep,
So round thy life, where I lie buried deep,
A thousand little tender thoughts shall spring,
A thousand gentle memories wind, and cling.
O, promise me, my own, before my soul
Is houseless,—let the great world turn and roll
Upon its way, unvext . . . its pomps, its powers !
The dust saith to the dust, . . . " The earth is ours."
I would not, if I could, be Queen again,
For all the walls of the wide world contain.
Be thou content with silence.   Who would raise
A little dust and noise of human praise,
If he could see, in yonder distance dim,
The silent eye of God that watches him ?
Oh ! couldst thou see all that I see to-night
Upon the brinks of the great Infinite !

" Come out of her, my people, lest ye be
Partakers of her sins ! " . . . . My love, but we
Our treasure where no thieves break in and steal
Have stored, I trust.   Earth's weal is not our weal.
Let the world mind its business—peace or war ;

Ours is elsewhere.   Look, look,—my star, my star!
It grows, it glows, it spreads in light unfurl'd;—
Said I "my star"? No star—a world—God's world!
What hymns adown the jasper sea are roll'd?
Even to these sick pillows!   Who enfold
White wings about me?   Rest, rest, rest . . . I come!
O love, I think that I am near my home.
Whence was that music?   Was it Heaven's I heard?
"Write 'Blessèd are the dead that die i' the Lord,
Because they rest,'" . . . because their toil is o'er.
The voice of weeping shall be heard no more
In the Eternal City.   Neither dying
Nor sickness, pain nor sorrow, neither crying,
For God shall wipe away all tears.   Rest, rest . . .
Thy hand, my husband,—so—upon thy breast!

THE DIRGE.

Pluck the pale sky-colour'd periwinkle,
That haunts in dewy courts, and shuns the light:
Gather dim violets and the wild eyebright,
That green old ruin'd walls doth oversprinkle:
And cull, to keep her company
In death, rue, sage, and rosemary,
And flowery thyme from the faint bed o' the bee;
For they, when Summer's o'er, make savour sweet
To cherish Winter: strew black-spikèd clove,
And mint, and marjoram, to make my love
A misty fragrance for her winding-sheet.
But pull not up red tulips, nor the rose,
For these be flaunting flowers that live i' the world's gay
*   shows.*

THOMAS MÜNTZER TO MARTIN LUTHER.

(FROM PRISON.)

I KNOW not if what now my spirit doth spend
This tortur'd frame's last strength in sore endeavour
To write to thee will reach thee, Luther, ever.
For I, whose crime is to have been man's friend,
No friend can claim, whose friendship's faith I may
Trust these, my life's last words, to thee to send,
After my death, which thou dost urge, men say.
I know not, Luther, if what's writ to-night
Be for thy reading, or for any man's.
'Tis as God wills.   But, since His own eye scans,
And answers, in my heart, what now I write,
Still I write on, while He withholds the end.
And, setting bare my spirit in God's sight,
I summon thine to witness.
                                        'Twere in vain
To urge the old sad difference o'er again.
Doom'd to an imminent death,—a dreadful one
In all save this,—that death, whato'er the shape
God gives it, is the event of life alone
Graced with God's last great gift to man,—escape
From men's tormenting,—I desire not now
To argue a long-talk'd theology.

How much mere knowledge with mere life may grow
Concerns not one that, being about to die,
Approaches Truth by no such process slow.
Too near death's hour of certainty am I.
But O the pity!   Had we two been one!
As once we might have been : who cannot be,
Henceforth, united, till by God's clear throne
We stand together, with Heaven's eyes to see
What Earth's miss'd miserably.
                                        O why, why
This woeful haste, that mars so much?   See here
The sad result.   For, Luther, while I die,
What ominous, incongruous faces leer
Beside thine own with laughing lip and eye?
What strange unholy helpmates share with thee
The sad bad joy of this false victory
O'er me and man?   Error on error! see,
Beneath the same soil'd banner at thy side,
Hand clasping hand, grim Saxon George allied
With him of Hesse! sworn foes erewhile, tho' now
George, who would think he did God service good
Could he but rend thee limb from limb, as thou
Bidd'st him rend me, red with thy brother's blood,
Thy right hand holds : who clasps the other? he,
The Landgrave, who hates him, as both hate me.
And thou, the while, art hugging each red hand!
What glues so fast the fratricidal Three
Together thus?   And what of such a band
The shameful central link makes Luther be?
My blood.   O shame, shame, shame, my brother,
        shame!
Is it not sad that God such things should see,
And thou the cause?   O worst disgrace of all!

That, when God asks, "Who did this?" men must name
Their noblest, and the blame of such deeds fall
On him whose scorn should brand them with the
    blame
Such deeds deserve.   Error beyond recall!
Yet, think, think, Luther, and be sad 'tis so.

Desirest thou man's good?   I wot thou dost.
But self hath film'd thy spirit's eagle eye.
Hear him not, heed him not, since cry he must,
The flattering fiend, that in thy heart doth cry!
I hear the plausible serpent tempting Dust
To mimic God! and thou dost taste his lie,
And in the sweetness of it take delight,
Murmuring, "Man's good? for what else have I striven,
Toil'd, dared, done battle, conquer'd?   Man's good, ay!
But man's good, by my gift, to mankind given,
Not man's good, man's hereditary right."

Consider, Luther ('tis Paul speaks, not I),
How all are members of the Body of Christ:
Where were the hearing, were the body all eye?
Were it all ear, in what would sight exist?
Were all one member, where the body then?
Many the members, tho' the body is one:
One Spirit of God in many lives of men:
Can the eye say to the hand, "Need have I none
Of thee"? or can the head say to the feet,
"I need ye not"?   Nay, rather they which be
The body's feeblest members most complete
The body's being: rather those that we
Esteem least comely claim the comeliest care,
Those least in honour honour most entreat:

Since to the body these most needful are :
The weaker parts chief cherishing demand :
The limbs crave clothing—not the head, the hand.
What gleam'd on Corinth, in the dawn of Faith,
Is Luther blind to, in Faith's noonday blaze ?
To thee, Apostle, still the Poor Man saith
The selfsame word that in the old proud days
Paul to the rich Corinthians cried.   They heard,
Believed, obey'd, and blest the Preacher's word.
To Corinth God one preacher sent : to thee
A thousand preachers cry aloud, my brother.
The fetter'd foot rebukes the hand that's free.
Should not we members cherish one another ?
For if one member suffereth pain or wrong
All suffer with it, and the whole frame ails :
Since each to each the bodily parts belong,
And none without his fellow's help avails
The body's use.   But is it so with us ?
The Rich oppress the Poor : the Strong the Weak :
The hand lops off the foot.   The body, thus
Self-mutilated, suffers, and doth shriek :
But the ear hears not what the tongue doth cry,
And the hand helps not, and Shame shuts the eye !

I sought to heal this sickness into health :
· To mitigate, not magnify, man's wrong :
For Want win justice, and give worth to Wealth :
To free the Weak, not to enslave the Strong :
'Mid gifts unequal, 'mid unequal powers,
Secure the equal happiness of all :
Maintain God's law in this mad world of ours :
Replace the force of mere material thrall
By force of love; the old empiry of Might,

Which is imposed upon unwilling hate,
By the serene sweet sovereignties of Right,
That are accepted, and secured i' the state
Of man's free spirit, by the loyal love
Of what the soul perceives to be Above.

I sought to attain this by no violent aids :
I preach'd not Justice from the cannon's mouth.
In humble hearts, not over crownèd heads,
I claim'd dominion, and 'twas granted.   Youth,
Hope's dawn-star trembling in his tear-lit eyes ;
Old Age, the twilight of his toilful day
Suffused with solemn joy—like evening skies
That promise watchful shepherds a fair morn—
Brightening his grave, calm, satisfied regard ;
And Womanhood—the maiden in her May,
The care-worn wife, with hungry eyes, grown hard
From grieving without hope—pale mothers, worn
With nursing breadless babes ; the wan array
Of this world's weary hearts ;—all these, no scorn
Could sneer to shame, no cares could keep away,
No want withhold, from Love's new-found domain.
Love shew'd his face, and was forthwith beloved !
No drop of blood was shed, no victim slain,
For love of all in each loved spirit moved,
And this man's pleasure was not that man's pain ;
But in Mulhausen God saw, and approved,
The bloodless triumph that bequeath'd no stain
To Love's least soldier.   And there rose on earth,
For Heavenly augury of human gain,
A glorious Form of innocent beauty and mirth,
—A little State like One large Family :
All members of one body at one birth :

And all were lowly, because all were high :
None poor : none idle : tyrant none, nor thrall :
Strong labour for the strong : light for the weak :
Labour for all : and food for all : for all
Hope that makes strong, and Reverence that makes
    meek,
Conscience that governs, Justice that allies,
Love that obeys, and Faith that fortifies.

And so, it grew, and grew : and so, I deem'd
It might grow yet—Earth's fruit of Heavenly seed!
But no! the vulture swoop'd, the eagle scream'd,
The roused hawk hunger'd, and the dove must bleed!
The banded anarchs of a brutal time
Hated us strongly, and were strong : their greed
Was made earth's god : their lust earth's law sublime :
We loved, and we were weak : that was our crime.
And where was Luther then ?   From town to town
Chasing grey-headed Carlstadt, his old friend :
Denouncing, persecuting, hunting down,
Down, to a noble life's disastrous end,
The man, to whom, in God's attesting name,
His solemn faith was pledged not long before :
The man he loathed because he could not tame
That old man's fearless spirit any more
To crouch to his!   Or to obedience old
Scolding Melanchthon's meeker nature back.
. . . Ah, dear Melanchthon, loved, tho' lost!   How,
    fold
On fold, the blurr'd Past lifts its vapour black,
To let emerge those melancholy eyes
Once more, which still my wrong'd heart loves! Alack,
Love is not always just, nor Memory wise.

May truer friends forgive me, that I cease,
A moment even, to list to their loud woes!
The thought of thee o'er all things breathes sad peace:
And, for a while, in sorrowful repose
The world's vast wail is husht, to let me hear
The old sweet fluteplaying . . . so faint, so clear!
Melanchthon, never play that flute again!

Back, heart, to Luther!   Where was Luther then?
Maligning Müntzer to the magistrate;
The rich man's friend, the friendless people's foe:
With frenzied rail, rebuking hope: elate
To lift the high-born, lay the low-born low:
Now this Elector, now that Landgrave, praising:
Thro' all Thuringia preaching scorn and strife:
In every Saxon burg crusaders raising
Against the hated Anabaptist's life!

Even then, the untaught patient peasant clung
To hope in justice from an unjust power.
Sharp was the cry which misery from him wrung,
But scant his asking even in that last hour.
He ask'd for leave to labour and to live,
—A free man's life and labour, not a beast's:
To honest Want what honest Wealth may give,
Wages for work: Christ's charity from Priests:
Justice from Law: and man's humanity
From Human Power.   His prayer was humbly urged:
Scorn was the guerdon, outrage the reply.
With hoot and howl, the importunate wretch was
    scourged
From field to forest, and from moor to fen.
Then, then at last, lash'd, famisht, to its lair,

The frenzied People, raving, rent its den :
Then savageries of nature seethed and surged
In manly breasts unmann'd by mad despair :
Brute hardship brutalized the hearts of men :
And beasts of burden changed to wild beasts then.

Ay! then, indeed, another voice was heard :
Not mine : and stormy listeners, lured by hate,
Welcomed the preacher of a wilder word,
With hearts whose love's last cry was strangled late.
Like rainless lightning thro' a wildwood ran
Stork's fiery utterance : where it dropp'd, it burn'd :
And all was flame. For each wrong'd heart of man
Caught fire and flared ; and, flaring, backward turn'd
Before the rushing wind of ruinous Wrath,
And pour'd that glare upon a blighted Past :
And each beheld, what barr'd the backward path,
Some mighty image of a monstrous wrong
Whereon the red revengeful light was cast.
This saw his son's back bleed beneath the thong :
That other his dishonour'd bride beheld,
Or ravisht daughter : one, the hunter's throng
Trampling his thrifty field : another yell'd,
" In Leipheim bleach my boys' unburied bones ! "
One saw his brother burning at the pyre :
One caught from bloody racks a comrade's groans :
One saw his father on the cross expire.
Then burst the dreadful shout, the dooming word,
And in the hand of Vengeance flash'd the sword.

And peace was pass'd away. To me, to all,
No choice survived, but action, and a cause
To fight for : man's oppressor, or his thrall :

The makers, or the breakers, of bad laws.
My choice was fixt, my part imposed: in me
No pause disloyal to the past allow'd.
Albeit strife's end I could not fail to see:
The certain slaughter of an unskill'd crowd,
Disaster, disappointment, death: fit ends
To false beginnings—war to vengeance vow'd,
And valour shamed by violent deeds.   My friends
To fancied victory, fool'd, with blindfold eyes,
Went forth: unblinded I, to sacrifice.

Yet, when the Armies of the Poor display'd
The Wheel of Fortune on their ensigns borne,
Which, in the turning of her hoodwink'd head,
Turns all things upside down with captious scorn,
" Not Chance, but Hope, be our device! " I said,
" For godless Fortune's gifts leave Faith forlorn,
But God's gift Hope stays fast when these be fled."
And on the People's flag I blazon'd then
Heaven's rainy bow, first rear'd o'er rescued men.

Ay! tho' that banner hath been beaten down,
That symbol trampled out in streams of blood,
While this contented world without a frown
Is praising faithless peace in festal mood,
Tho' all the friends for whom I hoped are slain
Like shambled sheep, and tho' myself must die
In some few hours, that hope I still retain:
Not with the same wild moment's flashing joy
That seized my soul when, in war's desperate hour,
I stood on the hill-top, and saw beneath
The all-surrounding hosts of hostile Power,
And mine own helpless sheep, ordain'd to death,

A faint and weary flock, which to devour,
The herded wolves, hoarse barking, bared sharp teeth ;
While high in heaven, athwart the thunder-shower,
Even as I lifted up my voice, and cried
To God, with stretch'd expostulating hand,
Sprang forth the sudden rainbow, basing wide
O'er battle strewn about the lower land,
Storm strewn in heaven, all its aery pride,
Triumphant on the everlasting hills !
Not thus I hope.   No gleam of promise thus
Visits this hour, which Heaven with darkness fills.
For men must wait.   God deigns not to discuss
With our impatient and o'erweening wills
His times, and ways of working out thro' us
Heaven's slow but sure redress of human ills.
When Christ was in the garden captived, they
That, till that hour, had talk'd and walk'd beside Him,
Hoping in Him, lost hope, and fled away,
And he that knew Him best ere dawn denied Him.
What wonder ?   All seem'd lost, i' the very eve
Of an immortal victory.   In man's sight,
All *was* lost.   What disciple could believe
Love's triumph in Life's failure, that sad night ?
But God makes light what men make dark : His fire
He frees where fall our ashes.   And, because
I feel God's power, still doth my spirit aspire :
Not fearing, even now, that unjust laws
By unjust force maintain'd, rack, stake, or cord,
The sign'd conventions of convenient Wrong,
The tyrant's sceptre, or the hireling's sword,
The servile pulpit, timorous to the strong,
To the weak truculent, or custom tough,
Can crush man's rights forever, or prolong

Man's pain an hour, whene'er God cries "Enough!"
And for this reason, and because I think
I never cared about myself since first
I cared for man,—from whom I dare not shrink,
Not even tho' he forsake himself,—nor aught
Hath Fancy nourisht, or Ambition nurst,
That was not featured in the womb of thought
By Hope's keen contemplation of man's face;
Because I cared not ever, care not now,
Which runner's foot be fleetest in the race,
Who, at the goal, assumes to grace his brow
The garland won, who takes the upper place,
Chief at the board, when festal wine-cups flow,
So long as, at the last, the goal be gained,
The garland got, the general table spread;
—Whoe'er the man by whom man's aim attain'd,
Joy crowns my heart, if victory crown his head!
Luther, because 'twas thus—'tis thus—with me,
And because, gazing with intentest gaze
Round each lost field where my life's ruins be,
A gleam of hope for man, in these dark days,
(—His last, perchance, for centuries long!—) I see,
Or seem to see, i' the spirit-power which stays,
Tho' stain'd—like sunrise o'er a stormy sea
Pour'd from a clouded crag with struggling rays—
On thy firm forehead's pride,—I write to thee.
Love mankind, Luther, if thou lovest not me!
For thou, great Spirit, art full-arm'd! a soul
Clothed with strong thunder by the hand of God:
Ardent to combat, potent to control:
Gabriel's spear, John's Angel's measuring-rod,
The Cherub's flaming sword, and Michael's shield,
Were given to thee—to conquer, not to yield.

Yield not the Devil his recaptured prey!
Conquer for all mankind!   Complete thy task!
The People, thou wast sent to save and sway,
Die in the Desert: thirsty lips, that ask
In vain for water! perishing feet that stray
Farther and farther from the Promised Land,
And sink 'neath weary loads along the way!
Mock not man's thirst with driblets pour'd i' the sand
From the scant leavings of Wealth's well-drain'd flask.
Cleave thou the stubborn stone with stern command.
Smite these rich rocks!   The rod is in thy hand.

Thou canst.   But if thou wilt not . . .
                                   Hark! give ear
To this sad prophecy of woes to be,
A dying voice to night-winds, moaning here,
Delivers, charging them to bear to thee
The burthen of Time's melancholy song:
The Church thou buildest, scorning first to free
Life's cumber'd field for Love's foundations, long
Shall be, herself, the slave of Power: and she,
Wed to the World, not Christ, the unchristian wrong
Of worldly Force with worldly Fraud shall share,
And so wax weak by scheming to be strong;
Till there shall be on earth a sight to scare
Earth's holiest hope from human hearts away:
A Priesthood, purchased for complacent prayer,
Leagued with Earth's Pomps, for profit and for pay,
Against Heaven's Love: praisers of things that are,
Scorners of good that's not: cleaving to clay,
Strangling the spirit; purblind, unaware!
Contracting, not enlarging, day by day,
The charities of Christ, with surly care:

Till man's indignant heart shall turn away,
And choose the champions of its faith elsewhere.
And champions shall it find.   Dread champions, they!
The impatient offspring of prolong'd despair:
A prayerless, pitiless, imperious brood,
Whose battle-cry shall be a cry for blood.

It may come soon, come late, come once for all,
Achieve its task, and pass, content, away,
That Hour of Fate, which God to life shall call:
It may come many times, and miss its prey,
And pass, dissatisfied, to come again,
More grimly arm'd with greed of greater sway,
To rescue from more wretchedness more men:
I cannot tell.   For unseen hands delay
The coming of what oft seems close in ken,
And, contrary, the moment, when we say
"'Twill never come!" comes on us even then.
I cannot tell the coming of that day,
If near or far, or how 'twill be, or when:
But come it will, and do its work it must,
So sure as moves God's spirit in man's dust.

Men call me Prophet.   And thou, too, in scorn.
Prophet I am.   For grief hath made me wise.
The night's lone watchman feels far off the morn,
And, till redress'd, all wrongs are prophecies.
This is no tortured fool's despairing curse,
No maniac menace from a murder'd man.
Luther, consider—ere man's need be worse,
If thou wilt help it, as none other can.
I claim not justice now, I do beseech
Compassion, for the Poor.   To thee, to all,

I would, indeed, my dying cry might reach :
—Place for the People's Cause ! in which I fall.

My sands run out. What else my soul would say
Must be said shortly. And these fingers write
But ill the struggling thoughts that force their way
Thro' tortured nerves, and speak in pain's despite.
Judge if 'tis pity for myself I crave.
Luther, one woman lives that loves me : one
Whose life I'd die ten thousand deaths to save :
I have no friends, and therefore she hath none,
Save God : I cannot shield her, from the grave
To which men doom me : worse than all alone
I leave her, compass'd with a world of foes !
That is the wife whose steps with mine have gone
Faithful thro' life, tho' led from woes to woes.
I have not breathed one prayer, not made one moan
To thee for her, that's as myself, Heaven knows !
Much less for this least self, that's soon to die ;
Tho' it hath suffer'd somewhat. Thrice they bound
This body to their rack. Thou wast not by.
Thy friends were. Each dictated some fresh wound,
And all applauded. Let that pass. For man,
Not for myself, I end, as I began,
This letter, and this life.
        With failing force,
But not with fainting faith, I lift the cry
That speeds my spirit on its sunward course
Beyond Death's night. And, as I lived, I die,
Man's friend : imploring—tho' it be in vain—
From thee, from all,—man's pity for man's pain !

v.   Q

ADOLPHUS, DUKE OF GUELDERS.

(FIFTEENTH AND SIXTEENTH CENTURIES.)

ADOLPHUS, Duke of Guelders, having died,
Was laid in pomp for men to see.   Priests vied
With soldiers, which the most should honour him.
Borne on broad shoulders through the streets, with
     hymn
And martial music, the dead Duke in state
Reach'd Tournay.   There they laid him in the great
Cathedral, where perpetual twilight dwells,
Misty with scents from silver thuribles ;
Since it seems fitting that, where dead kings sleep,
The sacred air, by pious aids, should keep
A certain indistinctness faint and fine,
To awe the vulgar mind, and with divine
Solemnities of silence, and soft glooms,
Inspire due reverence around royal tombs.
So, in the great Cathedral, grand, he lay.

The Duke had gain'd his Dukedom in this way :
Once, on a winter night, . . . these things were written
Four centuries ago, when men, frost-bitten,
Blew on their nails, and curst, to warm their blood,
The times, the taxes, and what else they could, . . .
A hungry, bleak night sky, with frosty fires
Hung hard, and clipt with cold the chilly spires,

Bent, for some hateful purpose of its own,
To keep sharp watch upon the little town,
Which huddled in its shadow, as if there
'Twas safest, trying to look unaware ;
Earth gave it no assistance, and small cheer,
'Neath that sharp sky, resolved to interfere
For its affliction, but lockt up her hand,
Stared fiercely on man's need, and his command
Rejected, cold as kindness when it cools,
Or charity in some men's souls.   The pools
And water-courses had become dead streaks
Of steely ice.   The rushes in the creeks
Stood stiff as iron spikes.   The sleety breeze,
Itself, had died for lack of aught to tease
On the gaunt oaks, or pine-trees numb'd and stark.
All fires were out, and every casement dark
Along the flinty streets.   A famisht mouse,
Going his rounds in some old dismal house,
Disconsolate (for since the last new tax
The mice began to gnaw each other's backs),
Seem'd the sole creature stirring ; save, perchance,
With steel glove slowly freezing to his lance,
A sullen watchman, half asleep, who stept
About the turret where the old Duke slept.

The young Duke, whom a waking thought, not new,
Had held from sleeping, the last night or two,
Consider'd he should sleep the better there,
Provided that the old Duke slept elsewhere.
Therefore (about four hundred years ago,
This point was settled by the young Duke so,)
Adolphus—the last Duke of Egmont's race
Who reign'd in Guelders, after whom the place

Lapsed into Burgundian line—put on
His surcoat, buckled fast his habergeon,
Went clinking up that turret stairway, came
To the turret chamber, whose dim taper flame
The gust that enter'd with him soon smote dead,
And found his father, sleeping in his bed
As sound as, just four hundred years ago,
Good Dukes and Kings were wont to sleep, you know.

A meagre moon, malignant as could be,
Meanwhile made stealthy light enough to see
The way by to the bedside, and put out
A hand, too eager long to grope about
For what it sought.   A moment after that,
The old Duke, wide awake and shuddering, sat
Stark upright in the moon; his thin grey hair
Pluckt out by handfuls; and that stony stare,
The seal which terror fixes on surprise,
Widening within the white and filmy eyes
With which the ghastly father gazed upon
Strange meanings in the grim face of the son.
The young Duke haled the old Duke by the hair
Thus, in his nightgear, down the turret stair;
And made him trot, barefooted, on before
Himself, who rode a horseback, thro' the frore
And aching midnight, over frozen wold,
And icy meer.   (That winter, you might hold
A hundred fairs, and roast a hundred sheep,
If you could find them, on the ice, so deep
The frost had fixt his floors on driven piles.)
From Grave to Buren, five and twenty miles,
The young Duke hunted thro' the hollow night
The old Duke, like a phantom, flitting white

Thro' darkness into darkness, and the den
Where great men falling are forgot by men.
There in a dungeon, where newts dwell, beneath
The tower of Buren Castle, until death
Took him, he linger'd very miserably ;
Some say for months ; some, years.   Tho' Burgundy
Summon'd both son and father to appear
Before him, ere the end of that same year,
And sought to settle, after mild rebuke,
Some sort of compromise between the Duke
And the Duke's father.   But it fail'd.

        This way
The Duke had gain'd his Dukedom.

         At Tournay,
Afterwards, in the foray on that town, :.
He fell ; and, being a man of much renown,
And very noble, with befitting state,
Was royally interr'd within the great
Cathedral.   There, with work of costly stones
And curious craft, above his ducal bones
They builded a fair tomb.   And over him
A hundred priests chanted the holy hymn.
Which being ended, . . . "Our archbishop" (says
A chronicler, writing about those days)
"Held a most sweet discourse." . . . And so, the psalm
And silver organ ceasing, in his calm
And costly tomb they left him ; with his face,
Turn'd ever upward to the altar-place,
Smiling in marble from the shrine below.

These things were done four hundred years ago,
After which time, the great Duke Charles the Bold
Laid hold on Guelders, and kept fast his hold.

Times change : and with the times too change the men.
A hundred years have roll'd away since then.
Such wrongs to right, such far truths to attain,
Time, tho' he toils along the road amain,
Is still behindhand ; never quite gets thro'
The long arrears of work he finds to do.
You call Time swift ? it costs him centuries
To move the least of human miseries
Out of the path he treads.   You call Time strong ?
He does not dare to smite an obvious wrong
Aside, until 'tis worn too weak to stand
The faint dull pressure of his feeble hand.
The crazy wrong, and yet how safe it thrives !
The little lie, and yet how long it lives !
Meanwhile, I say, a hundred years have roll'd
O'er the Duke's memory.

                    Now, again behold !

Late gleams of dwindled daylight, glad to go :
A sullen autumn evening, scowling low
On Tournay : a fierce sunset, dying down
In clots of crimson fire, reminds a town
Of starving, stormy people, how the glare
Sunk into eyes of agonised despair,
When placid pastors of the flock of Christ
Had finish'd roasting their last Calvinist.
A hot and lurid night is steaming up,
Like a foul film out of some witch's cup,
That swarms with devils spawn'd from her damn'd
        charms.
For the red light of burning burgs and farms
Oozes all round, beneath the lock'd black lids

Of heaven. Something on the air forbids
A creature to feel happy, or at rest.
The night is cursed, and carries in her breast
A guilty conscience. Strange, too! since of late
The Church is busy, putting all things straight,
And taking comfortable care to keep
The fold snug, and all prowlers from the sheep.
To which good end, upon this selfsame night,
A much-dismay'd Town Council has thought right
To set a Guard of Terror round about
The great Cathedral; fearing lest a rout
Of these misguided creatures, prone to sin,
As lately proven, should break rudely in
There, where Adolphus, Duke of Guelders, and
Other dead dukes, by whom this happy land
Was once kept quiet in good times gone by,
With saints and bishops sleeping quietly,
Enjoy at last the slumber of the just;
In marble; mixing not their noble dust
With common clay of the inferior dead.
Therefore you hear, with moody measured tread,
This Guard of Terror going its grim watch,
Thro' ominous silence. Scarce sufficient match,
However, even for a hundred lean
Starved wretches, lasht to madness, having seen
Somewhat too long, or too unworthily look'd
Upon, their vile belongings being cook'd
To suit each priestly palate. . . . If to-night
Those mad dogs slip the muzzle, 'ware their bite!

And so, perchance, the thankless people thought:
For, as the night wore off, a much-distraught
And murmurous crowd came thronging wild to where,

I' the market-place, each stifled thoroughfare
Disgorges its pent populace about
The great Cathedral.
                              Suddenly, a shout,
As tho' Hell's brood had broken loose, rock'd all
Heaven's black roof dismal and funereal.
As when a spark is dropt into a train
Of nitre, swiftly ran from brain to brain
A single fiery purpose, and at last
Exploded, roaring down the vague and vast
Heart of the shaken city.   Then a swell
Of wrathful faces, irresistible,
Sweeps to the great Cathedral doors ; disarms
The Guard ; roars up the hollow nave ; and swarms
Thro' aisle and chancel, fast as locusts sent
Thro' Egypt's chambers thick and pestilent.

There, such a sight was seen, as, now and then,
When half a world goes mad, makes sober men
In after years, who comfortably sit
In easy chairs to weigh and ponder it,
Revise the various theories of mankind,
Puzzling both others and themselves, to find
New reasons for unreasonable old wrongs.

Yells, howlings, cursings ; grim tumultuous throngs ;
The metamorphoses of mad despair :
Men with wolves' faces, women with fierce hair
And frenzied eyes, turn'd furies : over all
The torchlight tossing in perpetual
Pulsation of tremendous glare or gloom.
They climb, they cling from altar-piece and tomb ;
Whilst pickaxe, crowbar, pitchfork, billet, each

Chance weapon caught within the reckless reach
Of those whose single will a thousand means
Subserve to (terrible, wild kings and queens
Whose sole dominions are despairs), thro' all
The marble monuments majestical
Go crashing. Basalt, lapis, syenite,
Porphyry, and pediment, in splinters bright,
Tumbled with claps of thunder, clattering
Roll down the dark. The surly sinners sing
A horrible black santis, so to cheer
The work in hand. And evermore you hear
A shout of aweful joy, as down goes some
Three-hundred-years-old treasure. Crowded, come
To glut the greatening bonfire, chalices
Of gold and silver, copes and cibories,
Stain'd altar-cloths, spoil'd pictures, ornaments,
Statues, and broken organ tubes and vents,
The spoils of generations all destroy'd
In one wild moment! Possibly grown cloy'd
And languid, then a lean iconoclast,
Drooping a sullen eyelid, fell at last
To reading lazily the letters graven
Around the royal tomb, red porphyry-paven,
Black-pillar'd, snowy-slabb'd, and sculptured fair.
He sat on, listless, with spiked elbows bare.
When (suddenly inspired with some new hate
To yells, the hollow roofs reverberate
As tho' the Judgment-Angel pass'd among
Their rafters, and the great beams clang'd and rung
Against his griding wing) he shrieks : " Come forth,
Adolphus, Duke of Guelders! for thy worth
Should not be hidden." Forthwith, all men shout,
" Strike, split, crash, dig, and drag the tyrant out!

Let him be judged!" And from the drowsy, dark,
Enormous aisles, a hundred echoes bark
And bellow—"Judged!"

              Then those dread lictors all,
Marching before the magisterial
Curule of tardy Time, with rod and axe,
Fall to their work. The cream-white marble cracks,
The lucid alabaster flies in flakes,
The iron bindings burst, the brickwork quakes
Beneath their strokes, and the great stone lid shivers
With thunder on the pavement. A torch quivers
Over the yawning vault. The vast crowd draws
Its breath back hissing. In that sultry pause
A man o'erstrides the tomb, and drops beneath;
Another; then another. Still its breath
The crowd holds, hushful. At the last appears,
Unravaged by a hundred wicked years,
Borne on broad shoulders from the tomb to which
Broad shoulders bore him; coming, in his rich
Robes of magnificence (by sweating thumbs
Of savage artisans,—as each one comes
To stare into his deadly face,—smeared and smudged),
Adolphus, Duke of Guelders, . . . to be Judged!

And then, and there, in that strange judgment-hall,
As, gathering round their royal criminal,
Troopt the wild jury, the dead Duke was found
To be as fresh in face, in flesh as sound,
As tho' he had been buried yesterday;
So well the embalmer's work from all decay
Had kept his royal person. With his great
Grim truncheon propt on hip, his robe of state
Heap'd in vast folds his large-built limbs around,

The Duke lay, looking as in life; and frown'd
A frown that seem'd as of a living man.

Meanwhile those judges their assize began.
And, having, in incredibly brief time,
Decided that in nothing save his crime
The Duke exceeded mere humanity,
Free, for the first time, its own cause to try,
So long ignored,—they peel'd him, limb by limb,
Bare of the mingled pomps that mantled him;
Stript, singed him, stabb'd him, stampt upon him, smote
His cheek, and spat upon it, slit his throat,
Crusht his big brow, and clove his crown, and left
Adolphus, Guelders' last own Duke, bereft
Of sepulture, and naked, on the floor
Of the Cathedral. Where, six days, or more,
He rested, rotting. What remain'd, indeed,
After the rats had had their daily feed,
Of the great Duke, some unknown hand, 'tis said,
In the town cesspool, last, deposited.*

* "Et, comme ecrit Philippe de Comines (qui mêsmes a été
employé en ce different par le Duc Charles de Bourgongne) le
dit Adolph alla de nuict en plein hyver prendre son vieux pere
hors du lict, et lui fit faire pieds nus cincq lieues de chemin, et
le detint six mois prisonier en une profonde et obscure prison.
. . . Le Duc Charles de Bourgongne tacha par plusieurs fois
de reconcilier le pere et le fils, mais en vain. . . . Sur quoy le
fils repondit qu'il aymoit mieux jêter son pere en un puits, et
s'y precipiter apres luy, que de consentir à un tel accord, disant
que son pere avoit gouverné 44 ans, et que partant il estoit
maintenant temps qu'il gouvernait aussi quelque peu."—D.
Emanuel V. Meteren. Traduict de Flamend en Françoys par
I. D. L. Haye 1618.
"Il alla vers Tournay, où il fut tué par les Français en une
escarmouche, non obstant qu'il ne fit que crier Gueldre!
Gueldre! ce qui luy arriva selon le juste jugement de Dieu
pour sa grande rebellion."—*Ibid.*, Fol. 9.

JOHN PETER CARAFA.

(HONORES MUTANT MORES.)

A.D. 15—.

["Quelle . . . . che sono fatti per amministrare le cose spirituali non hanno bisogno di niente."—*Letters of Cardinal Carafa. Caracciolo MS.* "Tal era il furore e la cupidigia dei Carafa, che pareva fossero tornati i tempi dei Borgia."—BOTTA, *Storia di Italia*, lib. ix. p. 226.]

I.

JOHN PETER, Count of Madalone, son
  Of Count John Anthony Carafa, fled
From Rome, indignant at the evil done
  By wolves that on the fold of Christ were fed :

II.

And gave himself to Poverty and God :
  And with firm footstep, pure, severe, and sad,
The untrodden paths of abnegation trod,
  Poor amidst wealth, and grieved by evil glad.

III.

The fame of his fair life, and fervid faith,
  Grew with the growing evil of the time,
And sounded as the archangelic breath,
  Blown thro' Heaven's trump, in challenge to Earth's
    crime.

IV.

The Holy Father of the Faithful thought,
  "My counsellor shall be this saintly man,
As God is his:" and many a time besought
  John Peter's presence at the Vatican.

V.

But to the sinful city he had fled
  With feet that, wing'd by indignation, shook
Rome's dust away, the self-made exile said,
  "The spirit that is within me will not brook

VI.

"To breathe the breath of thy polluted air."
  Howbeit, when God's Vicegerent sent from Rome
Command to him to come, in place of prayer,
  Loyal to his high lord, he groan'd, " I come."

VII.

And, being at Rome, he cried, "I loathe this life,
  And call on Death to lead my spirit home.
Death hears me not.   God's will prolongs the strife
  My sad soul wages with the sins of Rome." *

VIII.

Sometimes the high hand of His Holiness
  Doth, for the ennobling of the Church, dispense
Honours whereby a good man's lowliness
  Is raised into a great man's Eminence:

---

* Letters to his Sister: selected by M. Charles de Samm
from the MS. collection of the Duke of Policastro.

IX.

But, in the Church's pious customs never
  (Nor the traditions, nor the usages
Of immemorial Rome, wherein forever
  As the tradition so the usage is)

X.

Prescription, precedent, or practice show'd
  That, if the head of its recipient
Were housed in Rome, to the man's own abode
  A scarlet hat might properly be sent.*

XI.

This pauper Priest was made a Cardinal:
  The Pope's own envoy bore the scarlet hat
To his poor house: and found not wherewithal,
  (Save the one stool where its lone inmate sat)

XII.

In that bare lodge, that wanted all save worth,
  To place the gift: whose stern recipient gazed
Ungladden'd, and from thankless doors drave forth
  The messenger unmoney'd and amazed.

---

* "Jamais Pape n'avait envoyé la barrette à un prélat présent à Rome." . . . "Tel était la pauvreté du nouveau Cardinal qu'il n'y avait dans sa petite chambre de meuble convenable pour y poser la barrette, et qu'il n'avait rien à offrir à l'envoyé du Pape chargé de la lui remettre. Tout Rome en parlait et s'en étonnait."—*Caracciolo MS.*

XIII.

At length one Pope, and then another, died :
　And Cardinal Carafa, after these,
Became a Pope, himself.　The whole world cried,
　" 'Tis well ! for he is worthy of the keys."

XIV.

Simple, austere, men knew him.　Pure his name,
　And praised his virtues.　Nobly born was he,
Yet not ignobly known.　His ample fame
　Was spotless.　Worthier Pope there could not be.

XV.

" The luxury of the new Pope's table " (writes *
　A Venice envoy to the Vatican)
" Is more than may be dream'd of.　All delights
　With all magnificences this proud man

XVI.

" Mingles in one.　The daintiest viands grace
　The costliest dishes, the most sumptuous wines
From the most gorgeous goblets flow to chase
　Care from the banquet where his splendour shines :

XVII.

" Good cheer he loves : and lustily he eats
　And deep he drinks : right royal is his tone :
The mightiest monarchs of the world he treats
　As clots of common dust beneath his throne :

* Relazione di Bernardo Navigero.

XVIII.

" His daily drink is butts of burning black
    Fierce Naples wine, and cups of Malvoisie.
Methinks his belly is but a Bacchus' sack.
    And his least meal meats five and twenty be.

XIX.

" Wondrous his wealth is.   Of his noble birth
    So proud is he, and of his present state,
That even as tho' he scorn'd to tread on earth
    Is the high going of his haughty gait.

XX.

" His nephews are the richest lords in Rome.
        And, for the greatness of the power they have,
Many there be that flatter them, and some
    That in dark wishes dig them a deep grave."

XXI.

Dame History is so old, she knows not well
    Present from Past.   She loves to say her say
Till it is stale, and the same story tell
    To-morrow as she told it yesterday.

CHRISTIAN, THE DOL-HARTZOG.

(SO CALLED FROM HIS FURIOUS BEHAVIOUR.)

1660.

CHRISTIAN, Duke of Brunswick, and Bishop of Halberstadt,
For a token of love, wore a lady's glove, in the loop of
  his riding-hat.
For he had seen the Bohemian Queen, whose gracious
  gift, they say,
Was the right to assume, in the place of a plume, the
  glove she had worn that day.
For Christian, the Dol-Hartzog, was half a brute at
  the best,
With but little space for a lady's face to lie and be
  loved in his breast.
Yet he may have loved well, for he hated well (tho' he
  showed his hate like a beast,
With tooth and claw), and the thing of things that he
  hated most was a priest.
He maul'd the monk, and flay'd the friar, nor left the
  abbot a rag,
And " *Gottes Freund und Pfaffen Feind,*" was the boast
  on his battle flag.
Yet he worshipt God in his own wild way—as a beast
  might worship too—

V.   R

Simply by thoroughly doing the work which God had
    set him to do :
With never a *Pater noster* said, never a candle burn'd,
And never a *Pleni gratia,* for any good gift return'd.
Worship no better than any beast's! yet with rever-
    ence, too, to spare,
Of its own dumb kind, in the silent mind, for what
    God made gentle and fair.
At least, from one touch I argue as much in this wild
    man of Halberstadt,
Since, for token of love, a pure lady's glove he wore in
    his riding-hat.

Christian, the Dol-Hartzog, came riding to Pader-
    born ;
And his men were dropping for lack of bread, and his
    horses for lack of corn,
Not a crown-piece in the coffer, either bread or corn to
    buy !
" What shall we do, Duke Christian ? " " Anything,
    friends, but die ! "
" The Saints us save," saith some one, " for we are
    weary and faint."
" 'Sdeath ! and so they shall, good fellows ! Who is
    the Paderborn Saint ? "
" The Paderborn Saint is the Saint Liboire ; and his
    image stands by itself
As large as life in the church, all cover'd with jewels
    and pelf."
" The Saint Liboire is a saint of saints, for he to our
    pious wishes
Shall accord a final miracle in the way of the loaves
    and fishes !.

Faith! since he hath jewels, and since he hath pelf, he
    shall buy us both bread and corn,
And if ever I swear by a saint, it shall be by the Saint
    of Paderborn."

Christian, the Dol-Hartzog, rode on into Munster
    town,
There, in the great Cathedral (greater for their
    renown!)
Carven in silver, and cover'd with gold (truly a glorious
    band!)
Round the altar, all in a row, the Twelve Apostles
    stand.
Christian, the Dol-Hartzog, call'd his captains of war—
" We will visit these Twelve Apostles, and see how
    their worships are,"
Then they all went clanking together (godless knaves
    as they were)
Over the sacred flintstones, up to the altar stair :
Never a *De profundis* was heard, never an anthem
    sung,
But where, thro' great glooms, 'twixt the solemn tombs,
    those iron footsteps rung,
Each priest, like a ghost, from that grisly host,
    patter'd off o'er the pavement stone,
And the iron men and the silver saints stood face to
    face and alone.
To that Sacred Dozen, thro' a silence frozen, strode the
    wild man of Halberstadt,
As when Brennus the Gaul stalkt into the hall where
    the Roman senators sat.
The Duke loves little speaking; but he made, that
    day, a speech

To those Twelve Apostles, as pregnant as any the
    preacher can preach;
For, " You Twelve Apostles," said he, "for many a
    year and a day
How is it that you have dared your Master to dis-
    obey—
Who bade you '*ite per orbem*,' go about the world where
    ye can,
From city to city for ever, succouring every man ?
But you, yet unmoved by the mandate, you slothful
    and rascally crew !
Stand there stock-still, letting others be stript to give
    succour to you.
Therefore, about your business! down instantly all,
    and disperse !
Comfort the needy! circulate freely! profit the uni-
    verse !
The better to serve which purpose, divinely ordain'd
    from of old,
I hereby will and command both ye and your ill-gotten
    gold
To assume the shape of Rix-thalers!' "
                         The Apostles had nothing to say,
As it seems, in defence of themselves. They at least
    were obliged to obey.
At dawn they were down from their niches; ere night
    on their mission they sped;
And the broken were bound up and heal'd, and the
    hungry were speedily fed.

This way Duke Christian affirm'd, little heeding
    Apostles or Priests,
That the first great need of a man is—*to feed:* after
    the fashion of beasts !

But, since even the beasts must work, Duke Christian
    thought, I suspect,
If Apostles are made to work also, Apostles mustn't
    object.*

---

* " On nommoit ce Duc de Christian, communement l'Halber-
stat, parce qu'il en êtoit Evêque, ou le Dol Hartzoch, c'est à
dire qu'il faisoit des actions d'un furieux. C'êtoit un Prince
de fort belle taile, et puissant de sa personne. Il etoit três-
brave, mais son courage tenoit plûtôt de la brutalité. . . . Il
faisoit alors le passioné de la Reyne de Bohéme à qui il avoit
pris un Gant d'Angletere que je luy ay veu porter atachè au
cordon de son chapeau, et pendant sur le bord comme un Plumet.
. . . N'ayant pas dequoy payer cette Armée il fit monnoyer
un saint Liboire bien plus grand que le natural . . . il marcha
droit à la grande Eglise appellée le Dome accompagné de tous
ses colonels et Capitaines, où il harangua ces Apôtres leur
réprochant leur paresse, etc. . . . Il avoit pris pour sa dévise
Gottes freindt, und der Pfaffen feint : c'est à dire Ami de Dieu
et Ennemi des Prêtres, qu'il tuoit, ou du moins châtioit sans
remission."—*Aubery du Maurier' Memoires,* p. 192.

THE DAUPHIN.

A PALACE here, a People there,
Face to face, i' the rainy air :
For the rain is raining heavily,
And the sick day shutting a bloodshot eye.
The People, nowhere a while ago,
Now here, now there, now everywhere.
And, of all in the Palace, none doth know
Where the People may be, ere is done
This last of two disastrous days,
Now waning fast, with watery rays.
Quick, Fancy ! ere its light be gone,
From out of the many 'tis darkening on
Save me a single face.   This one.

Broider'd of satin, as best befits,
Is the gilded chair where the urchin sits,
Whose grandsires all earth's greatest were
In grandeur, when the grand were great.
For the childhood of this child is heir
To monarchy's old age.

                              The late
Sunbeam, now sinking in his hair
(Weary of strife with a rainy sky),

Faintly, solemnly, lingers there
With a sorrowful glory, soon to die :
As all things must, some day, whene'er
Time disavows them : Time knows why.

O'er kingdoms twain thou wert born to reign,
Bourbon child of the Habsburg mother!
Life's fairest, one : and earth's, the other :
France, and Youth.   Of all the train
Of those the wondering world admires,
Lords and Ladies, Knights and Squires,
Long-robed Senator severe,
Royal Duke, and Princely Peer,
—They whose heads be Heads of France,
To whom, with a sullen countenance,
Hungry hundreds crook the knee,
None but boweth the head to thee,
Little child!   Whose face is one
Of a group that all are gone.

For, since thou, O child, didst flee,
Who knows where? from human sight;
Never child, kingborn, like thee,
Hath been born to absolute right :
Sons of kings no more can be
Guaranteed, as thou wert then,
Of the servitude of men.

Hearest thou the sounds outside?
Hearest thou the sounds within?
In the neighbouring chamber Pride
Stoops, in colloquy with Fear :
Mounier's loyal cares begin:

Prudence plucks at Lafayette :
Orleans with sulky stride
Is philosophising yet :
Chartres hath Louis by the ear :
Necker rubs a ruminant chin.
Outside in the twilight drear
Swells the ominous surly din.

See ! the child is playing now
With his sister's silky tresses :
To whose infantine white brow
Lips as white a mother presses.
Are not children safe from harm,
　　　Circled by a mother's arm ?

In the chair where sits the child
Smiling, long since sat and smiled
Him men named the " Grand Monarque."
Ah, the light is fading dark !
Thro' the palace windows wide
What is still so dim descried
In the pale persistent rain ?

Is the deluge back again ?
And what wreckt world's groaning ark
There emits its monstrous train
To new-people earth with pain ?
Men or beasts ?　What are they ?　Mark
Seest thou ? hear'st thou, little child ?
Haggard faces : women wild :
Men red-handed, blood-defiled :
Heroism, and Hope, and Hate,
Hunger, Horror, Wrath, and Crime,

Mingling in the march of Fate,
Life's grotesque with Love's sublime !
Ragged wretches grim and stark,
Smiling as they never smiled
Till this moment : jaw of shark
Gaping at a drowning ship :
Eye of tiger : lion's grip :
Stormy starvelings, smutcht and soil'd,
Thick thro' garden, court, and park,
Round that palace terrace-piled,
Teeming, tossing, trampling . . . Hark !
First a growl, and then a howl,
Voice of a vast tormented soul,
And then a shrill heart-breaking bark,
And now an immense murtherous roar,
Nearer, drearer, more and more,—
The famisht wild beast's roar for bread !
Suddenly the child's hand ceased
Its sport among the tiny tresses
Of the little golden head
Backward bent to its caresses ;
All those tumbled curls released ;
While the pouting child-lips said,
" MOTHER, I AM HUNGRY ! "

                                 Cry
Of the Poor man's child, supprest
In a People's starving beast,
For so many wicked years !
Cry, no law could longer smother
In the lawless lifeless past !
By what strange revenge of chance
Didst thou thus ascend so high,

From what depths of woe upcast,
As to smite the heart of a mother,
Heard in the unwilling ears
Of a listening Queen of France,
From a Dauphin's lips at last ?

MISERY.

I.

'TWAS neither day nor night, but both together
Mix'd in a muddy smear of London weather,
And the dull pouring of perpetual
Dim rain was vague, and vast, and over all.

She stray'd on thro' the rain, and thro' the mud,
That did the slop-fed filmy city flood,
Meekly unmindful as are wretches, who,
Accustom'd to discomfortings, pursue
Their paths scarce conscious of the more or less
Of misery mingled with each day's distress.
Albeit the ghostly rag, too thin to call
Even the bodily remnant of a shawl,
As, at each step, the fretful cough, in vain
By its vext victim check'd, broke loose again,
And shiver'd thro' it, dripping drop by drop,
Contrived the flaccid petticoat to sop
With the chill surcharge of its oozy welt.

The mud was everywhere. It seem'd to melt
Out of the grimy houses, trickling down
Those brickwork blocks that at each other frown,
Unsociable, tho' squeezed and jamm'd so close
Together; all monotonously morose,

And claiming each, behind his iron rail,
The smug importance of a private jail.
She stray'd on thro' the mud : 'twas nothing new :
And thro' the rain—the rain ? it was mud too !
The woman still was young, and Nature meant,
Doubtless, she should be fair ; but that intent
Hunger, in haste, had marr'd, or toil, or both.
There was no colour in the quiet mouth,
Nor fulness ; yet it had a ghostly grace
Pathetically pale.   The thin young face
Was interpenetrated tenderly
With soft significance.   The warm brown eye,
And warm brown hair, had gentle gleams.   Perchance
Those gracious tricks of gesture and of glance,
Those dear and innocent arts,—a woman's ways
Of wearing pretty looks, and winning praise,
—The pleasantness of pleasing, and the skill,
Were native to this woman,—woman still,
Tho' woman wither'd.   There's a last degree
Of misery that is sexless wholly.   She
Was yet what ye are, mothers, sisters, wives,
That are so sweet and lovely in our lives ;—
A woman still, for all her wither'd look,
Even as a faded flower in a book
Is still a flower.

II.

       Dark darker grows.   The lamps
Of London, flaring thro' the foggy damps,
Glare up and down the grey streets ghostily,
And the long roaring of loud wheels rolls by.
The huge hump-shoulder'd bridge is reach'd.   She
    stops.

The shadowy stream beneath it slides and drops
With sulky sound between the arches old.
She eyed it from the parapet.   The cold
Clung to her, creeping up the creepy stream.
The enormous city, like a madman's dream,
Full of strange hummings and unnatural glare,
Beat on her brain.   Some Tempter whisper'd,
                                                        " There,

Is quiet, and an end of long distress.
Leap down! leap in!   One anguish more or less
In this tense tangle of tormented souls
God keeps no strict account of.   The stream rolls
Forever and forever.   Death is swift,
And easy."
                    Then soft shadows seem'd to lift
Long arms out of the streaming dark below,
Wooingly waving to her.
                                    But ah no,
Ah no!   She is still afraid of them to-night,
Those plausible familiars!   Die?   What right
Is hers to die?—a mother, and a wife,
Whose love hath given hostages to life!

The voices of the shadows make reply,
" Woman, no right to live is right to die.
What right to live,—which means, what right to eat
(What thou hast ceased to earn) the bread and meat
That's not enough for all,—what unearn'd right
Hast thou to say, ' *I choose to live* ' ? "
                                                    With might
The mocking shadows mounted, as they spoke,
Nearer, and clearer; and their voices broke
Into a groan that mingled with the roar

Of London, growing louder evermore
With multitudes of moanings from below,
Mysterious, wrathful, miserable.

                    "Ah no,"
She moan'd!   "For Willie waits for me at home,
And will not sleep all night till I am come.
'Tis late . . . and no good news!" . . .

                      A drunken man
Reel'd past her, stared, and down the dark began
To troll a tavern stave.

                 Up stream'd again
The voices of the shadows, in disdain :

"A mother? and a wife?   Ill-gotten names,
Filch'd from earth's blisses to increase its shames!
What right have breadless mothers to give birth
To breadless babies?   Children, meant for mirth,
And motherhood for rapture, and the bliss
Of wifehood crowning womanhood, the kiss
Of lips, whose kissing melts two lives in one :—
What right was thine, forsooth, because the sun
Is sweet in June, and blood beats high in youth,
To claim those blessings?   Claim'd, what right, for-
    sooth,
To change them into curses : craving love,   .
Who lackest bread?   There is no room above
Earth's breast for amorous paupers.   Creep below,
And hide thyself from failure!"

                 "Is it so?"
She murmur'd, "even so!" . . .

                Three tiny elves
As plump as Puck, at all things and themselves
Laughing, ran by her in the rain.   They were

Chubby, and rosy-cheek'd, with golden hair,
Tossing behind: two girls, a boy: they held
Each other's hands, and so contrived to weld
Their gladnesses in one.   No rain, tho' chill,
Could vex their joyous ignorance of ill.
Then, sorrowfully, her thoughts began to stray
Far out of London, many a mile away
Among the meadows:
                    "In green Hertfordshire
When lanes are white with May, the breathing briar
Wafts sweet thoughts to our spirits, if we pass
Between the hedges, and the happy grass,
Beneath, is sprinkled with the o'erblown leaves
Of wild white roses.   In the long long eves
The cuckoo calls from every glimmering bower
And lone dim-lighted glade.   The small church tower
Smiles kindly at the village underneath.
Ah God! once more to smell the rose's breath
Among those cottage gardens!   There's a field
Past the hill-farm, hard by the little weald,
Was first to fill with cowslips every year;
The children used to play there.   Could one hear
Once more that merry brook that leaves the leas
Quiet at eve, but thro' the low birch trees
Is ever noisy!   Then, at nutting time
The woods are gayer than even in their prime,
And afterwards, there's something, hard to tell,
Full of home-feelings in the healthy smell
Wide over all the red plough'd uplands spread
From burning weeds, what time the woods are dead.

" We were so young! we loved each other so!
Ah yet, . . . if one could live the winter thro'!

And winter's worst is o'er in March . . . who knows?
The times might mend."
                     Then thro' her thoughts uprose
The menacing image of the imminent need
Of this bleak night.
                     " Two little mouths to feed!
No work! . . . and Willie sick! . . . and how to pay
To-morrow's rent?" . . .
                     She pluck'd herself away
From the bewildering river; and again
Stray'd onwards, onwards, thro' the endless rain
Among the endless streets, with weary gait,
And dreary heart, trailing disconsolate
A draggled skirt with feeble feet slip-shod.
The sky seem'd one vast blackness without God,
Or, if a god, a god like some that here
Be gods of earth, who, missing love, choose fear
For henchman, and so rule a multitude
They have subdued, but never understood.
The roaring of the wheels began anew.
And London down its dismal vortex drew
This wandering minim of the misery
Of millions.

III.

              Grey and grisly 'neath this sky
Of bitter darkness, gleam'd the long blind wall
Of that grim institute, we English call
The Poor-House.
                     We build houses for our poor,
Pay poor-rates,—do our best, indeed, to cure
Their general sickness by all special ways,
If not successful, still deserving praise.

Yet misery increases faster still
Than means to feed it, tho' we tax the till
To cram the alms-box. Which is passing strange,
Seeing that this England in the world's wide range
Ranks wealthiest of the nations of the earth.
But thereby hangs a riddle which is worth
The solving some day, if we can. That's all.

This woman, passing by that Poor-House wall,
Shudder'd, and thought . . . no matter! 'twas *a thought
Only* that made her shudder,—till she caught
Her foot against a heap of something strange,
And wet, and soft; which made that shudder change
To one of physical terror.
                                'Twas as tho'
The multitudinous mud, to scare her so,
Had heap'd itself into a hideous heap,
Not human sure, but living. With a creep
The thing, whate'er it was, her chance foot spurn'd,
Began to move; like humid earth upturn'd
By a snouted mole, disturb'd; or else,—suppose
A swarm of feeding flies, when cluster'd close
About a lump of carrion, or a hive
Of brown-back'd bees. It seem'd to be alive
After this fashion. A collective mass
Of movement, making from the life it has,
Or seems to have, in common, tho' so small,
A sort of monstrous individual.
For, from the inward to the outward moved,
The hideous lump heaved slowly; slowly shoved
Layer after layer of soak'd and rotting rags
On each side, down it, to the sloppy flags
Beneath its headless bulk; thus making pace

v.   s

For the upthrusting of the creature's face,
Or creature's self, whate'er that might have been.
Whence, suddenly emerging,—to be seen,
One must imagine, rather than to see,
Since it look'd nowhere, neither seem'd to be
Surprised, or even conscious,—there was thrust
(As tho' it came up thus because it must,
And not because it would) a human head,
With sexless countenance, that neither said
To man, nor woman . . . " I belong to you,"
But seem'd a fearful mixture of the two
United in a failure horrible
Of features, meant for human you might tell
By just so much as their lean wolfishness
Contrived more intensé meaning to express
Than hunger-heated eye or snarling jaw
Of any real wolf.
            Stricken with awe,
The woman, only very poor indeed,
Recoil'd before that creature past all need,
And past all help, too, being past all hope.
For, stern and stark, against the stolid cope
Of the sad, rainy, and enormous night,
That sexless face had fix'd itself upright
At once, and, as it were, mechanically,
With no surprise ; as much as to imply
That it had done with this world everywhere,
And henceforth look'd to Heaven ; yet look'd not
    there
With any sort of hope, or thankfulness
For things expected, but in grim distress,
From the mere wont of gazing constantly
On darkness.

London's Life went roaring by,
And took no notice of this thing at all.
It seem'd a heap of mud against the wall.

IV.

She who had stumbled on it shrank away
Abasht; not daring, at the first, to say
Such words as, meant for comfort, might have been
Too much like insult to that grim-faced Queen,
Or King, whiche'er it was, of Wretchedness.
Her own much misery seem'd so much less
Than this, flung down before her,—by God sent,
It may have been, for her admonishment.
But, at the last, she timidly drew near
And whisper'd faintly in the creature's ear,
" Have you no home ? "
                            No look even made reply,
Much less a word.   But on the stolid sky
The stolid face stared ever.
                            " Are you cold ? "
A sort of inward creepy movement roll'd
The rustled rags.   And still the stolid face
Perused the stolid sky.   Perhaps the case
Supposed was too self-evident to claim
More confirmation than what creeping came
To crumble those chill rags; subsiding soon,
As tho' to be unnoticed were a boon,
All kinds of notice having proved unkind.
Such creatures as men hunt are loth to find
The hole discovered where they hide; and, when
By chance you stir them out of it, they then
Make haste to feign to be already dead,

Hoping escape that way.
                 The woman said
More faintly, " Are you hungry ? "
                    There, at once
Finding intensest utterance for the nonce,
With such a howl 'twould chill your blood to hear
The wolf-jaws wail'd out, " Hungry ? ha, look here ! "
And, therewith, fingers of a skeleton claw
Tearing asunder those foul rags, you saw
. . . Was it a woman's breast ?   It might be so.
It look'd like nothing human that I know.
She, whose faint question such shrill response woke,
Stood stupefied, stunn'd, sick.

v.

                  Just then there broke
Down the dim street (and any sound just then,
Shaped from the natural utterance of men,
To still that echoed howl, had brought relief
To her sick senses) a loud shout . . . " Stop, thief !
Stop, thief ! "
          A man rush'd by those women,—rush'd
So vehemently by them, that he brush'd
Their raggedness together,—as he pass'd,
Dropp'd something on the pavement,—and was fast
Wrapp'd in the rainy vapours of the night,
That, in a moment, smear'd him out of sight,
And, in a moment after, let emerge
The trampling crowd; which, all in haste to urge
Its honest chase, swept o'er those women twain,
Regardless, and rush'd on into the rain,
Leaving them both, upon the slippery flags,

Bruised, trampled,—rags in colloquy with rags,
And so,—alone.

VI.

              Meanwhile the wolfish face,
Resettled to its customary place,
Was staring as before, into the sky,
Stolid.   The other woman heavily
Gather'd herself together, bruised, in pain,
Half rose up, slipp'd on something, and again
Sank feebly back upon her hand.
                        But now
What new emotion shakes her?   Doth she know
What this is, that her fingers on the stone
Have felt, and, feeling, close so fiercely on!
This pocket-book? with gold enough within
To feed . . . Alas! and must it be a sin
To keep it?   Were it possible to pay
With what its very robber flings away
For bread . . . bread! . . . bread! . . . and still not
    starve, yet still
Be honest!
              " Were one doing very ill
If . . . One should pray . . . if one *could* pray, that's
    sure,
The strength would come at last.   We are so poor!
So poor . . . 'tis terrible!   To understand
Such things, one should be learn'd, and have at hand
Ever so many good religious books,
And texts, and things. And then one starves. It
    looks
So like a godsend.   What does the Book say
About ' the lions, roaring, seek their prey '?

And the young ravens? 'Ye are more than these.'
Ah, but one starves, tho'!"

                Crouch'd upon her knees
She dragg'd herself up close against the wall,.
And counted the gold pieces.

                  "Food for all?
And leave to live . . . till one can work, of course.
Why else should God have sent it? Which is worse—
To starve, or . . . 'Tis as long as it is broad.
And then, consider this, I pray, dear God!
This that was born a human soul! Ah me,
God's creatures to be left like this! Just see
How thin she is!"

                Her hands about the thing
They clutch'd began to twitch. Still fingering
The gold convulsively, again she thought,
Or tried to think, of lessons early taught,
Easy to learn once, in the village school,
When to be honest seem'd the simple rule
For being happy; and of many a text
That task'd old Sundays; growing more perplext,
As, more and more, her giddy memory made
Haphazard catches at the words.

                  " Who said
' Therefore I say unto you ' (ah! 'twere sweet)
' Have no thought for your lives, what ye shall eat '
(If that were possible!)—'nor what to wear '?
Have no thought? that should mean, then, have no
      care!
And elsewhere . . . 'Ask, and ye shall have.'"

                      She stopp'd,
And trembled. And the tempting treasure dropp'd
From her faint hand.

She snatch'd it up again,
And cried, " Mine ! mine ! be it the Devil's gain
Or God's good gift ! Sure, what folks must, folks may,
And folks must live."
          She gazed out every way
Along the gloomy street. In desert land
To tempted saints mankind was more at hand
Than now it seem'd to this poor spirit pent
In populous city.

VII.

       Hurriedly, she bent
Above her grim companion, in whose car
She mutter'd, hoarse and quick . . . " Make haste !
    see here.
There's bread enough for all of us. Get up !
Quick ! quick ! and come away. To-night we'll sup,
To-morrow we'll not starve . . . another day,
Another . . . and then, let come what come may !
Off ! off ! "
       No answer.
           To the stolid sky
The stolid face was turn'd immovably.
The sky was dark : the face was dark. The face
And sky were silent both : you could not trace
The faintest gleam of light in the dark look
Of either.
       Vehemently the woman shook
That miserable mass of rags. It let
Itself be shaken : did not strive to get
Up, or away : said nought. A worried rat
So lets itself be shaken by a cat

Or mastiff, when the vermin's back, 'tis clear,
Is snapp'd, and there's no more to feel, or fear.
Then o'er the *living* woman's face there spread
Death's hue reflected.

         " Late ! . . . too late ! " she said.
"O Heaven, to die *thus!*"

         With a broken wail
She turn'd, and fled fast, fast.

         Fled whither?

VIII.

         Pale
Thro' the thick vagueness of the vaporous night,
From the dark alley, with a clouded light,
Two rheumy, melancholy lampions flare.
They are the eyes of the Police.

         In there,
Down the dark archway, thro' the greasy door,
Passionately pushing past the three or four
Complacent constables that cluster'd round
A costermonger, in the gutter found
Incapably, but combatively, drunk,
The woman hurried. Thro' the doorway slunk
A peaky pinch'd-up child with frighten'd face,
Important witness in some murder case
About to come before the magistrate
To-morrow. At a dingy table sat
The slim Inspector, spectacled, severe,
Rapidly writing.

         In a sort of fear
Of seeing it again, she shut her eyes
And flung it down there. With sedate surprise

The man look'd up.
> "Because I do not know

The owner, sir" . . . she said. "A while ago
I found it. And there's money in it . . . much,
Oh, so much money, sir!"
> A hungry touch

Of the defeated Tempter made her wince
To see him count it. Such a short while since
She, too, had done the same.

> "Your name? address?"

She gave them. Easy, from the last, to guess
Their wretchedness who dwelt in such a place!
The shrewd and practised eye perused her face
Contented, not surprised; for they that see
Crime oftenest, oftenest, too, see honesty
Where most of us would seldom look for it,
Or find it with surprise . . . in rags, to wit.

"Honest and poor. Deserves a large reward.
No doubt there'll be one."

> "Ah, the times are hard,

So hard, God help us all! and, sir, indeed
We are so poor. Two little mouths to feed.
If one could only get some work to do!"

"Ah . . . married? out of work? and children? two?
Mem. Let the owner know, if found. Good night."

But still she stood there. He had turn'd to write.
She stood, and eyed him with a dreary eye,
And did not move. He look'd up presently.

" Not gone, yet? eh? what more?"

                          " And, sir " . . . she said,

" There's by the Work-House wall a woman . . .
     dead.
There was no room within, sir, I suppose.
There are so many of them.   Heaven knows
'Tis hard for such as we to understand
How such things happen in a Christian land."

Her face twitch'd, and her cough grew fierce again,
As she pass'd out into the night and rain.

LAST WORDS

OF A SENSITIVE SECOND-RATE POET.

WILL, are you sitting and watching there yet?   And I
    know, by a certain skill
That grows out of utter wakefulness, the night must
    be far spent, Will:
For, lying awake so many a night, I have learn'd at
    last to catch
From the crowing cock, and the clanging clock, and
    the sound of the beating watch,
A misty sense of the measureless march of Time, as he
    passes here,
Leaving my life behind him: and I know that the
    dawn is near.
But you have been watching three nights, Will, and
    you look'd so wan to-night,
I thought, as I saw you sitting there, in the sad mono-
    tonous light
Of the moody night-lamp near you, that I could not
    choose but close
My lids as fast, and lie as still, as tho' I lay in a dose:
For, I thought, "He will deem I am dreaming, and
    then he may steal away,
And sleep a little: and this will be well." And truly,
    I dream'd, as I lay

Wide awake, but all as quiet, as tho', the last office
    done,
They had streak'd me out for the grave, Will, to which
    they will bear me anon.
Dream'd; for old things and places came dancing about
    my brain,
Like ghosts that dance in an empty house: and my
    thoughts went slipping again
By green back-ways forgotten to a stiller circle of time,
Where violets, faded for ever, seem'd blowing as once
    in their prime:
And I fancied that you and I, Will, were boys again
    as of old,
At dawn on the hill-top together, at eve in the field by
    the fold;
Till the thought of this was growing too wildly sweet
    to be borne,
And I oped mine eyes, and turn'd me round, and there,
    in the light forlorn,
I find you sitting beside me. But the dawn is at hand,
    I know.
Sleep a little. I shall not die to-night. You may
    leave me. Go.
Eh! is it time for the drink? must you mix it? it
    does me no good.
But thanks, old friend, true friend! I would live for
    your sake, if I could.
Ay, there are some good things in life, that fall not
    away with the rest.
And, of all best things upon earth, I hold that a faith-
    ful friend is the best.
For woman, Will, is a thorny flower: it breaks, and
    we bleed and smart:

The blossom falls at the fairest, and the thorn runs
    into the heart.
And woman's love is a bitter fruit; and, however he
    bite it, or sip,
There's many a man has lived to curse the taste of that
    fruit on his lip.
But never was any man yet, as I ween, be he whosoever
    he may,
That has known what a true friend is, Will, and wish'd
    that knowledge away.
You were proud of my promise, faithful despite of my
    fall,
Sad when the world seem'd over-sweet, sweet when the
    world turn'd gall :
Therefore, fair weather be yours, Will, whether it
    shines or pours,
And, if I can slip from out of my grave, my spirit will
    visit yours.

O woman-eyes that have smiled and smiled, O woman-
    lips that have kissed
The life-blood out of my heart, why thus for ever do
    you persist,
Pressing out of the dark all round, to bewilder my
    dying hours
With your ghostly sorceries brew'd from the breath of
    your poison-flowers ?
Still, tho' the idol be broken, I see at their ancient
    revels,
The riven altar around, come dancing the selfsame
    devils.
Lente currite, lente currite, noctis equi !
Linger a little, O Time, and let me be saved ere I die !

How many a night 'neath her window have I walk'd in
     the wind and rain,
Only to look at her shadow fleet over the lighted pane!
Alas! 'twas her shadow that rested, 'twas herself that
     fleeted, you see,
And now I am dying, I know it:—dying, and where
     is she?
Dancing divinely, perchance, or, over her soft harp
     strings,
Using the past to give pathos to the little new song
     that she sings.
Bitter?   I dare not be bitter in the few last hours
     left to live.
Needing so much forgiveness, God grant me at least to
     forgive.
There can be no space for the ghost of her face down in
     the narrow room,
And the mole is blind, and the worm is mute, and
     there must be rest in the tomb.
And just one failure more or less to a life that seems
     to be
(Whilst I lie looking upon it, as a bird on the broken
     tree
She hovers about, ere making wing for a land of love-
     lier growth,
Brighter blossom, and purer air, somewhere far off in
     the south,)
Failure, crowning failure, failure from end to end,
Just one more or less, what matter, to the many no
     grief can mend?
Not to know vice is virtue, not fate, however men
     rave:
And, next to this, I hold that man to be but a coward
     and a slave

Who bears the plague-spot upon him, and, knowing it,
    shrinks or fears
To brand it out, though the burning knife should hiss
    in his heart's hot tears.
Yet oh ! the confident spirit once mine, to dare and to
    do !
Take the world into my hand, and shape it, and make
    it anew :
Gather all men in my purpose, men in their darkness
    and dearth,
Men in their meanness and misery, made of the dust of
    the earth,
Mould them afresh, and make out of them Man, with
    his spirit sublime,
Man, the great heir of Eternity, dragging the conquests
    of Time !
Therefore I mingled among them, deeming the poet
    should hold
All natures saved in his own, as the world in the ark
    was, of old ;
All natures saved in his own to be types of a nobler
    race,
When the old world passeth away, and the new world
    taketh his place.
Triple fool in my folly ; purblind and impotent worm,
Thinking to move the world, who could not myself
    stand firm !
Cheat of a worn-out trick, as one that on shipboard
    roves
Wherever the wind may blow, still deeming the con-
    tinent moves.
Blowing the frothy bubble of life's brittle purpose
    away ;

Child, ever chasing the morrow, who now cannot
ransom a day:
Still I call'd Fame to lead onward, forgetting she
follows behind
Those who know whither they walk thro' the praise or
dispraise of mankind.
Friend, lay your hand in my own, and swear to me,
when you have seen
My body borne out from the door, ere the grass on my
grave shall be green,
You will burn every book I have written. And so
perish, one and all,
Each trace of the struggle that fail'd with the life that
I cannot recall.
Dust and ashes, earth's dross, which the mattock may
give to the mole!
Something, secure of achievement survives, as I trust,
with the soul.

Something? . . . Ay, something comes back to me . . .
Think! that I might have been . . . what?
Almost, I fancy at times, what I meant to have been,
and am not.
Where was the fault? Was it strength fell short! And
yet (I can speak of it now)
How my spirit sung like the resonant nerve of a
warrior's battle bow
When the shaft has leapt from the string, what time,
her first bright banner unfurl'd,
Song aim'd her arrowy purpose in me sharp at the heart
of the world!
Was it the hand that falter'd, unskill'd? or was it the
eye that deceived?

However I reason it out, there remains a failure time
    has not retrieved.
Comfort me not. For if aught be worse than failure
    from over-stress
Of a life's prime purpose, it is to sit down content with
    a little success.
Talk not of genius baffled. Genius is master of man.
Genius does what it must, and Talent does what it
    can.
Blot out my name, that the spirits of Shakspeare and
    Milton and Burns
Look not down on the praises of fools with a pity my
    soul yet spurns.
And yet, had I only the trick of an aptitude shrewd of
    its kind,
I should have lived longer, I think, more merry of
    heart and of mind.
Surely I knew (who better?) the innermost secret of
    each
Bird, and beast, and flower. Failed I to give to them
    speech?
All the pale spirits of storm, that sail down streams of
    the wind,
Thro' the cloven thunder-cloud, with wild hair blowing
    behind;
All the soft seraphs that float in the light of the
    crimson eve,
When Hesper begins to glitter, and the heavy wood-
    land to heave:
And the white nymphs of the water, that dwell 'mid
    the lilies alone:
And the buskin'd maids for the love of whom the
    hoary oak-trees groan;

They came to my call in the forest; they crept to my
    feet from the river:
They softly look'd out of the sky when I sung, and
    their wings beat with breathless endeavour
The blocks of the broken thunder piling their stormy
    lattices,
Over the moaning mountain walls, and over the sobbing
    seas.
So many more reproachful faces around my bed!
Voices moaning about me: " Ah! couldst thou not
    heed what we said?"
Peace to the past! it skills not now: these thoughts
    that vex it in vain
Are but the dust of a broken purpose blowing about
    the brain
Which presently will be tenantless, when the wanton
    worms carouse,
And the mole builds over my bones his little window-
    less house.
It is growing darker and stranger, Will, and colder—
    dark and cold,
Dark and cold! Is the lamp gone out? Give me thy
    hand to hold.
No: 'tis life's brief candle burning down. Tears?
    tears, Will! Why,
This which we call dying is only ceasing to die.
The hard thing was to live, Will. With flowers and
    music, life,
Like a pagan sacrifice, leads us along to this dark High
    Priest with the knife.

Wherefore, if man be immortal (which faith in the days
    that are done

I have ever upheld 'neath the weight of that Present,
    which now is this Gone)
Should he fear lest his feeble unfolding from this cramp
    and chrysalis world
Of forces sheathed in himself, by the strongest not
    wholly unfurl'd,
This first of man's efforts at growth, howsoever it fail
    or succeed,
Be the last of his dealings with time, and the spirit
    stop short with the deed?
Pray for my soul, that she may find and fashion some
    fairer way
From the manifold modes of expression as yet unfound,
    unattempted, to say
The word within, which that handful of earth the hard
    sexton will shovel anon
On the lips of a buried man can surely not check, when
    its meaning is gone
To work on the world that death opens. I wait.
    There are ages in store.
But the love . . . ah, the love, Will? the fair human
    face that I follow'd of yore,
It eludes me at last, and for ever! for ever I lose it!
    the most
I can gain from the grave, is—not this, but the know-
    ledge of why it was lost.

SIDE BY SIDE.

I.

(FRIEND AND FRIEND.)

MAY we, then, never know each other ?
  Who love each other more, I dare
Affirm for both, than brother brother,
    Ay ! more, my friend, than they that are
      The children of one mother.

A look—and lo, our natures meet !
  A word—our minds make one reply !
A touch—our hearts have but one beat !
    And, if we walk together—why,
      The same thought guides our feet

The selfsame course !   The flower that blows
  A scent unguess'd in hedgerow green,
Slim spiders, where the water throws,
    The starry-weeded stones between,
      Strange light that flits and flows,

Were charged by some sweet spirit, sure,
  (Love's minister, and ours !) to strike
Our sense with one same joy, allure
    Our hearts, and bless us both alike
      With memories that endure.

True friend! I know you : and I know
  You know me too.   And this is well.
Yet something seems to lie below   ·
  All knowledge, which is hard to tell.
    The world, where hands let go,

Slips in between.   The warmth yet stays
  Where, twelve safe hours ago, no more,
Your soul touch'd mine.   But days and days
  Make callous what one day leaves sore,
    Ichoring the wound they graze.

Not ours the change, if change must fall,
  Nor yours the fault, nor mine, my friend!
Life's love will last : but not love's small
  Sweet hourly lives.   That these should end
    It grieves me.   That is all.

This is time's curse.   Since life began
  It hath been losing love too fast.
And I would keep, while yet I can,
  Man's faith in love, lest at the last
    I lose love's faith in man.

But something sighs, "Be satisfied.
  Ye know no more than ye can know."
And walking, talking, side by side,
  It sometimes seems to me as though
    Love did to love provide

(How shall I say?) a man, in fine,
  A ghostly Third,—who is, indeed,
Not you nor I, though yours and mine;
  The creature of our mutual need,
    The friend for whom we pine.

You call him Me: I call him You:
  Who is not either you nor I:
This phantom friend, whom we pursue,
  Released by Love's fine alchemy,
    Mere product of us two!

The man that each in each hath sought,
  And each within himself hath found:
The being of our separate thought,
  To each by his own nature bound,
    From his own nature wrought.

Heed well our friend, while yet we may!
  There are so many winds about,
And any wind may blow away
  Love's airy child.   O never doubt
    He is the common prey

Of every chance, while love remains:
  And every chance which he survives
Is something added to love's gains.
  Comfort our friend whilst yet he lives!
    Dead, what shall pay our pains?

If cold should kill his heart at last,
   Regret will idly muse, and think
In at what window blew the blast?
   Or how we might have stopp'd that chink.
     What mends a moment past?

II.

(MAN AND WIFE.)

Nay, Sweet! no thought, not any thought,
   At least not any thought of you,
But what must thank dear love. Nor aught
   Of love's mistrust between us two
Can ever creep. Thank God, we keep
   Too close to let thin doubts slip through,

And leave a scar where they divide
   Hearts meant by Heaven to hold together.
So, soul by soul, as side by side,
   We sit. Thought wanders hither, thither,
From star to star, yet not so far
   But what, at end of all its tether,

It feels the beating of your heart,
   To which mine bound it long ago.
Our love is perfect, every part.
   Love's utmost reach'd at last, must so
Henceforth abide. And, if I sigh'd
   Just now, I scarcely wish to know

The reason why.　Who feels love's best,
　　Must feel love's best can be no more.
We see the bound, no longer guess'd,
　　But fix'd for ever.　Lo, the shore !
On either hand, 'twixt sea and land,
　　How clear and fine does sight explore

That long-drawn self-determined line
　　Of difference traced !　My Own, forgive
That, sitting thus, your hand in mine,
　　Glad that dear God doth let us live
So close, my Own, so almost one,
　　A thought that wrongs repose should strive

With pure content.　So much we are,
　　Who are no more . . . could I explain !
Ah, the calm sea-coast !　Think, how far
　　Across the world came land and main,
Endeavouring each to find and reach
　　The other,—well, and they attain

Here !　And just here, where they unite,
　　The point of contact seems to be
The point of severance.　Left and right,
　　Here lies the land and there the sea.
They meet from far : they touch : yet are
　　Still one and one eternally,

With still that touch between—that touch
　That joins and yet divides—the shore.
Oh, soul to soul, dear love, 'tis much !
　Love's utmost gain'd can give no more.
And yet . . . Well, no ! 'tis better so.
　Earth still (be glad !) holds Heaven in store.

.

.

SPRING AND WINTER.

I.

Was it well in him, if he
  Felt not love, to speak of love so ?
If he still unmoved must be,
  Was it nobly sought to move so ?
—Pluck the flower, but not to wear it—
Spurn it from him, yet not spare it ?

II.

Need he say that I was fair,
  With such meaning in his tone,
Adding ever that her hair
  Had the same tinge as my own ?
Pluck my life up, root and bloom,
To make garlands for her tomb?

III.

And, her cheek, he said, tho' bright,
  Lack'd the lucid blush divine
Of that rose each whisper light
  Of his praises waked in mine
But 'twas just that he loved then
More than he can love again.

IV.

Then, if beauty could not bind him,
    Wherefore praise me, speaking low ?
Use my face just to remind him
    How no face could please him now ?
Why, if loving could not move him,
Did he teach me still to love him ?

V.

"Yes!" he said, "he had grown wise now :
    He had suffer'd much of yore :
But a fair face, to his eyes now,
    Was a fair face, and no more.
Yet the anguish and the bliss,
And the dream too, had been his."

VI.

Ah, those words a thought too tender
    For the commonplaces spoken !
Looks whose meaning seem'd to render
    Help to words when speech came broken !
Why so late in July moonlight
Just to say what's said by noonlight ?

VII.

And why praise my youth for gladness,
    Keeping something in his smile
That changed all my youth to sadness,
    He still smiling all the while ?
Since, when so my youth was over,
He said, "Seek some younger lover !"

VIII.

Well, the Spring's back now ! the thrushes
    Are astir as heretofore,
And the apple-blossom blushes
    As of old about the door.
Doth he taste a finer bliss,
I must wonder, in all this,

IX.

(Winning thus what I have lost)
    By the usage of my youth ?
—I can feel my forehead crost
    By the wrinkle's fretful tooth,
While the grey grows in my hair,
And the cold creeps everywhere.

IMPERFECTION.

I.

Whom first we love, we lose before we wed.
  Time rules us all. And life, indeed, is not
.The thing we plann'd it out ere hope was dead.
  And then, we women cannot choose our lot.

II.

'Much must be borne which it is hard to bear:
  Much given away which it were sweet to keep.
The deed that never hath been done, the tear
  That never hath been wept,—who knows how deep

III.

These lurk in unlived lives? Ourselves behind
  Ourselves we leave, and miss what most we seek:
In our own memories our graves we find.
  Strong is the burden, but the back is weak.

IV.

My little boy begins to babble now
  Upon my knee his earliest infant prayer.
He hath his father's eager eyes, I know,
  And, they say too, his mother's sunny hair.

v.

But when he sleeps and smiles upon my knee,
　　And I can feel his light breath come and go,
The thought of one comes o'er me (woe is me!)
　　Who loved me, and whom I loved, long ago.

vi.

Who might have been . . . ah, what I dare not think!
　　The thing which must be, must be for the best.
God help us do our duty, and not shrink,
　　And trust His mercy humbly for the rest.

vii.

But blame us women not, if some appear
　　Too cold at times; and some too gay and light.
The life unlived, the deed undone, the tear
　　Unshed, . . . not judging these, who judges right?

viii.

Were we but judged by what we might have been,
　　And not by what we are, too apt to fall!
My little child—he sleeps and smiles between
　　These thoughts and me.　In Heaven we shall know
　　　all!

A MAN OF SCIENCE;

OR, THE BOTANIST'S GRAVE.

"Here lie the mortal remains (I may spare you the limitless list
Of academies, institutes, colleges, orders, whereof he was member)
Of Doctor Theophilus Timothy Bloom, the renown'd botanist,
Deceased (so his gravestone instructs you) the fourteenth day of December,

In the Year of Our Lord, One Thousand Eight Hundred and Sixty-two."
See! the lichens, already revenging themselves on their former tormentor,
Sprawl over his new-cut name, and have hidden it half out of view.
Meanwhile, I that knew the man, mourning my mild-eyed Mentor,

Gràced in his dust by this epitaph lean and bald as
    himself,
    Whom I fancy I still see spreading his specimens
        dry in the sun
He has taken his final farewell of, bequeathing, at
    least, to my shelf
    Full forty folios in print, and a manuscript newly
        begun

On the carbonaceous compounds found in botanical
    tissues,—
    Cellulose, glucose, lignine, dextrine, inuline, starch,—
A treatise laboriously written, and raising remarkable
    issues
    On all questions of cellular structure, commenced
        but a year back in March,—

For the honour and glory of Science, as well as my
    old friend's sake,
    I, that knew him, I say, here relate you his life
        from beginning to end.
—Hark! how the throstle is singing! and yonder
    bluebells in the brake,
    How they nod on the noontide airs! . . . Peace be
        to the soul of my friend!

Man's life dwindles apace, while the world grows
    vaster and vaster,
    And Nature, pleasing herself, smiles heedless of
        simple or sage.
Be it known, then, that Doctor Theophilus Timothy
    Bloom, our master,
    Who has left us forlorn of his lights in the sixtieth
        year of his age,

He, too (who could imagine it?), under that lean
    leathern hide of his
    Once bore about the high-beating and bountiful
        heart of a boy,
A heart full of wonder and worship! Was passionate,
    too, in the pride of his
    New-born belief in himself as a being capacious for
        joy.

Bright you may image the eye of him (long since dull
    as a paste eye),
    Bright with a brilliant hope in a July morning sweet,
When the boy's blithe step thro' the college cloister
    bounded hasty,
    And, proud, at the door of the Teacher the passionate
    boy's heart beat.

"Speak, my Pupil!" "O Master, I burn with a
    boundless impatience TO KNOW."
    "For this must I praise thee, my Pupil. For know-
    ledge is joy to the creature
Created to know the Creator. Yet patience! since
    knowledge is slow,
    Being infinite. *What* wouldst thou know?" And
    the boy, unabash'd, answer'd, "Nature."

"Nature is vaster than knowledge. What wouldst
    thou know *of* her, my son?"
    "Not, O Master, the *act*, which I see, but the *thought*,
    which I cannot discern:
I stand in the centre, gaze round me, see everywhere
    action alone,
    And find nowhere the source of the thought found
    in action wherever I turn."

v.   U

Said the Teacher, "In order, my Pupil, to reach to the
    source of the thought,
  We must follow the act in succession.   The thought
    may be one, once for all,
All at once; but the action is many and diverse, to
    unity brought
  In the mind by slow aggregates growing alike from
    the great and the small.

"There is but one vast universal dynamic, one mover,
    one might,
  Variously operant under the various conditions it
    finds:
And we call that by turns electricity, friction, caloric,
    and light,
  Which is none of these things, and yet all of them.
    Ask of the waves and the winds,

"Ask of the stars of the firmament, ask of the flowers
    of the field,
  They will answer you all of them, naming it each by
    a different name.
For the meaning of Nature is neither wholly conceal'd
    nor reveal'd,
  But her mind is seen to be single in her acts that are
    nowhere the same.

"Each of these acts is a spy and informer upon her:
    and any
  Of the separate sciences, following these, may be
    follow'd by man:

For the goal of man's mind is one, but the goings of
    men's minds many,
    And each, by his own way going, must get to the
        goal as he can.

"By the hundred ways that await you are waiting a
    hundred guides :
    Yet you can but walk one way at a time, follow one
        guide, use
One chart, in despite of the ninety-nine others each
    comer decides
    At the outset to take or renounce, as his choice may
        predominate.   Choose ! "

Heavy, then, hearing this, was the heart of the student,
    whose soul
    But a moment before on her wing was uplifting the
        world's light load,
And, "How can I choose me, O Master, the road, since
    I see not the goal ?
    Or how can I choose me the guide, since I see not
        even the road ? "

The Master, smiling, answer'd . . . " Of the works of
    Nature, those
    Wherein her method of working is easiest found of
        detection,
Are certain living bodies whose life can but feebly
    oppose
    The life-seeking, life-slaying process of scientific
        dissection :

" These bodies are vegetal bodies : the dealing of
     Science with these
   Is the least of her difficult labours.   Begin, then,
     with Botany . . . Stay !
Open the door before you, and turn to the right, if you
     please.
   You are in the Botanical Class, now.   Stay here,
     friend.   I wish you good day."

So sitteth Theophilus perch'd on the brim of the beaker
     of knowledge,
   Poor fly ! sipping . . . Nature ? no, Botany,—
     merely one kind of ingredient
Of the complex Elixir he thirsts for :—the blue-eyed
     hope of the College,
   A maiden-minded student, humble of heart and
     obedient.

But O what a hopeless confusion doth Order at first
     sight appear !
   Unwearied Theophilus, sitting, and conning the
     grammar of Nature,
Thro' the whole of the humming hot noon with the
     cuckoo's note cleaving it clear,
   Is it knowledge thou seekest ?   Then patience, and
     master, meanwhile, nomenclature.

So, like a drunken bee, you behold him, bewilder'd,
     floundering,
   Foot-deep, faint in the pollen ; or, now, climbing
     filaments, high on

The polypetalous whorl; now, wandering round and
    around a ring
  Rotate, campanulate, ventricose, valvate . . . O
  wheel of Ixion!

Day after day, and still darkness. At length a light
    breaks on the labour.
  For Linnæus, the Lecturer tells us, has classified
    plants, single-handed.
"Classification of plants?" . . . All hail! bid the
    pipe and the tabor
  Be joyful! the chaos grows cosmic: at length on
    firm ground we are landed!

No! for this classification's imperfect. No cause for
    dejection.
  Here's a new house, where the first thing is simply
    to stow away lumber;
Make yourself room to look round you; in time, after
    farther reflection,
  Doubtless you'll hit on some better arrangement;
    and, once disencumber

The ground that you stand upon, presently things will
    drop into their places,
  Each his appropriate corner find out, and most fitting
    relation:
So, till the fates find a fitter one, let us, not making
    long faces,
  But thankful enough to Linnæus, put up with his
    classification.

Still, tho', the infinite found in the finite dismays our
    endeavour.
  To the unknown perforce we abandon this vast starry
    sphere (sad confession!)
As baffling our bounded embrace : but it surely is hard
    when forever
  The least grain of sand we approach, growing reach-
    less, eludes our possession.

Worlds beyond worlds without end, we may make up
    our minds to relinquish :
  But worlds within worlds without end make the
    heart of a man faint within him ;
To be mock'd by a mite! and to feel that the lamp of
    our life must extinguish
  Its light, ere, exploring, we measure immensity
    pack'd in a minim!

To be crusht by a crystal of salt! to be foil'd by a
    film, or a flinder!
  To be stopped like the merest, minutest of emmets,
    whose poor little progress
To the goal, where she drops underground, the least
    hump of a molehill may hinder!
  A fortress to find in each fungus! in each lady Fly-
    trap an ogress!

" *One* group, but one, from the million learn first to
    know something about, now,"
  Says the Lecturer, leaving the pulpit, his brain for
    a while pump'd powerless,

" I propose to begin with the most elementary class,
    and give out now,
  As the theme of our next day's discourse, the class
    call'd Cryptogamic, or Flowerless."

Deep, then, we plunge into Acrogens, Ætheogams,
    Amphigams, still:
  Hope to get on by degrees into Exogens, Endogens:
    meantime
Moons wax and wane; summers fleet; from the
    Student, as patient he crams still
  Dry leaves under tin lids, steals sighing the glad and
    the green time.

Sad! For I fancy . . . at times, as the moist eye
    wanes ever meeker,
  And the lank yellow locks by degrees fell scant from
    the pure bald brow,
Much-tried Theophilus (still a sad-thoughted, unsatis-
    fied seeker)
  Startled, perchance, by the cuckoo, or vext by green
    buds on the bough,

Lifting those wide wan looks, with an unslaked grief
    in the gaze of them,
  Into the high blue stillness of heaven, so still, and
    so high !
Watching the white clouds roll'd on the unreturning
    ways of them,
  Murmuring among his books, with a deep dejected
    sigh,

" Ah, but all this, after all, is not what I pined for!
     Up there
    The veilèd Mystery sits on the solemn mountain
     peak:
The vast clouds form and change at her feet: and my
     heart's despair
    Cries aloud where no answer is heard: for this
     Silence never will speak.

" Yonder, up there, as of old, when he play'd on my
     heart's harp-strings,
    The wind, with a surly music, is moaning aloof in
     the tree:
Yonder, up there, in the blue and the breezy mid-sky
     swings
    The lanneret hawk, as of old, when my heart went
     higher than he.

" Could one leap all at once to the end! not doom'd,
     like a grub, to grope
    About in the blinding earth, looking up never more
     from one's load!
Well, never mind!   One is laying up knowledge, at
     least, one must hope;
    And one cannot afford to leap over the knowledge
     that lies in one's road."

Intermediate methods! importance of every detail!
    Say we, consoling ourselves; and again pick up
     heart to persist.

Ha, but cryptogams grow by the hundred, and books
    by the bushel,—*men* fail!
Here the door opens. In steps the Botanical
    Archivist,

Asking . . . whom else but Theophilus? what better
    man could you wish?
To catalogue all the collection of dried plants
    recently sent
From the Himalayan range by Commander Cornelius
    Fish;
And Theophilus cannot decline an appeal where an
    honour is meant.

Friend! when a man to one purpose the whole of his
    will hath awarded,
He will justly be jealous of all other claims on the
    time given to it:
He will lock up his life in a turret of tall triple brass,
    dragon-guarded,
Hide himself close in a strong central thought, and
    let nothing break thro' it:

Beauty peeps in at the casement, he savagely fastens
    the shutter:
Pleasure trips light at the threshold, he pushes the
    bolt in the door:
Fortune, red gold in her right hand, comes fearless with
    good news to utter,
He seals up his ears like Ulysses, and laughs at her,
    proud to be poor:

But one foe, the most unforeseen, the most dangerous,
    deadliest of all,
  Sure, if it finds, to o'erthrow him—the child of a
    word or a glance,
The tenant of emptiest nothing—he cannot exclude, nor
    forestall,
  Nor contend with, how wary so ever : and that foe
    is Innocent Chance.

Theophilus, most conscientious, most scrupulous scraper-
    together
  Of crumbs dropt from other men's trenchers, labo-
    riously much annotating,
Sorting, reviewing, arranging,—assigning its true
    whence and whither
  To this plant, and that plant, of each plant the
    family history stating,

In the hap-hazard, higgledy-piggledy ship-load of riches
    from Nature
  Robb'd by Commander Cornelius Fish, the illustrious
    sailor,
Lights, by ill luck, on a milk-white gnaphalium,
    foreign in feature,—
  Petals more pointed and definite, sepals profuser and
    paler

Than those of its kindred in Europe,—in short, a new
    specimen, clearly
  Distinguish'd. Whereat, as in conscience compell'd,
    for mankind's information

The Doctor (alas! now no longer mere student, but
    straighten'd severely
Into sedate middle age) then and there, after due
    consultation

Of all that botanical writers have said on gnaphalia in
    general,
    Sits down, and indites a small treatise, this specimen
        specially treating;—
Its structure, morphology, system, and elements,
    gaseous or mineral,
    Thus, in respect of the race of gnaphalia, our know-
        ledge completing.

Which done now, . . . no sooner the Doctor's small
    treatise, exciting sensation,
    Is read by the learnèd, than straightway three
        scandalized *savants*, dissenting
In toto, determined to deal with what calls for severe
    reprobation,
    Hurl at him and the public three passionate pam-
        phlets, objecting, commenting,

Suggesting, appealing, opposing, inveighing, reproach-
    ing, regretting;
    Whereunto, nothing daunted, he feels himself bound
        to make answer minutely,
Disclosing, expounding, disputing, affirming, denying,
    upsetting,
    Proving himself no mere tiro, attacking the main
        points acutely.

Back to the charge, each opponent, tenacious returning, with rage hacks
    Hard at the Doctor, and fights every inch with the heart of a Roman:
Not to be vanquish'd by numbers, the Doctor, as valiant as Ajax,
    Buckles the tighter his breastplate, and rushes in wrath on the foeman.

Religion, meanwhile, and Theology fly to the rescue of something,
    No man precisely knows what, with emphatical protest on all things.
O what a strepitant contest, to make a man envy the dumb thing
    Gifted by God with the grace to be silent, whatever men call things!

Thus the learnèd defunct we lament grew at last (for humanity's sake too!)
    Nothing more than, himself, a mere human gnaphalium, sapless and wither'd;
Till Death, for his own choice collection of dried things, was minded to take to
    Himself such a notable specimen. Bloom, with the bloom off him, gather'd

By Dis, gloomy gatherer! catalogued, pack'd up, disposed of for ever,
    Lies (here you have him!) named, dated, and done with. Meanwhile the great question

He started, surviving the Doctor, who died of his latest ·
    endeavour,
    Continues to puzzle our Pundits with cart-loads of
    precious suggestion.

Suppose, now, some man with one object in life—to
    construct a steam-engine :—
    First, say you, study dynamics; then metals; learn
    smelting and founding ;
Off with you, next, to the cog-wheel department ; cog-
    wheels ; you may then join
    The cylinder-makers ; and so forth ; in this way the
    full circle rounding ;

Meanwhile the man dies. Our friend here,—what now
    is he doing, I wonder ?
    Chasing a phantom gnaphalium, worlds beyond worlds
    wanly straying ?
Or simply, with palms cross'd at ease on his cool narrow
    couch, lying under
    This pother, and laughing alone in his grave-sleeve
    at what I am saying ?

Anyhow, here lie the mortal remains (with a limitless
    list too
    Of academies, institutes, colleges, orders, whereof he
    was member)
Of Doctor Theophilus Timothy Bloom, the renown'd
    botanist, who
    Died in the year Sixty-two, on the fourteenth day
    of December.

Well! sitting here on the grave of my master, while
    under the stone
  The red worm is picking his brains, there's a notion
    comes into my mind :—
(Was it the throstle that sung it, up there where the
    blackthorn is blown ?
  Or here, in the long grass, was it let fall by the
    whispering wind ?

What, if the grey cricket chirrup'd it, chasing yon
    seed-ball enchanted?
  What, if the wild bee humm'd it, ruffling the rich
    guelder rose ?)
The world, perchance after all, knows already enough :
    what is wanted
  Is, not to know more, but know how to *imagine* the
    much that it knows.

A GREAT MAN.

I.

THAT man is great, and he alone,
Who serves a greatness not his own,
   For neither praise nor pelf:
Content to know, and be unknown:
    Whole in himself.

II.

Strong is that man, he only strong,
To whose well-order'd will belong,
   For service and delight,
All powers that, in the face of Wrong,
    Establish Right.

III.

And free he is, and only he,
Who, from his tyrant passions free,
   By Fortune undismay'd,
Hath power upon himself, to be
    By himself obey'd.

IV.

If such a man there be, where'er
Beneath the sun and moon he fare,
   He cannot fare amiss.
Great Nature hath him in her care—
     Her cause is his:

V.

Who holds by everlasting law
Which neither chance nor change can flaw:
   Whose steadfast course is one
With whatsoever forces draw
     The ages on:

VI.

Who hath not bow'd his honest head
To base Occasion: nor, in dread
   Of Duty, shunn'd her eye:
Nor truckled to loud times: nor wed
     His heart to a lie:

VII.

Nor fear'd to follow, in the offence
Of false opinion, his own sense
   Of justice unsubdued:
Nor shrunk from any consequence
     Of doing good.

VIII.

He looks his Angel in the face
Without a blush : nor heeds disgrace,
   Whom nought disgraceful done
Disgraces.   Who knows nothing base
    Fears nothing known.

IX.

Not morsell'd out from day to day
In feverish wishes, nor the prey
   Of hours that have no plan,
His life is whole, to give away
    To God and man.

X.

For tho' he live aloof from ken,
The world's unwitness'd denizen,
   The love within him stirs
Abroad, and with the hearts of men
    His own confers :

XI.

The judge upon the justice-seat :
The brown-back'd beggar in the street :
   The spinner in the sun :
The reapers reaping in the wheat :
    The wan-cheek'd nun

XII.

In cloister cold : the prisoner lean
In lightless den : the robèd Queen :
  Even the youth who waits,
Hiding the knife, to glide unseen
  Between the gates :—

XIII.

He nothing human alien deems
Unto himself, nor disesteems
  Man's meanest claim upon him :
And, where he walks, the mere sunbeams
  Drop blessings on him :

XIV.

Because they know him Nature's friend,
On whom she doth delight to tend
  With loving-kindness ever,
Helping and heartening to the end
  His high endeavour.

XV.

Therefore, tho' mortal made, he can
Work miracles.   The uncommon man
  Leaves nothing commonplace.
He *is* the marvellous.   To span
  The abyss of space,

XVI.

The orb of time, is his by faith,
And his, whilst breathing human breath,
   To taste, before he dies,
The deep eventual calm of death,
     Life's latest prize.

XVII.

If such a man there be, where'er
Beneath the sun and moon he fare,
   He doth not fare alone.
He goeth girt with cohorts, powers,
The monarch of his manful hours,
     Whose mind's his throne :

XVIII.

He owes no homage to the sun :
There's nothing he need seek or shun :
   All things are his by right :
He is his own posterity :
His future in himself doth lie :
     His soul's his light :

XIX.

Lord of a lofty life is he,
Loftily living, tho' he be
   Of lowly birth : tho' poor,
He lacks not wealth : nor high degree
     In state obscure.

XX.

The merely great are, all in all,
No more than what the merely small
   Esteem them.   Man's opinion
Neither conferr'd, nor can recall,
   This man's dominion.

EPILOGUE.

Speed thee well, noble soul, gallant heart,
　Who unscared goest forth to the strife !
Speed thee well, wheresoever thou art,
　In the ranks of the armies of life,
Who dost battle for Good to the death,
　In that battle which never shall cease :
And whose truth, long as Falsehood hath breath,
　Will not parley with Falsehood for peace !
Who aloud, tho' unheard, criest No,
　When earth's clamorous Yes doth assent
To the evil that's easy to do
　In a world that's with evil content.
Yet restrain the exuberant sense
　Of the strength that is theirs who are strong
In the Right : which, however immense,
　Is not yet more immense than the Wrong.
Look behind thee, and scan what is lost :
　And around thee, behold what doth rest.
Lo, how little earth saves at the most
　Of the life of her bravest and best !
Of what mighty endeavours begun
　What results insufficient remain,
And of how many victories won
　Half the spoils have been taken again !

For in scum this hot passion of life,
　　Seething over, is spent: and so loses
The possession of that which the strife
　　Of its turbulent impulse diffuses :
Until, self-defeated, it sinks
　　Back again to a lowlier level,
As, from bubbles that burst at the brinks,
　　Fall the lees of each lingering evil.
By evangel and angel from Heaven
　　Unto Earth's many mourners below,
Long of yore, the "Glad tidings" were given :
　　But earth's gladness, O where is it now ?
Long of yore, on the mountain, the voice
　　Of the merciful Master was heard
To the mourners proclaiming "Rejoice : "
　　And, rejoicing, they welcom'd His word :
To the hand of the rich man "Restore,"
　　To the heart of the poor man "Be fed,"
And "Be heal'd," to the souls that were sore,
　　And to all men "Be brothers," it said.
But since Christ has been nail'd to the tree,
　　Fruits unripe have our hands gather'd of it :
Noisy worship of lip and of knee,
　　Niggard love, not of love, but of profit.
For the poor is opprest as of old :
　　And of all men is no man the brother :
And the Churches but gather their gold,
　　While the nations destroy one another :
Only, all of these things are now done
　　In another than Cæsar's name :
And all wrongs that are Christless go on
　　Unashamed of all Christian shame :

O the infinite effort that seems
  But in infinite failure to finish!
Man's belief in the good that he dreams
  Must each fact, he awakes to, diminish?
God forbid! Whom thank thou for whatever
  Of evil remains—understood
As *good* cause for continued endeavour
  In the battle 'twixt Evil and Good.
Old Experience—the bourne and the grave
  Of the Sluggard's self-sepulchred mind—
Is the stronghold whence issues the Brave
  To acquire new realms for mankind.
For had man's ever-widening will
  No domain but Experience, his sons,
Like his sires, would be savages still,
  Chewing acorns and worshipping stones.
Deep in Nature's undrain'd Cornucopia
  Every good that man seeks he shall find:
And to fools, only fools, is Utopia
  The abode of the hopes of mankind.
For whate'er God hath made for man's good,
  He hath granted man means to attain:
Say thou therefore "I will," not "I would,"
  Undeterr'd by the coward's disdain.
All unblest would our fate be, indeed,
  If yet all that can bless it were ended,
And we had but to write and to read
  Of the deeds which the great buried men did!
Did they plant? what they planted we grow,
  Every grain shall be ground into bread.
Every virtue that's in us we owe
  To the unborn no less than the dead:

·For ere born yet, Posterity breathes
    In our being : and shapes by its breath
The incentives (worth more than the wreaths)
    Of the men that win wreaths after death.
God be thank'd that the dead have left still
    Good undone, for the living to do—
Still some aim for the heart and the will
    And the soul of a man to pursue !
God be thank'd for the ills that endure,
    With the glory that's yet to be won
From the hurts we may hope yet to cure
    By the deeds yet reserved to be done !
And thank God for the foes that remain,
    If they hearten us, Friend, for the fight ;
And the mercy that grants to man's gain
    Yet a new gain forever in sight !
Forth ! Rejoice in the Good that God gives
    By the hand of beneficent Ill,
And be glad that He leaves to our lives
    Means to make them heroical still.

THE END.

PRINTED AT THE CAXTON PRESS, BECCLES.